FOURTEEN
STORIES
BY

PEARL S. BUCK

By Pearl S. Buck

FRIEND TO FRIEND [with Carlos P. Romulo]

MY SEVERAL WORLDS

THE CHILD WHO NEVER GREW

AMERICAN ARGUMENT

TALK ABOUT RUSSIA

WHAT AMERICA MEANS TO ME

OF MEN AND WOMEN

HOW IT HAPPENS

TELL THE PEOPLE

AMERICAN UNITY AND ASIA

FIGHTING ANGEL

THE EXILE

*

THE CHINESE NOVEL

[NOBEL PRIZE LECTURE]

*

COMMAND THE MORNING

LETTER FROM PEKING

IMPERIAL WOMAN

GOD'S MEN

FAR AND NEAR

PAVILION OF WOMEN

COME, MY BELOVED

THE HIDDEN FLOWER

KINFOLK

PEONY

PORTRAIT OF A MARRIAGE

THE PROMISE

DRAGON SEED

TODAY AND FOREVER

OTHER GODS

THE PATRIOT

THIS PROUD HEART

A HOUSE DIVIDED

THE MOTHER

THE FIRST WIFE AND OTHER STORIES

SONS

THE GOOD EARTH

EAST WIND: WEST WIND

*

VOICES IN THE HOUSE

BRIGHT PROCESSION

THE ANGRY WIFE

THE TOWNSMAN

THE LONG LOVE

*

ALL MEN ARE BROTHERS

[SHUI HU CHÜAN]

TRANSLATED FROM THE CHINESE

*

CHRISTMAS MINIATURE

MY SEVERAL WORLDS [Abridged for Younger Readers]

THE BEECH TREE

JOHNNY JACK AND HIS BEGINNINGS

ONE BRIGHT DAY

THE BIG WAVE

YU LAN: FLYING BOY OF CHINA

THE DRAGON FISH

THE WATER-BUFFALO CHILDREN

THE CHINESE CHILDREN NEXT DOOR   STORIES FOR LITTLE CHILDREN

THE CHRISTMAS GHOST

FOURTEEN

STORIES

BY

PEARL S. BUCK

THE JOHN DAY COMPANY
NEW YORK

Contents

A CERTAIN STAR   11

THE BEAUTY   35

ENCHANTMENT   54

WITH A DELICATE AIR   65

BEYOND LANGUAGE   81

PARABLE OF PLAIN PEOPLE   105

THE COMMANDER AND THE COMMISSAR   112

BEGIN TO LIVE   132

THE ENGAGEMENT   151

MELISSA   175

GIFT OF LAUGHTER   192

DEATH AND THE DAWN   210

THE SILVER BUTTERFLY   222

FRANCESCA   233

FOURTEEN

STORIES

BY

PEARL S. BUCK

A Certain Star

HE WOKE AT DAWN this Christmas morning. For a brief instant he could not remember where he was. Then the warmth of childhood memory crept into his drowsy mind. He was here at the farm, in his old home, the broken rafters of his old room above his head. It was yesterday, only yesterday, that he had insisted upon this homecoming and against the subdued but massive revolt of his family he had carried it through.

"Oh, Dad," his daughter Anne had wailed. "Go to the farm now? On Christmas Eve? But we've planned—"

She had protested with such sparkling anger that he had turned on her with like anger.

"It's been years since I asked anything of you!"

His son spoke. "I have a date, Dad."

"You'll break your date, Hal," he had said firmly.

He had turned then from his two mute and furious children to Helen, his wife.

"Christmas has departed from this house," he told her.

She had smiled patiently. "I'm used to your large announcements, darling. And things are about as they have been, since the war ended. Everything's changed. It's inevitable."

11

"The foundations don't change," he had insisted. "We must get back to being a family. I'll have the car ready in an hour."

He was aware of the command in his voice. He had grown used to command during the war, and no less in these years of continuing atomic research. He was accustomed to obedience in his great laboratory of scientists and he did not stay to hear more protest in his house. And knowing his punctual ways, they had assembled in an hour, and in total silence, for the long drive to the farm.

Well, they had obeyed him, at least. They were here together, miles away from late dancing and much drinking and the time-wasting frivolities that he detested. And it was Christmas. During this day surely he would win them back again. For he had lost them somehow during these years which had been absorbed in his work.

His name, his fame, Arnold Williams, nuclear scientist, one of the top three in the world, had overwhelmed them—and, to some extent, him. Scientists of every country turned to him for advice and argument and, compelled by the rapid growth of knowledge, he had dedicated his whole being to his researches.

This was his duty, of course, during the war, when his experiments had belonged to his government, but the line between duty and the pleasurable excitement of successful work was not so clear after the war ended.

While he pursued his separate way, his children had grown up, and Helen was certainly older than she should be. The old joy between them was gone. Yesterday, in his own home within easy distance of his laboratory at the university, he had suddenly realized that whatever was going on, in spite of last-minute shopping and an artificial, modernized tree, it was not Christmas. . . .

He remembered Anne, his daughter, so pretty, so feverish, not at all gay, flying to the telephone, always to be disappointed. It was never the right voice. . . . So whose was the voice for which she listened? Oh, Anne, beloved child, it was for her sake above all that he wanted to be alone today with his family. . . .

And what of the star? On Christmas mornings, when he was a boy lying here in this bed, there had been a certain star, high over the barn. He saw it always when he rose, earlier than usual, so that he could get the milking done before they opened the doors to the parlor where the Christmas tree stood. The Christmas Star! He threw back the covers and leaped out of bed—nonsense, probably, for the star might not be there now.

As he fumbled in the closet for his old clothes, it occurred to him that in a way this star was responsible for the direction of his life. It had led him to the heavens.

"What do you want for Christmas, boy?" His father had asked the question the year he was fourteen.

"I want a telescope," he had said.

His father had stared at him, his small blue eyes sharp and inquisitive above his ragged beard.

"What for?"

"To look at stars with."

His father had grunted, without sympathy it seemed, but on Christmas morning there was a mail-order telescope under the tree. It was the only gift he wanted. Impatient for the night, he had been compelled to wait until darkness fell. Then lifting his telescope to his eye, he peered at the star. What disappointment! It was larger, more glowing, but as far off as ever.

The next day, in sheer experiment, he had looked at the sun, and to his astonishment he saw spots upon it, and this had led to the buying of a book, an introduction to the sky, and so had begun his interest in cosmic rays.

He was dressed now in ski pants, sheepskin coat and fur boots. He slammed the door as he left the room, then winced, for Helen was still asleep, he hoped. If he had waked her, she would be patient with him, as indeed she had always been ever since his dark prowlings (begun long ago because his famous hunches came by night as well as by day) made it necessary for him to sleep alone. He could bear no interruption when he was seized by a theory and knew no peace until he had pursued it.

"When you marry me," he told Helen the day they were engaged, "you don't marry a man. You marry a sort of—of monster."

13

She had only laughed. Then one day during the war, when they were living in a barracks at Los Alamos, she had looked at him thoughtfully.

"What does that look mean?" he had inquired.

"Perhaps you *are* a sort of monster," she had said.

He had laughed, but the words came back to him now as he stepped outside the kitchen door into the darkness. The cold was solid enough to cut, the colder because the house was warm. He had put in an oil burner years ago when the children were small, but when he was a boy there was only the huge wood range in the kitchen. It was still there, for memory's sake. . . .

The snow creaked under his boots as he walked toward the barn. The sky was clear, the stars luminous and twinkling through the icy air. He looked up, searching the heavens. Ah, his star was plain! There it hung over the ridgepole of the barn, not so large as he had imagined, but unmistakably the same.

The years had painted it bigger and more golden than it was now, or perhaps his boy's imagination had seen it so. Yet there it shone, steady and true, as he had remembered it.

His feet found the familiar groove in the path under the snow and as he stood in the windless air the old wonder came flooding back again, the wonder of the universe. He had known it years ago, distilled through the single star. He had lost it in the hurry and excitement of his youth, in the years when he had been working for a living by day in the laboratory of a great industry. In his own small laboratory, by night, he had explored the secrets of the explosive rays of the sun, and using his meager holidays he had made pilgrimages to Einstein in Germany and Rutherford in England.

Skeptic and daring, he had wandered far from this humble place upon which he now stood to gaze again at a star on Christmas morning. He had been a proud and argumentative man, until the day when he had found terror and a new humility in the nucleus of an atom, laid bare before him in a hidden place in the desert. Infinite energy, encased in a shape so small that eyes could not see it!

14

Yes, this star upon which he now gazed had guided his life. What next? Where would the path lie from this Christmas morning?

He shivered suddenly and remembered that he was standing halfway to his knees in snow. It had fallen during the night, the soft stuff clinging to every branch and twig, and the air from the lake was icy. He turned reluctantly and followed his own tracks back to the house and into the kitchen.

The light was on when he opened the door and Helen, wrapped in her red flannel bathrobe, was standing at the gas stove, making coffee.

"Merry Christmas," he said and kissed her cheek. "Did I wake you?"

"You're as cold as a snowman," she said, rubbing that cheek. "And you didn't wake me. I couldn't sleep."

"Christmas in your bones?"

She shook her head. "I don't sleep as well as I used to." She set two cups on the table and poured the coffee. "You want breakfast now?"

"No, but I'll have coffee."

They sat down. She sipped her coffee slowly, but he took a hot gulp.

"That's good—I was cold all the way through."

"What were you doing outside at this hour?" she asked.

"What would you say if I told you I went out to see a star?" he replied.

"It's been a long time since you were interested in stars," she said.

He glanced at her. She looked too tired, this slender wife of his. "Maybe we shouldn't have come here to the farm. Maybe it's too much for you. Don't you feel well, Helen?"

"I'm all right," she said. "Just getting old, I suppose."

"Nonsense! You're worried about something."

She got up to make more coffee. "I heard Anne crying in the night."

He stared at her in consternation. "Why should Anne cry?"

"They don't say anything," she told him. "You know they never

15

say anything nowadays. One doesn't know what goes on in anybody."

She threw him a strange, sad look which he did not comprehend.

"Anne seemed perfectly willing to come here yesterday," he reminded her. "She was more willing than Hal was—he had a dance or something."

"They both had parties." She stirred her coffee thoughtfully. "It isn't like Anne to give up so easily—not if she wants something."

"That's true."

Anne never gave up easily when she wanted something very much. So yesterday obviously there wasn't anything she wanted very much.

"I hope she wants the bracelet I've bought her for Christmas," he grumbled. "It cost enough."

"I don't know what they want any more. Everybody's changed somehow." She sighed and began sipping her coffee again, holding her cup in both hands as though they were cold.

He examined her face, still so pretty in spite of its pallor. It had been a long time since he had seen her in the morning before she made up her face. He was an early worker, and she slept late.

"Are you all right?" he asked again.

"Tired," she said. "My time of life, maybe."

"Woman's retreat," he declared. He got up and kissed her cheek. "Remember how you used to climb Mont Blanc with me when we were measuring cosmic rays? That wasn't so long ago."

She smiled faintly and did not reply. He tousled her hair to tease her and she caught his hand and slapped it gently. "I'll bet that your Christmas presents aren't wrapped."

"You're wrong! I had them wrapped at Tiffany's," he said.

She looked shocked. "Did you get everything there?"

"Everything," he said, "and when I said I wanted them gift-wrapped, the clerk said stiffly that the usual Tiffany wrapping *is* a gift wrapping."

That made her laugh and he felt victorious.

16

"And now," he said. "I am going upstairs to the attic to bring down my precious parcels for the tree."

"Why on earth did you take them to the attic?" she inquired. "The children won't snoop—you forget they're grown up."

"Habit. Before I knew it last night I was in the attic, putting my small expensive packages in the corner where we hid Anne's doll house and Hal's bicycle . . . How many years has it been since we spent Christmas here?"

"Not since you fell in love with the nucleus of an atom," she said. There was a glint of old mischief in her blue eyes. "I wish I knew the enchantment in a nucleus!"

"Ah, there's enchantment!" he retorted. He left her then and climbed the stairs to the attic and found his gifts in the brown paper bag in which he had thrust them for safekeeping yesterday. Halfway down the stairs again to the second floor he heard Anne's voice in the upper hall as she talked to someone—a man, of course.

"What's the use of my coming into town tonight? . . . Yes, I could come with Hal—he's got a date—but what's the use? It would be midnight before you could get away from your family and we'd have fifteen minutes—well, half an hour then—and you uneasy all the time. What good is that?"

He heard the passion and the pain and, his heart suddenly aching, he saw her there at the telephone. She was still in her pink flannel nightgown, her yellow hair curling about her head, a mere child in spite of her twenty years. No man had the right to hurt this child he had begotten! How could he persuade her to tell his name so that he could defend her from the fellow?

"Anne," he said.

She hung up instantly. Then she turned and looked up at him with huge, startled blue eyes.

"It's early for you to be up on Christmas morning, isn't it?" he asked.

"I couldn't sleep," she said. "It's terribly cold here by the lake."

"It's just as well you're up," he said. "We have the tree to cut, Hal and I, and we'll trim it and get dinner together the way we

17

used to do. I'll bring in some branches for you to decorate the house with—maybe some ground pine, eh?"

He deposited the brown paper bag on the stairs and came toward her.

"Feeling sentimental, aren't you, Santa Claus?" Anne crossed the hall to meet him and standing tiptoe, she kissed his cheek. "You're a sweet old thing," she said suddenly.

"Thank you," he said. "I haven't heard even that for a long time."

"I haven't said anything to you for a long time," she agreed. "You've been away somewhere these ten years, haven't you?"

She was tracing the outline of his eyebrow with a delicate forefinger.

"It's you," he said, capturing the forefinger. "You've grown up without asking me. I get only glimpses of the daughter I used to have."

All the same, he was thinking, if he hadn't insisted on being here today there would not have been even this interchange. She'd have been asleep in her bed, exhausted by dancing and carryings-on. She leaned her head against his chest unexpectedly.

"I wish I were little again," she whispered. "I wish I had never grown up!"

He pressed her soft hair. "Why, Anne—why, Anne—"

"Silly, isn't it!" She lifted her head and shook the tears from eyes that smiled up at him too brightly. Then running to her room she shut the door against him.

"Merry Christmas," he called after her, but she did not answer.

He opened Hal's door then. There, sprawled across the bed, lay his dear and only son—eighteen, a six-footer, handsome, brilliant— and a total stranger.

He tiptoed across the floor and looked down at his sleeping child. A man, this child—a child, this man. Tall, thin with youth, big bones, fresh skin and dark hair too long, here was his son, holding within the new shape of manhood a thousand memories of boyhood.

Hal it used to be who could not wait to get to the lake in summer, to swim, to fish, to sail. Twice he was nearly drowned in the

18

deep, still waters, the first time swimming beyond his strength, the second time by a blow on the head against a rock when he dived. Twice he was saved, both times by his father. Three times, then, this son had been given to him alive, the first time fresh from his mother's womb.

Now he was a stranger who drove wildly into the night, who danced crazy dances with persons unknown, who came home, sometimes drunk, to break the hearts of parents. How could his son be saved? For inside that noble skull there was a brain worth saving. His own old professor at Harvard had written him about Hal. "If you can pull him through this pretentious youthfulness, this cult of 'beat,' you'll have a man."

Suddenly Hal opened his eyes and looked at him.

"What do you want, Dad?"

"Merry Christmas," he said.

Hal yawned. "Is it time to get up?"

"We have the tree to cut after breakfast."

Hal turned and burrowed into his pillow. "Okay—okay—"

He stood an instant longer, stifling his sudden impatience. Christmas, and the boy wanted to sleep! He remembered other mornings when Hal came into his room at dawn, shouting for the day to begin. And he had cut short his own sleep and had got out of bed so that his son could be happy.

He turned abruptly and left the room, closing the door just short of a bang. Patience! He was exhausted with being patient. Hal had no self-discipline. Why did men have children?

He went into his own room and stood by the window. The snow was falling again in a flurry from a sky overcast with gray clouds. The star was gone.

The day was clear again when he and Hal went tramping through the snow after breakfast. His spirits rose in spite of himself. Filled with warm and nourishing food, encouraged by the sight of a pretty flush on Helen's cheeks, though it might be no more than the heat of the old wood range which he had insisted upon lighting

19

in honor of the day, and softened by Anne's sporadic tenderness, he inclined his heart anew to this tall and silent youth who was his son.

"When I was a kid," he said, "we always had a white Christmas. We took it for granted. And I believe that you and Anne always took snow for granted, too, in the years when we came here for your Christmas holidays. Snow isn't so important in the city."

Behind him he heard Hal's crunching tread, but there was no answer to his small talk. He glanced over his shoulder, breathing out his frosty breath, and saw Hal's blank face. The boy was not listening. Then he caught his father's sharp glance.

"Did you say something, Dad?"

"Nothing important," he said shortly.

They tramped on. Why talk to a son who heard nothing? And he had a great deal to say to a son, a very great deal.

He longed to share with Hal something of his own life, the excitement of being a scientist in the atomic age when a scientist had suddenly become the most important man in the world.

In the past, isolated in his laboratory, working alone, often experimenting haphazardly, and usually in vain, a scientist had been scarcely human, a magician, or a crank. Now, with the knowledge of the energy that was in the core of the universe, that infinitely small core, he was respected—and feared. . . . Did Hal dream of such things? There was no way of knowing, no communication between father and son.

He paused to examine the spruce woods in which they stood. The trees had grown too tall. They would have to look for young growth beyond.

"How far are you going?" Hal asked.

"We must find a tree of reasonable size," he said. "We'll go to the edge of the forest."

"We could cut the top out of any tree," Hal said.

He shook his head. "I'm too good a woodsman for that. My father's ghost would rise. Kill a whole tree for its top?"

"It's getting late," Hal urged.

"What's your hurry?"

Hal stopped in the snow. "Dad, I want to get back to town by eight o'clock tonight."

He turned and faced his son. "One thing I asked of my family this Christmas—the one gift I really want—that we spend the day together here. And the day includes the evening. It will be six o'clock before we get dinner over. Then we'll have the tree."

He saw a strange look in Hal's eyes, a muted rebellion. If the boy felt that way, why didn't he fling out his anger? Once when he himself was eighteen, he had fought his father first with words, and then with fists. It had concerned a day, too, a summer's day when he had wanted to go to the state fair, and his father had forbidden it.

"Hay's fit to cut," his father had said roughly. "Nobody's goin' nowheres."

"I'm going," he had said.

"Try it!" his father had shouted.

They had glared at each other. Suddenly his father had bellowed at him, "If you feel like you look, we'll fight it out—see who's the better man—"

They had fought, wrestling like bulls, young and old, and he had downed his father. He had watched his father get to his feet, pride and shame tearing his heart in two.

"All right," his father had said sullenly. "I'll make hay alone."

"I'm not going," he said and the two of them had worked side by side throughout the long hot hours until sunset. . . . Yes, that boy—himself—had been someone he could understand. Why didn't Hal defy him?

"You're the boss," Hal said. "Guess you'll always be the boss now."

He stared at his son's bitter face. "What the hell do you mean by that?"

"Just what I said. You're the boss. You've been the big boss ever since the war, haven't you? Atomic killer!"

He stared at the dark young giant, who glowered at him. Then rage ran over his body like fire and he hit his son on the jaw, a clean right-hander that amazed him. In the same instant he recognized pride in the blow—a low male pride that shocked him. His hand dropped.

"Hal!" he stammered. "Hal, I didn't mean—I don't know what got into me. But you called me an evil name. Still, I shouldn't have done it."

Hal pulled his handkerchief out of his pocket and mopped his face.

"Is it bleeding?" he asked casually.

"Yes, a little. It's a bad bruise. . . . What made you call me that name, boy?"

"It's what you are, aren't you? A sort of master killer—"

"No!"

Hal inspected the handkerchief spattered with blood. He rolled it up and put it back in his pocket.

"Okay . . . Let's cut the Christmas tree."

"Hal, I can't just let this pass."

"I said okay—okay."

"Okay, then!"

He was furious again and he stalked grimly ahead of his son for fifty paces. Then he stopped before a graceful young spruce.

"Here's our tree," he said.

"I'll cut it," Hal said.

He swung the ax three times against the trunk, each time missing the groove. Then he threw down the ax.

"I'm dizzy, Dad."

"Let me look at your face." He cupped his hand under his son's chin and examined the blackening bruise. "I'll ask you to forgive me for such an act on Christmas Day," he said abruptly.

"It's all right," Hal said. "I called you a name."

"Which I don't deserve," he maintained. "But rest yourself—I'll chop down the tree."

He struck four clean blows and the tree fell away with a long groan. He lifted the stump end and Hal took the top. In silence they carried it down their tracks and across the meadow to the front porch of the house.

"I'll brush the snow off," Hal said.

"Let's go into the house and get warm first."

He led the way into the kitchen. The room was warm and fragrant with sage and roasting turkey.

"Hi there, you two," Helen called cheerfully. She was basting the bird in the oven, her face rosy and her hair a tumble of silvery curls.

"There's no oven like this one," she went on. "I wonder that we were ever willing to give up wood ranges."

"Wait until you have an atomic oven," he retorted. "A couple of minutes and your turkey is done. We sit down to the table and you press a button. We exchange a little small talk, pass the time of day, and the bird will be ready to carve."

Nobody answered. He was pulling off his boots and did not notice the silence. At the kitchen table Anne was polishing the old farmhouse silver.

"Any telephone calls?" Hal asked.

"None," Anne said. She looked up and gave a cry. "What's the matter with your face?"

"Your face," Helen echoed. She closed the oven door. "Why, it's awful!"

"I hit him," Arnold said harshly. He got up and drew a glass of water and drank it.

"I called Dad a name," Hal said.

Helen sat down on the kitchen stool. "Oh dear, oh dear—what is the matter with us—"

"A Christmas gift!" Anne said, and laughing hysterically, she buried her face in her hands.

"Anne!" he shouted. "Stop it! Stop laughing. Stop it, I tell you—"

He seized her shoulders and shook her. She lifted her face to him, broken with laughter or weeping, he did not know which.

"Are you going to hit me, too, Dad? Is that the sort of man you are now?"

23

He stepped back. "What do you mean?" he demanded. He looked from one face to another. "What do any of you mean?"

It was Anne who answered. She was the fierce one, the little fierce one who flew at him and bit him one day when she was seven. In all justice, he had been compelled to spank her for unparalleled naughtiness because she had drawn pictures of lambs and daisies over his sheets of equations. The scars of her little teeth were on his thumb still.

"We don't know you," Anne said distinctly. "You're changed. You've become a stranger to us."

He contemplated these three whom he loved. For a moment he felt helpless and driven to escape. He thought of flight—anywhere to get away from them. Why had he ever left the comfort of his laboratory? Yet he could not escape them, wherever he was. He loved them, each of them differently and all too well. Wherever he went he carried them with him because he loved them. . . . And now he must face them as he had faced the other terrifying decisions of a scientist's life.

Should he pursue this knowledge to the uttermost, too, as he had pursued the quest of the energy locked in the nucleus of the atom? There had been times when he longed to escape that ultimate knowledge, yet he had been stern with himself. There could be no escape for the scientist.

Even while he knew that a secret energy could and might destroy the world, he had pursued the knowledge of it as his duty. It could, rightly used, bring life instead of death.

In a strange way love was like that, a power for evil or for good. Everything depended upon the human being. . . . So why were these three strangers to him now when he loved them so much? On this Christmas morning, he was conscious only of love. What could he say to make them understand?

He sat down at the kitchen table and looked from one face to another. They were watching him and he made himself gentle before them.

"Anne," he said at last, choosing her face among the three. "You're as honest as the Christmas star. I appreciate it. You say I'm a stranger to you, my family . . . and all the time I've been thinking that *you* were the strangers—you and Hal, and even you, Helen. I've felt lost here. But I've felt lost for a long time—in my own house."

Anne was embarrassed. He saw it. He must take it more slowly. "You've been busy, Dad—" she said.

"I've been busy, of course," he agreed. "Too much away from you all, too busy about what I thought was my duty—my job. But I can't live without you, my—my dears, whatever I am."

He yearned for understanding but, searching their faces, he saw them still wary. . . . They didn't know him as he was now. Other memories crowded their minds. He could guess what they were thinking: That he'd make love to them, try to win them back again, prove that he was still the gay and tender father, the passionate lover and husband.

But he wouldn't plead. He spoke to Anne again.

"Go on being honest. . . . Why do you feel I am a stranger?"

Her lovely little face seemed to be shut tight against him. "People ask me how it feels to have a father who—who made the atomic bomb. They ask me what you're making now. And I say I don't know. Because I don't. You never tell us anything."

Hal broke in. "Don't blame Dad for the bomb. Whatever he had to do about that, I guess he had to do it. Besides, it's all over—long ago."

In the big, warm kitchen the delicious smells of pine branch and roasting turkey combined. Outside the day had changed. The sky was darkening again and snow was beginning to fall in the windless air, great soft flakes. To the outer eye it was a Christmas scene as traditional as the turkey in the oven, the spruce tree waiting on the front porch.

He remembered it the same on every Christmas of his childhood, and yet today there was something in this house that had never been here before. A fear had unfolded itself, a human fear of a

25

future—hideous but possible—because of what he and his fellow scientists had done.

And if the fear were here, was it not in every other house, in every other heart, a secret unspoken, a shadow unexplained? He who had discovered a miracle had failed to share it with these he loved. They knew only the fear.

He lifted his head. "Let me try," he said. "Let me try to explain myself. I think I understand why you are afraid of me."

Anne could not bear this. "Dad, not afraid of you, exactly. But nobody feels safe any more. That's why we rush around—we don't want to think about it. None of us do. . . . So we just keep rushing around, not thinking."

His wife took pity. "I know you can't help it, Arnold. . . ."

"I have a fear, too," he said at last. "The fear you have is a fear I share."

They were listening to him as they had not listened before. He was saying something new.

"Are you afraid of yourself?" Anne asked.

"No," he said strongly. "I know myself. Yes, I am changed, but not as you think. No one can discover the things I've discovered and not be changed. I am a humble man as I was never humble before. I believe in God. . . ."

He spoke the words simply, aware of their significance. He had never spoken the Name before. Agnostic and skeptic, he had taken pride in disbelief.

"Not the God of my fathers, perhaps," he went on, trying to be plain and not sentimental, "but yes, I believe in the eternal Creator, maker of heaven and earth. How can I not believe? I have met creation at work in the center of the atom—invisible, but full of purpose, immeasurable in power and energy. . . . I believe where I cannot see."

They were so still that they seemed not to breathe. It occurred to him now that he had never spoken to them of his serious thoughts. The days of their years together had skimmed by upon the surface of life. He had been too shy, perhaps, to uncover the hidden realities. And they had starved for reality.

They were relaxing, listening, Anne on the floor, her hands clasped about her drawn-up knees, Hal leaning against the door, hands in his pockets, and Helen sitting at the table, her head bent. She was listening, he knew, but skeptically, perhaps? Perhaps they were all skeptical.

He faltered. He tried to laugh. "Sounds big, doesn't it? Maybe I'm fooling myself . . ." He let the words trail off.

"I must baste the turkey again," Helen said suddenly.

He suspected, from the look on her too sensitive face, that the moment was more than she could bear. They waited while she opened the iron door of the oven. They watched while she dipped the fat juice with a big spoon and poured it over the huge bird. In these ways, he thought, were the vast, the small, mingled in their lives today. Christmas star and atomic fears.

She drew a glass of cold water, drank it and sat down again at the table.

"Go on, Dad," Anne said.

"I don't know how to go on now," he said abruptly. "It's true I've been away for years. Even though I sleep and eat at home a good deal of the time—I'm somewhere else. Maybe I can't get back. Maybe we'll never really meet again, you three and I.

"It's lonely, being a scientist—a lonely life. We don't make contact except with one another in our own world. That's why we keep going to conferences and meetings, I suppose—trying to find people who speak our language—with whom we can communicate through equations. . . . You've got to meet me halfway, you three!"

"Suppose we can't," Anne said in a low voice.

"Then I suppose I'll have to go my way alone," he said somberly.

Helen got up and went to the window and stood there watching the drifting snow. "We're all in the atomic age together," she said. "You got there first, that's all."

"That's very perceptive of you, darling," he said gratefully.

27

The telephone rang. Hal went into the hall to answer it and they waited.

"I don't know whether I'm coming," they heard him say. "I won't know for a while yet . . . I'll be late if I do come."

He came back into the room. He threw himself down on the shaggy rug before the kitchen range, crossed his hands under his head and stared at the ceiling.

"Go on, Pop," he said.

"I can't go on," he said to his son. "You'll have to take me on faith. You can believe in me whatever I do, or you can't believe in me. All I can say is that I have seen a vision as truly as those men of old who followed the star—the wise men. They believed that a child would bring in a new and better age . . . and so do I."

"Plenty of people were afraid of that new age, too," Helen said.

"Right again," he said, and again was grateful.

She had been peering out the window and now she went to the bread box and found a crust and crumbled it. Then she opened the window and put the crumbs on the outside sill.

"I see a belated wood thrush," she said.

"Herod tried to kill the child, remember?" This was Anne, remembering the old story.

He turned to her. "He wanted to stop the new age. But nobody can do that—nobody and nothing. There's no going back to what we were—Herod couldn't kill the child . . . and we can't destroy the creative nucleus of the atom. It's eternal. It's there. We have to learn how to use it—for good and only for good."

He got to his feet restlessly and began pacing the floor, from the window to the south to the window to the north while the snow drove white against the panes. The big old kitchen stretched the width of the solid house. And he mused aloud . . .

"I wish it could have begun differently—in peace instead of in war. I wish I could have lighted cities and made houses warm and perfected a fuel for wonderful machines that aren't even invented yet. . . . But it couldn't begin that way, it seems. First of all we had to stop a subhuman man from destroying the world."

He paused and faced them.

"You understand? Hitler would have destroyed us! He was after the bomb, too. We were only months ahead."

"But Germany had surrendered," Anne said.

"Japan hadn't," he retorted. "And there were subhumans there who wanted to keep on fighting. It's the subhumans we have to watch."

He was pacing the floor again. "The only thing I fear in life is the subhuman. I trust the energy in the atom—you can know it and learn to use it—it's predictable. And I trust a good man as I trust God. But the subhuman—no! He's the enemy—the only one we have. And he may live next door as well as across the sea. He might be alive in one of us—even in me!"

He stopped in front of Anne and jabbed his long forefinger at her. "That's why you're afraid of me!"

His hand dropped. "Good God, child—you *should* be afraid of me! I was afraid of myself this morning." He turned to Hal. "Son, why did I hit you?"

"Forget it," Hal said under his breath. "I was mad at you, too."

"I can't forget," his father said. "There's something subhuman in me, too."

He was talking aloud to himself, putting his soul into words this Christmas morning. But they listened. Even though it was too much for them, they knew what he was talking about. Helen held out her hand to him and he grasped it. Anne laid her forehead against her hunched knees and he saw her body tremble. Was she weeping? He did not know.

Hal leaped up from the floor and clapped him on the back. "Enough talk! I guess we understand each other a little, anyway. . . . We'd better get the tree up, Dad. I'll drag it into the living room through the front door."

"I'll find the Christmas tree trimmings," Helen said.

She stopped on her way and kissed his cheek. But Anne sat crouched on the floor, her head bent. He glanced at her and went to the window and looked out. The snow had ceased to fall and between the wintry gray of the sky he saw lines of blue again. A variable sort of day, he thought, and it was not half over. Getting up early, even to see a star, was beginning to tell on him. And all this commotion in his family—who knew how deep it went? He had lost too much time to retrieve in one day.

And then Anne lifted her head and began to talk. "I've wanted for weeks to tell you . . . I'm terribly unhappy."

He felt his heart leap. Then he had not utterly failed!

"Tell me why you're unhappy, Anne."

"I've fallen in love."

He drew up the hassock and sat down within reach if she put out her hand to him.

"But that's wonderful," he said gently.

"It's not," she said. "I love someone who doesn't love me."

"Not possible," he declared. "I don't believe there's a man on earth who can't love you. Even if he's blind and can't see the way you look."

She laughed brokenly and scrambled to her feet. She came to him and leaned her cheek on top of his head so that he could not see her face.

"He doesn't love me enough," she said. "Not enough to give up anything for me—only enough to kiss me—and so on."

"And so on . . ." he repeated. "That's not enough, I agree."

"No," she said. "Because I love him too much. So it's got to be everything or nothing—Dad, he's married. So it's nothing."

"That's bleak," he agreed gravely. "That's very bleak."

She broke at his tenderness. "Oh, Dad, the world's empty!"

He pulled her to his knees, a child again as she used to be and a child still. She buried her face against his shoulder and began to weep soundlessly, as a broken heart must weep. No, she was not a child. A child sobs aloud. . . .

He held her, waiting. He could not throw out the usual snips and bits of comfort. You are only twenty—there are other men, young and handsome. This will pass, my child, this will pass. He would speak only the truth.

30

She lifted her distraught face. "Shall I ever get over this, Dad?"

"Never," he said. "One never gets over these big things. They stay in you. Other things will come—other loves. You'll live in them, too. You'll live in everything. We must—there's no escape from living."

Her head dropped to his shoulder again but she was not weeping now. He felt the heart in agony but her mind was working, her will assembling itself. She sat up and smoothed her hair.

"What would have happened to me if you hadn't made us come here for Christmas?" she asked.

"Tell me," he said.

"I planned to run away—with him—for a weekend. And this morning I couldn't. I heard you get up and go outside. I went to the window and watched you tramp through the snow and stand there by the barn a long time."

"I had to see the star again," he said.

"The star?"

He told her then of what the Christmas star had meant to the child he had once been, here in this old house, and how yesterday in the city he had longed intolerably to come back, to get his bearings once more by the star.

She slipped from his knees, no more the child. "That's what I need—to get my bearings."

"Sense of proportion," he said. "What's important and what isn't."

She walked to the window as he spoke and now she, too, stood looking out upon the snowy scene.

"Don't tell anyone about me, Dad—"

He was shocked. "How can you think I would?"

"I thought you might say something to Mother."

"You haven't?"

"No. She has enough to worry her."

"Something I don't know?"

"She thinks nobody knows. The doctor told me."

He went cold. "I should have been told at once, Anne."

"She didn't want *you* told, especially, and none of us until after

31

Christmas. That's why the doctor told me. Somebody ought to know, he said."

"She doesn't want me told," he repeated, stupefied. "But the doctor ought not to have listened to her!"

"She wouldn't even let him give her the tests until after Christmas. That's why he told me—in case she didn't feel well meanwhile."

He groaned. "All these doors shut between us!"

She came back to him and put out her hand and he clasped it for comfort. "You've opened one door today, Dad. And one open door helps the rest of us. Now we can communicate."

"But will you?"

"I will—I promise."

She smiled at him, a wise and sad smile. Some of the brightness of youth was already gone from her face.

"You'll be all right," he said. "Not at once, but step by step, a day at a time."

"Yes . . ."

She paused and sniffed. "Dad—the turkey!"

She flew to the oven and he grinned and went away. Out in the hall he called, "Helen, where are you?"

From afar off, from behind a closed door, her voice answered indistinctly.

"She's upstairs," Hal said from the living room.

The tree was up and fastened in its stand and he was pounding a last nail. "She went up to get the tree decorations and she hasn't come down. Maybe she can't find the star for the top. She couldn't remember where she put it."

He did not wait for Hal to finish. Up the stairs he leaped and to her door. It was locked. He tried the handle again.

"Let me in, Helen!"

"Just a minute, dear."

Her voice came faintly through the panels, but in less than a minute she turned the key and opened the door. She did look faint. Her eyes were enormous in her white face.

32

"Darling, what is the matter?" he cried.

He took her in his arms and she clung to him without answer.

"Why did you come up here all by yourself and lock the door?" he demanded.

"I don't want to tell you," she whispered after a time. "I don't want to spoil our Christmas."

"It's a day for telling," he said. "It's a day for trust."

"I'm not well," she faltered. "Something is wrong with me."

He looked down at the beloved face, pressed against his chest. The eyes were closed.

"Why didn't you tell me?"

"I couldn't—you were so far away."

"You went to the doctor by yourself?"

"Yes." The word was a sigh.

"What did he say?"

"The tests aren't complete."

"Am I far away now?"

"No."

"Never again?"

"Never."

"I'm going with you to the doctor tomorrow—and I'm staying with you."

She lifted a face suddenly bright. "Oh, Arnold, will you?"

"And maybe nothing is wrong," he said, "nothing that can't be mended."

"I can believe it possible—now."

She looked up at him, in her eyes a trust renewed. He bent his head and kissed her with a passion deeper than he had known in years. They were close again.

Downstairs Hal was telephoning.

"Hi, kid! Say, I can't get there tonight . . . No, not even late . . . I'm just not coming, see? . . . We're having our tree and everything."

The receiver slammed and he yelled up the stairs. "Dad—Mom—

you two up there! Are you bringing the Christmas stuff down? And don't forget the star!"

They drew apart and smiled. It was impossible not to hope on this Christmas day. That indeed was the whole meaning of the star.

The Beauty

Mrs. OMURA GLANCED at the kitchen clock. The hour was five, but the winter darkness had already fallen upon the city of Tokyo. The children would be home now at any moment, and let it be hoped that Setsu's feet were not wet. Though she was twelve and should know better, she was always in a dream, the way girls were nowadays. In the old days it could not happen that a child left school without her shoes, for she would have taken them off at the door and could not step outside until she had slipped her feet into geta. Now that schools were western in their habits the children wore their shoes indoors and outdoors. There were no distinctions anywhere.

Her son's voice shouted at this moment from the garden gate. "Mama-san!"

"Here I am, Toru!"

He ran in, kicking off his shoes at the door. At least the house was still Japanese. She did not allow shoes in here. She went to the faucet and wet a clean towel in the gush of hot water.

"Come here, Toru."

He stood before her, books hanging in a strap from his right hand while she wiped his face thoroughly with the warm cloth.

"Now your hands. How dirty you are!"

"It's the chalk. Is Father here?"

He asked the same question every day until it had become a dagger in her heart. The boy was growing up and wanted his father.

"You know your father is very busy. He cannot come home just because you are here."

"Where does he go?"

"I have told you."

"The bar. That is where he goes."

"Put away your books. We will eat our supper as soon as Setsu comes."

He went out and she heard him in the next room behind the sliding paper-covered shoji. He was a good child, quiet for his ten years, and too thoughtful. She must speak to her husband tonight.

"Good evening, Mother."

It was Setsu. The tall slender young girl had come silently into the kitchen, her shoes off, and her hair brushed neatly behind her ears.

"You are late, Setsu."

"The traffic was bad. Our bus stopped again and again."

"Worse than usual?"

She asked the question as carelessly as she could, but she glanced sharply at the pretty girl who was her only daughter. Twelve was still to be a child, but Setsu was maturing early. All the girls grew up too soon in this new Tokyo. They went out freely, they saw western films, they imitated American young people. Thus far, however, she had been able to refuse to allow Setsu to go to the rock-and-roll theater. She had gone there herself one day, when Setsu had first begged to go.

"All the girls go," Setsu had pouted.

"I will go," she had said. "I will see."

What she had seen had frightened her. There in a huge theater she had found herself surrounded by thousands of young people—

mostly girls, she had been shocked to see. On the stage the singers, young men, stood behind a microphone and sang, if it could be called singing, the wailing of western music, cowboy music, love songs that made her blush, old as she was. Yet the music was nothing in comparison to the screams and moans that came from the girls. Were they indeed Japanese? She saw that they were, for when the songs ended, first one girl, then twenty and more, rushed to the stage to hang garlands of flowers on the necks of the singers and even to kiss their cheeks. She had covered her eyes with her hands and stolen away.

"No, Setsu," she had said firmly. "Never will I allow you to go to that place."

She was not sure whether Setsu did go, in spite of this command. No mother could be sure of her children in this new Tokyo—or of her husband. She thrust aside the disloyal thought of her husband. "A woman may not be disloyal to her husband even in thought," her mother had taught her.

She looked up from the stove where she was turning the fish in a pan. Setsu was washing her hands. Now she set the bowls on the table and the chopsticks.

"Shall I set a place for Father?" she asked.

"You know he will not be here."

Silence fell between mother and daughter. It was broken again by Setsu.

"I don't see why you let Father go to the bar every evening."

Mrs. Omura paused in her task. She was slicing a raw carrot into flower shapes for the clear soup with which the meal began.

"I let him? I have nothing to do with it. He has always gone to bars."

"Not before the war."

"Before the war it was a geisha house. Nowadays the geisha are the bar girls. You know that."

"Mother, why do you stand it?"

Mrs. Omura put down the knife. "But men must go to bars now that we have no geisha houses. Where else would they go?"

37

"They could stay home."

Mrs. Omura allowed herself a bit of pretended laughter, stifled behind her palm, denying the pain of hearing her daughter speak aloud what she herself had only dared in thought.

"Mother, I wish you wouldn't giggle behind your hand! It is so old-fashioned." Setsu's cry was strangely passionate.

Mrs. Omura's hand dropped. "Your father stay home? He stopped that as soon as you children were born. He couldn't endure the crying and noise. Besides, he does have business."

Setsu was scornful. "Business! In bars? Such business!"

Mrs. Omura took up the knife. She spoke with regained dignity. "I do not allow this manner toward your father. Men go to bars to talk business over a cup of sakè. All big business deals, your father says, are—"

Setsu broke in, "And he comes home at two in the morning and expects you to be waiting for him with smiles and pity. 'My poor one, you are so tired. You have been working for our family all these hours. Here is your tea. I have drawn the hot water for your bath. Sleep late until the children are gone to school—'"

Setsu's imitation of her mother's voice was so perfect that Mrs. Omura was aghast. The child had lain awake to listen!

"You are a very naughty girl," she said severely.

Setsu stamped her foot. "Think of us, if you won't think of yourself! He is our father, isn't he? When do we see him? A few hours, perhaps, on Sunday, or on a holiday. Is that good for Toru? It doesn't matter about me, of course—"

She shrugged and turned away. "I don't know what he looks like any more. I could pass him on the street and not know him."

She left the room but Mrs. Omura called after her. "Setsu, come back!"

The girl came back reluctantly and stood in the half-open shoji.

Mrs. Omura walked toward her shyly. The girl looked a woman —and a stranger.

"What would you do if you were I?"

"I would go to the bar with him," Setsu said firmly.

"I?" Mrs. Omura said faintly. She was aware of appearing absurd as she stood there, knife in one hand and carrot in the other.

"Young women do go to bars," Setsu said. "They go with their husbands. Then the husbands stop going."

"How do you know this?"

"We talk about it at school. Some of the girls have older sisters who are married."

Mrs. Omura was horrified. "Such talk in school!"

"Yes," Setsu said. "Why not? It is only a few years until we are grown up and we will not allow our husbands to go to bars as you do."

Mrs. Omura looked at her daughter's round pretty face. She had not noticed before how firm were the lines of the childish mouth, how direct the gaze of the dark eyes. Girls were different nowadays, very different. She sighed and returned to the kitchen sink.

"Change your clothes and call Toru. We will have supper and then you must both do your homework. I have almost finished your pink dress."

The evening proceeded as usual. They ate in silence and Mrs. Omura cleared away. The children, wearing their home kimono, sat down at the low table with their books. Mrs. Omura sat at the table too with the pink dress she was making for Setsu. The girl was pretty in pink, her eyes and hair so dark. Let it be hoped that Setsu would not want some day to dye her hair in rusty blond streaks as young girls were doing nowadays. Strange fashion, when only a few years ago beauty lay in the darkness of a woman's hair! But everything was strange these days. The bars, for example—she preferred the old geisha houses where women were of one class and wives of another. These bar girls—

At this moment she thought of what Setsu had said. Perhaps the child was right. Why should she not go and see for herself what took place in bars? She had the right, surely, to know how her husband spent his evenings, these long evenings, endless after the children had gone to bed. It seemed, of a sudden, that she could not sit through one more evening waiting for his return, watching the hours pass until midnight and counting two more hours to wait. And as Setsu had said, so sharply true, when at two o'clock, or even half past, he came home at last, she must force a smile, she must bravely lie, she must welcome him tenderly and speak no word to him of her weariness or of the problems of her life in the home. He must be spared everything as men are always spared.

The young girl's words had sunk into her long wounded heart. Perhaps she was old-fashioned. Perhaps there was no reason why she should go on living this stupid life. Thus it came about that when the children were in bed and asleep, she amazed herself by what she did. She went to the closet where her clothes were folded and she took out her one western dress, bought during the Occupation. "You should have one western dress," her husband had said, "to please the Americans." So she had bought a two-piece suit of blue silk, but after the Occupation ended she had not worn it. The skirt was short and revealed her slightly bowed legs. She put it on now and combed her hair freshly, knotting it at the back, and clasped her string of pearls about her neck. After a moment, she even touched her lips with lipstick and looked at herself in the glass. She was neither pretty nor ugly, as such words go, but she looked as she wished to look, a woman of breeding and delicacy in spite of the grotesque costume. Kimono was far more flattering, but it would be conspicuous in a bar. She had once asked her husband if the bar girls wore kimono and he had answered shortly no, they did not.

She let herself out of the garden gate quietly, fastening the padlock since the children were alone. Then she stopped a taxicab.

"The Golden Moon Bar," she said.

It was one of the three best bars in the city and the taxi driver swung his cab into the heart of the night traffic. As usual with cab drivers he talked.

"You go alone, miss?"

"I am meeting my husband there," she said.

She was astonished at the calmness with which she spoke such words.

The man laughed.

"Old Japan is gone," he said, turning abruptly in order to avoid collision with a crowded bus. "Women go to bars with the men. What becomes of the children?"

She did not answer the question. It was none of his business.

He continued his prattle. "Everything is changed. The homes are empty and the offices and bars are full of women. All the women are looking for men. A man can have any woman he wants nowadays, except the old ones. Who wants them anyway? It's a great new world for the men."

He gave a coarse laugh and she shrank into deeper silence. When he perceived that she was not willing to talk he began to sing raucously and she had not the courage to protest. She had never before been alone in a taxicab. After a few minutes he turned sharply to the left and squeezed his way through a long alley. She knew at once when they reached the bar, for three girls in fluffy red dresses stood outside the door, smiling and waving. They crowded to the cab and fell back when they saw a woman.

"She is coming to find her husband," the driver explained. "Look out, you three!"

The girls tittered. Mrs. Omura paid no heed to them or to the man. She was stupefied with fright and could only go doggedly on. She paid off the man and turned to the girls, who stood across the doorway.

"Excuse me," she said. "I have come to meet my husband."

"Who is he?" the tallest girl inquired.

"He is Mr. Omura, vice-president of the Sakura Manufacturing Company."

The girls fell back. "Ah, Mr. Omura—we know him very well. A fine man—"

At the mention of her husband's name they changed. They looked at her with respect, they led her into the entrance hall of the bar and called:

"Mama, here is Mrs. Omura!"

Madame came out at once. She was a pretty woman, perhaps

41

thirty-five, but still slender and vivid. She wore a yellow satin dress of western style, low in the neck, without sleeves, and full-skirted. She put out both hands warmly. "Mrs. Omura," she cried in a hearty voice. "We are so glad to see you. Mr. Omura is having a drink at the bar. He enjoys whiskey very much. We always give him what he likes. Is he expecting you?"

Mrs. Omura did not answer at once. She would have liked to lie, but she was not accustomed to doing so, and she was afraid she might blush and betray herself. She could only tell the truth.

"He does not expect me. I just—I just came."

Madame understood. "Ah yes. We welcome ladies, too. Would you like to sit in the other room and have a quiet drink before you go into the main bar?"

"I would like that very much," Mrs. Omura faltered. Now that she was here she was glad to delay the meeting with her husband. She followed Madame into a small room, quite empty, where there were only a table and two chairs.

"Sit down," Madame said cheerfully. "I will have one of our girls bring you something nice to drink, something sweet, and she will keep you company for a while. I think I have just the girl for you—our very best."

She smiled brightly and bustled away, her full skirt swinging. Mrs. Omura sat motionless and waiting. She had not long to wait. In less than five minutes a beautiful woman came in. That was what Mrs. Omura noticed instantly—she was a beauty. Then she saw that she was not a young woman—not a young girl, that is. She was perhaps twenty-eight. She wore a red western dress, but her hair was long and smoothly coifed into a high knot instead of cut short and brushed into every which way. She set down on the table a tray bearing two tall glasses. Then she bowed deeply. Mrs. Omura rose and bowed only slightly less deeply and they sat down. The beauty began the conversation.

"Mrs. Omura?"

"I am she."

"Our Mama asked me to sit with you."

42

"Thank you."

"When you are ready, I will ask Mr. Omura to join us. Or you can join him at the bar."

"Are there other ladies at the bar? Like me, I mean."

The beauty smiled. She had a pale oval face in the classic style, and her mouth was small and exquisitely shaped. When her lips parted, her teeth showed even and white.

"Not quite like you, but the young wives sometimes come with their husbands. It is a new custom."

"Why do they come?" Mrs. Omura asked.

She was surprised to find that she was drawn to this woman. This was a warm beauty, a friend by intention, and not an enemy, as she had supposed all women in bars must be.

The beauty laughed, softly. "Ask yourself why you have come."

Mrs. Omura was surprised to discover at this moment that she wanted to weep.

"You—you cannot imagine," she stammered, "what it is to sit alone evening after evening, year after year, to wait for two o'clock, when he comes home. And then to be compelled to smile and pretend to welcome him, never asking a question, for fear he will be angry and not come home at all!"

The beauty nodded. "I know. Other wives have told me. And yet count yourself fortunate. Mr. Omura never makes an assignation. He comes here, he drinks and tells a few jokes, he talks to businessmen now and then. That is all."

At this point the beauty seemed somewhat embarrassed and invited Mrs. Omura, by a graceful gesture of her right hand, to drink a sip of wine. They drank and the beauty continued.

"Of course Mr. Omura has a favorite and it is understood that she sits by him and keeps his glass full and watches that he does not become drunk. But that is all. He never takes her to an hotel."

"An hotel?"

The beauty spoke with dignity. "This is a very decent bar, Mrs. Omura. Mama never allows assignations to take place here. Such

43

arrangements are made afterhours and in some hotel. We always close at two. Mama is very strict."

Mrs. Omura listened, gazing at the beautiful face.

"It is not fair," she said at last. "It is not at all fair."

"What is not fair, Mrs. Omura?"

"That women like you—"

"Women like me?"

"So beautiful—"

"Can I help that? You are quite pretty yourself."

"I have no chance—in comparison to you."

"Mrs. Omura, I promise you—"

"No, don't promise. I am only asking you—a question."

"Yes?"

"What shall I do?"

And then before she could stop herself it all came pouring out, the sadness, the wounded love, repressed by long habit and ancient tradition. The soft face, the tender dark eyes, the gentle hands, these attributes of the beauty drew it out from her, and she sobbed as she talked.

"How can women like you—you should think of us, you women— It's we who have all the weariness—the housekeeping—bearing the children— We are like servants, but we are not servants. We are women and we long for our husbands. But you steal him from me. You take his best—his thoughts—his talk—his laughter. He comes home silent, empty. I am even more lonely when he comes home."

The beautiful face changed from surprise to defense, to pain. The rose lips trembled, tears hung on the long dark lashes, the delicate hands fluttered and clasped themselves together under the soft chin. Above these hands the beauty looked at the sobbing wife as though she had never before seen a woman weep.

"I didn't think—Mrs. Omura, it has not occurred to me to imagine— You see, dear Mrs. Omura, I hate him!"

Mrs. Omura wiped her eyes and swallowed a sob. "How can you hate him?" she demanded indignantly. "He is good."

"He is a man," the beauty said. *"I hate all men."*

Mrs. Omura stared into the dark eyes. "You hate *men?*"

The beauty nodded. Her hands fell to her lap and lay there like loosely petaled flowers. "There are—so many of them and they are all the same. They are quite stupid. Each thinks himself—irresistible."

Mrs. Omura began to feel angry with the beauty. "It is you who make him believe this," she retorted. For her there was only one man, Mr. Omura.

The beauty drew a fan from her sleeve and fanned herself. "Can he not see that we behave the same toward any man who pays us? Why does he think it is only for him? I am so tired of them all. Do you know how many years I have been in this bar? Twelve years! Will you believe that I was only sixteen when I first came here? But it is true. Twelve years of flattering and coaxing and pretending and listening to stupid jokes! You have known only one man. I have known hundreds. There is not a straw's difference between them—vain, conceited, selfish, stupid—"

Mrs. Omura interrupted. "It is because you have no children."

The beauty shrugged her shoulders. "For this one thing I give thanks."

She folded the fan and put it in her sleeve again. She leaned her elbows on the table and spoke earnestly, her face close to Mrs. Omura's. "If I were free, as you are, I would have a little shop—a dress shop. I would employ six girls, four to sew the dresses I design, two to tend the shop. I would never receive a man—never!"

"Why don't you do what you want to do?" Mrs. Omura asked. She could feel anger rising hot under her breastbone. "Why do you make women like me miserable? Have your dress shop—leave my husband alone! We need him, the children and I. As a matter of fact—"

Here she felt suddenly shy. She had never used the word "love." There are no such words as "I love you," in Japanese but she knew them from English, because she had been to American motion pictures. There also she had heard such words as "sweetheart" and "darling," for which also there are no words in Japanese. Love for a husband, her mother had taught her, was too deep to be spoken. It can only be shown through tender and unselfish actions.

"As a matter of fact," she went on bravely, "we—love him."

The beauty sighed. She seemed not to notice Mrs. Omura's emotion. "I should do what you say, Mrs. Omura, but the truth is—I am very lazy. After all these years I have learned to sleep late in the day. When I have eaten a little food, my maid bathes me and dresses me. Then I have nothing to do except to look—as I am—and pretend that I admire a man. It is an easy way to earn a living. It is too late now for me to change."

"So because you are lazy," Mrs. Omura said bitterly, "I am to spend my evenings alone and my children without a father."

The beauty rose and began to walk back and forth as gracefully as a lazy cat. She smoothed her soft dark hair away from her cheeks, she bit her lip, she shrugged, smiled and sighed again. Then she sat down across the room from Mrs. Omura.

"Why don't you have the dress shop? You rise early every day. Your children go to school, you are alone in the evening."

"I don't want a dress shop," Mrs. Omura said.

"Then something else," the beauty urged. "Let him see that you have your own life, and therefore whether he comes home is of no importance."

"And compel him to turn more than ever to you? No, thank you! At least I am not stupid."

With this Mrs. Omura rose indignantly and left the room and the bar. In the alleyway she turned once to look back, uncertain whether she should let Mr. Omura know. The beauty was standing in the doorway, gazing wistfully toward her. When she saw Mrs. Omura turn she smiled and waved, but Mrs. Omura did not wave back or smile. Instead she went into the street, summoned a cab, and sat silent in the back seat. Two sentences remained clearly in her mind, one that the beauty hated all men, and the second that she, Mrs. Omura, could live a life of her own.

This life became so quickly clear to her, so possible, that when

Mr. Omura entered the house at a quarter past two, she met him with a real smile.

"The tea is fresh," she said. "You look tired. You should not have to do business at night as well as in the day. You are so faithful to your conscience."

He groaned mildly and sat down before the low table while she poured tea for him and went on talking.

"I have not been a good wife to you. I enjoy myself here at home when I should be working at something to earn money so you need not go to bars."

"What could you do?" he inquired without interest.

"I have been thinking of a dress shop," she said. She knelt on the mat across the table from him.

"A dress shop," he repeated. "Where would you get the capital? It is an absurd idea, the sort of thing a bar girl does with her savings when she grows old. But you have no savings."

"True," she said thoughtfully. "I have no savings. I am not so fortunate as a bar girl."

He raised his eyebrows. "What does that mean?"

"Nothing," she said, "nothing at all."

The evening proceeded as usual. He yawned and went to bed and she put away the teapot and bowls and went to bed, also.

Nevertheless the idea persisted that she could have a life of her own, although nothing changed. Mr. Omura continued to go to the bar and she continued to spend her evenings in solitude after the children were in bed. After about two months once more she sought out the beauty. This time she did not feel at all strange about going to the bar. She could even refuse to increase the tip to the cab driver and she entered the bar with assurance. "If you please," she said to the girls fluttering on the doorstep. This time Madame did not appear, and the beauty came immediately.

"Mrs. Omura," she said warmly. "I am so happy. You have come on a good day. Do you know how you helped me? After you left I began to think how shameful that I am so lazy while you slave in your household, and your husband always here in the evenings

47

and leaving you alone. The result is I have taken my savings and I have bought a dress shop. It is small, only one room for the shop and behind it a smaller room for me to live in. Now I need someone to help me. Will you be that one? I am afraid to begin alone."

Mrs. Omura was startled. She sat down at the table in the same room where she had sat before and considered.

"I cannot leave my house," she said at last.

"While Mr. Omura comes to the bar, you could come to my shop," the beauty suggested.

She looked so touchingly helpless, so exquisitely beautiful, that Mrs. Omura was moved. Seeing this, the beauty put out her little hand and took Mrs. Omura's hand. "It would only be for a short while, until I am accustomed to being alone. Then one by one I can find my six girls, as the business grows. It is not forever. Nothing is forever."

"Have you no mother?" Mrs. Omura inquired. "No older sister or friend?"

"None," the beauty said sadly. "They are far away in Hokkaido. I have lost them. They are only farm people and they sold me in a hungry winter. I do not belong to them now."

A long look passed between the two women. Mrs. Omura was the one to speak.

"Then I will help you."

In this way, simply and swiftly, Mrs. Omura's life changed. For a few weeks and then into months she went every evening to the dress shop. The beauty had chosen the site well. The shop was on the edge of the Ginza, where many people came and went. The beauty herself was a good saleswoman. She had only to linger in the doorway or to be busy at the window to have people stop to watch what she was doing. Men stopped because she was so beautiful and women stopped to see what the men were looking at. Then, forgetting the men, they went into the shop to buy the dresses. The beauty was clever and the dresses were unusual and very soon the shop was doing so well that the first two girls were employed, one to sew and one to serve.

Meanwhile Mrs. Omura and the beauty had become like sisters, elder and younger. For a while Mr. Omura was ignorant and innocent. One evening, however, he did not go to the bar. Mrs. Omura was first surprised and then impatient. She was especially eager to get to the shop. Some new fashion books had come in from America and she had planned to study them this evening with the beauty. There Mr. Omura sat, smoking a cigar while he read the newspaper.

"Are you not going to the bar?" Mrs. Omura inquired at last.

"No," Mr. Omura said.

"It there something wrong?" she asked.

He put down the paper. "Can I not spend the evening quietly in my own house?"

"Certainly," she said, alarmed at his frown. "But it is so unusual."

To this he said nothing. He was reading his paper again, the smoke drifting slowly in two streams from his nostrils. She glanced at the clock. She was half an hour late, and she could not telephone, for the instrument was on the small table at Mr. Omura's elbow. She grew desperate and brave.

"Since you are at home," she said, "may I go out?"

He looked over top of the paper. "Where?"

"To see a friend."

He stared at her. "The first evening I am at home you go out?"

"When you are not here, I must stay with the children. Now that you are here—"

"Go on," he said shortly, "go on—go on. Leave me to solitude. I will be the nursemaid. Suit yourself first."

She knew that he was asking for pity and her heart hardened against him. How many evenings through the years had she not sat here alone?

"Thank you," she said and went away.

In the shop she confided the whole conversation to the beauty, who listened with profound interest. Observing the enchanting face, it now occurred to Mrs. Omura why Mr. Omura no longer went to the bar.

"It is because you are not there," she said. She felt guilty as she

49

spoke. Here she was, enjoying the company of the woman whom perhaps her husband loved.

"Hush," the beauty said. "I never want to see a man again. I need not lie, I need not tell him how wonderful he is—"

Mrs. Omura interrupted. "In some ways he is wonderful."

The beauty laughed. "How funny you are! But let us waste no more time talking about men. Let us look at the new fashions from America."

The rest of the evening they spent in delightful discussion of American women and how they looked, and from the pictures the beauty designed several dresses suited to the Japanese female figure, combining the daring of the American and the subtlety of the Japanese. "To reveal innocently," the beauty said, "without seeming to reveal—"

Mrs. Omura received these words of wisdom gratefully, "I learn so much from you," she told the beauty.

The two women exchanged a look of sisterly affection and continued their work. It was two o'clock before Mrs. Omura reached home. She had hoped that the house would be dark, but no, the light was still burning in the living room. When she entered, Mr. Omura was waiting for her without a smile and certainly without a pot of hot tea. He sat on his folded legs beside the low table in the middle of the room, and he looked at her with accusing eyes.

"While you have been gone," he announced with majesty, "your son Toru has nearly died of a stomach-ache. He says the fish was not fresh."

She gasped and fled into the next room. Toru lay asleep on the tatami mat, his hand on his cheek. She felt his forehead. It was cool, but at her touch he opened his eyes.

"Does your stomach ache?" she asked anxiously.

"It did," he said, "but my father made me some hot ginseng tea and I am well."

"Oh, what a good father," she murmured.

The boy smiled and his eyes closed.

Mrs. Omura went back into the living room. "It was very good of you to make the ginseng tea— How did you know to make it?"

"I am not a fool," Mr. Omura said. He rose with a loud sigh. "But I am exhausted with waiting for you."

"You should not have waited," she said, apologetically.

"Of course I should," he declared. "I was anxious about you at this time of night—a woman still young and good-looking." He did not look at her as he spoke these astounding words. He rearranged the folds of his kimono and looked at her sidewise.

Mrs. Omura stared at him. She did not know what to say. In all the years of their marriage he had never praised her looks or her behavior and she yearned now to thank him, to speak a few words, perhaps even of love. But there are still no such words in Japanese, and if she said said "I love you" in English he would be startled and suspicious. Where could she have learned such English words? Impulsively she decided to tell him the truth.

"You remember the dress shop?"

He was sliding back the shoji and he paused, he turned and looked at her. "What dress shop?"

"You said I had no capital for a dress shop."

"Have you capital?"

She shook her head and looked back at him bravely.

"So there is no dress shop," he said.

"Yes, there is."

He returned to face her across the table. "How can you be at a dress shop until two o'clock in the morning?"

"I was designing dresses—with my business partner."

"Business partner!" He was suddenly furious. He strode to her side and seized her by the arm. "Who is the man?"

She stared at him, astounded.

"What man?" she asked.

"Your business partner!"

He glared into her wide eyes and seizing her by both arms he shook her. "I might have known! No woman is to be trusted. But you, my wife—coming home at two in the morning—"

She wrenched herself free of his arms. A lifetime of anger rushed

51

through her memory. Now was the moment for revenge. Now she could pour it all out on him like acid. You, you who came home year after year at two o'clock in the morning, you who went to geisha houses as soon as we were married and then to bars, always to bars, giving your time, your thought, to other women. It was all there to be said, but she did not speak it. Who was there to love him if she did not—he, poor man, who had wasted so many evenings of his life at a bar where no one loved him!

"Dear sir," she said softly and in deep pity. "Dear sir, my business partner is a woman. She had the capital."

"How could a woman have capital?" Mr. Omura demanded.

"She used to be a bar girl," Mrs. Omura said simply.

Husband and wife looked at each other, she with the pity, he with a dawning comprehension.

"How did you two meet?" he demanded.

"I was so lonely in the evenings. I missed you. One evening I went to—to find you."

"You went to the bar?" Mr. Omura asked, unbelieving.

"Yes."

"I never saw you."

"No, but a beautiful woman came to entertain me."

"What did she say?"

"She said she wanted to start a dress shop."

"Why?"

"Because she hates all men."

Mr. Omura seemed suddenly to collapse. He sat down on the table and held his head in his hands. "So that is why she went away."

"Yes."

"Of course I knew she did not care for—for any of us. None of them do."

"Why did you keep going there, year after year?"

"It was pleasant," he muttered. "Very pleasant. So pleasant to be surrounded by pretty women, hearing only pleasant things—a man can almost believe himself to be what he knows he is not—"

Too much was being said and Mrs. Omura knew it. A wife must not allow her husband to humiliate himself before her. She knelt beside him.

"I cannot believe that she did not love you. To me it is impossible that any woman could be near you, night after night, and not—love you."

His hands dropped away from his face. "You think so?"

"Impossible," she repeated.

He coughed, he got up, he walked around the table and stopped to look down at her. She continued to kneel before him as she had been taught that a wife should kneel before her husband. When he did not speak, however, she lifted her head to look up at him, and suddenly they both smiled. For a moment they looked at each other in silence. Then he spoke.

"From now on you need not kneel in my presence. In these modern times it is no longer the fashion."

And putting out his hands he took hers and lifted her to her feet.

Enchantment

THE TRAIN WAS CROWDED and he was late. At the first hasty glance up and down the car he thought there was no seat left. Then midway he saw a woman sitting alone. He hesitated, disliking by instinct to sit beside a strange woman. But at the end of one of his busiest days he did not feel he could stand up for an hour. The train jerked and pulled forward. He was the last passenger and this was the last seat. He had already been through three cars. He stood swaying a little, his briefcase heavy in his hand, and thought of the easy days when he stepped out of his office building into a quiet air-conditioned car. Poor Dixon, the chauffeur, lay dead somewhere in a jungle, probably—dead, anyway. He had been a good driver and a restful sort of fellow, young and serious and silent.

He suddenly felt quite too tired to stand and he made his way down the aisle. "Is this seat taken?" he asked the woman without looking at her.

"No, it isn't," she answered in a clear voice.

He lifted his briefcase and tried to find room for it on the rack. But packages crowded it and he was uncertain about its safety.

Leaning over her, he looked down. She was looking up, and their eyes met. He felt a shock of surprise. She was absolutely beautiful. "I'm afraid this isn't safe," he stammered.

"I am sure it isn't," she said with decision.

He lifted the briefcase from the rack, sat down, and put it between his knees.

He had no intention of speaking to her. He was tired and anxious to get home where Ruth was waiting for him. His home in these war-harassed days remained his refuge. He leaned back and closed his eyes and thought of it and of her. Together, Ruth and home, made the background of his life—no, the earth in which were his roots. He could endure the crass annoyances of his overcrowded days because he knew that outside the city, set far back from the tree-shaded streets of Lynnton, his own house stood in inviolable quiet, filled with beauty and composure. He and Ruth were still young. They had married young and had had their two children almost at once, the two boys who were now across the sea, one in Europe, one in the Pacific. He had the evening paper in his briefcase but he never read it until after dinner, when he and Ruth had the evening together. Fortified by her presence, he could face the news.

Thinking of her and of his home, he became aware of some influence playing upon his face as though it were a strong light and involuntarily he opened his eyes. The woman was looking at him. She was fantastically beautiful. Living happily with Ruth all these years, he had simply not thought of how women looked. But without emotion he now saw the soft full oval of this woman's face and her big black eyes, fringed and shaded by her long lashes. Her hair was gently disheveled about her face, and she wore a wide black hat put on carelessly. Her black coat she held about her shoulders, without slipping her arms in the sleeves.

"Will you help me?" she asked in a whisper.

He sat up surprised. He had been riding back and forth to Lynnton on this train ever since the war began and had spoken to no one and been spoken to by no one, unless by a chance man acquaintance. He would have distrusted this woman at once except that she looked so honestly into his eyes.

"Where do you get off?" she urged, leaning to him. She drooped her head so that the big hat screened her face from everyone except him.

He was wary about telling her. Perhaps she knew him for Roger Kentwell, of Kentwell, Bates, Incorporated, manufacturers of processed metals.

"What can I do for you?" he asked evasively.

"Just let me walk beside you, wherever you get off," she said softly. "As soon as we leave the station I shall not need you. It is only to get off the train."

He was the last man possible to be involved in anything. He felt his hair bristle slightly. "You had better tell me a little more."

She broke in. "You can simply say that you have no idea who I am—even that you did not notice me."

He smiled. "That would be rather difficult for anyone to believe," he said and then cursed himself for leading her on. For now her face softened and warmed.

"That's a very nice thing to say," she exclaimed. "I believe you are a kind man."

He wished then to retire again into silence, but he had made it impossible. He said curtly, to cut off her warmth, "Of course, if it will help you. My wife usually meets me in the car on the other side of the station."

"Oh, thank you," she said, and subsided into silence.

He glanced at her unwillingly once or twice after that. She sat motionless, her lovely profile outlined against the black brim of her hat, and her cream-white hands folded against the black stuff of her coat. He resisted the creeping curiosity that stirred in him. He looked away, and then was unable to keep from looking at her again, merely because he had never seen until now, he told himself, a really beautiful woman. Not that he cared for such beauty, he thought loyally. He of all men knew that beauty was the last essential to happiness between man and woman. Ruth was not beautiful.

He closed his eyes again and dreamed of her, half smiling. Ruth was so utterly honest, even about herself. She had never made any effort to hide her plainness. She did not laugh at herself for it, she seemed simply not to care. And she was so rich in all other ways that he had not missed beauty in her face.

The train clattered into Lynnton and he leaped to his feet. He was intensely conscious of the woman, but he made his usual dash down the aisle. The car had run beyond the platform and he had to jump to the cinder path. He had taken two long strides when he heard her calling him.

"Please—your hand!"

He turned and saw her swaying on the step. The train was already beginning to move. He dropped his briefcase. Involuntarily he put up his arms and she jumped into them. For an instant he felt her soft body and smelled a perfume. She moved away from him quickly and glanced around them.

"Nobody else got off?" she asked.

"No," he said shortly. He picked up his briefcase and began to walk quickly toward the platform, but she followed him easily.

They did not speak. She walked with her head up and her shoulders straight. Now that the light of late afternoon fell upon her he saw that she was young but not a girl. She was perhaps twenty-five or six. One hand was bare and he saw a twisted plain gold ring upon her finger, not a wedding ring. He felt again the influence of her intense beauty. A pretty woman, merely pretty, might claim her prettiness, but when a woman was as beautiful as this one, it was of her beauty one thought, not of her. Her beauty was as much her chance possession as her finding a diamond or her possession of an inherited estate.

Nevertheless he was uncomfortable when he saw Ruth walking down the platform toward them. Usually she waited in the car. He saw a look of amazement upon her face as she came near to him but he paid no heed to this. He bent and kissed her fondly as he always did. "Well, dearest," he said in his usual greeting.

"It was cold waiting in the car," she said, "and I've been walking up and down to keep warm. Your train was a few minutes late."

"I nearly missed it at that," he said.

He paid no attention to the woman. She fell back a step but still she was close enough so that to a stranger she might seem to be with them.

Ruth looked at her.

They walked the length of the platform and through the station. Two or three people they knew were there waiting for the next train into town. They called out greetings and stared at the woman. But Roger walked on, oblivious, Ruth at his left, the woman at his right. Outside the door on the other side, the woman turned warmly to him.

"Thank you," she said, in her rich voice, "I will never forget you." He felt a strange reluctance to let her go. "Are you sure you'll be all right?"

She laughed softly. "Oh yes—the man I'm afraid of isn't here—and the other one is."

"Your husband?"

"The one I'm afraid of is my husband." She put out her hand and took his and pressed it in both of hers, and stepped into a waiting car. Was it a waiting car? Roger stood staring after it. The driver was young and in love. It was quite evident that he was in love with the beautiful woman. He was kissing her hand, palm up.

"Well?" Ruth said lightly.

"I haven't the faintest idea who she is," he replied. "I took the only seat in the car and it happened to be beside her. Then she asked me where I was getting off and if she could get off with me. That's all."

"She was terribly pretty, wasn't she!" Ruth said pleasantly.

They got into the car and she took the wheel as she often did when he was tired.

"I suppose so," he said vaguely.

"Certainly so," Ruth said. "I always notice a really beautiful woman." She was guiding the car skillfully across a sharp turn and over the tracks into the main street. "I suppose, because I am so ugly."

She said this casually, lightly, but he knew her too well. His ears caught the undertone of pain. "You are not ugly," he said fondly. "You are the dearest woman in the world and the only one I have ever thought of."

She smiled. He saw her plain profile, and the smooth sweep of her straight ash-gray hair. She had never curled her hair, had never indeed made any pretenses. She had carried her plainness with a sort of pride. Now he perceived that this pride might also hide pain. She did care!

"You believe me when I say I don't know that woman?" he asked sharply.

"Of course, Roger," she replied calmly.

The car was running smoothly along the street. She began talking in her soothing pleasant fashion. "I found blue closed gentians down by the woods. Do you remember we found them three years ago and then not since? It was as though someone dropped them by accident that one year. But they have come back. I picked a big bunch of them and put them on the hall table—you'll see."

"Good," he murmured. The restfulness of her presence relaxed him. After the crises of the day, the decisions that he had had to make that might affect the very war itself, to hear of blue closed gentians was like music. She never met him with trouble but always with something good and pleasant. She made his whole life pleasant. That was a lovely word and it described her. Pleasant Ruth!

They were driving in the gate now and up their own lane. The house was softly lit for his homecoming and the big setter dog clattered down the front steps and stood waiting for him. Long ago Ruth had trained the dog to carry his briefcase and now she whined.

"All right, Trixie," he said and gave the dog his briefcase. She carried it proudly to the doorstep and pushed the door open and went in and laid it on the low settle. Ruth laughed and he laughed, too. Her laughter was always delicious, low and hearty and real.

He shut the door behind him and smelled the clean fragrance of his house. "God, I'm glad to get home," he said. "I've never had a harder day. The gentians—lovely! What smells so good?"

"I was lucky enough to find roast beef," she said cheerfully. She helped him take off his top coat and hung it up for him in the closet. "Dinner when you want it, dear heart," she said gently. He climbed the stairs, every muscle and nerve letting down its tautness. He was able to do all he did simply because of Ruth, he thought. He took his time, bathed, and put on his lounging suit, and went downstairs, content to the heart of him. He depended on her and he knew he could always depend on her. What if he had been husband to the beautiful woman—the husband whom she feared because another man was in love with her! For a moment he pitied her. Then he congratulated himself. Ruth could never love another man.

He smiled as he entered the living room, his slippered feet silent upon the deep rugs. Then he saw Ruth's face in the mirror opposite the door and the smile was gone. She was standing there, staring at herself and with fright and repulsion, as though she saw a stranger.

"Ruth!" he cried sharply.

He saw her face change before his eyes, the calm face he had always thought was her own. She was smiling. But he could not accept what he had seen. He stood looking at her gravely.

"Now," he said, "what were you thinking?"

They had always been honest with one another and she was honest now. "Simply, that I am so ugly," she admitted. She spoke cheerfully enough and she put her hand into his arm and drew him to the dining room. "It's nothing new," she went on as they sat down.

The table was set as perfectly as ever, and the soup was served by the maid who had taken the butler's place when he went to war. Across the table the candlelight shone on Ruth's face, and did not spare her. He had held her so dear for all these years that he had not even seen her face separate from his love. Now when she called

60

herself ugly it separated her face and he saw with a shock that she was ugly. The knowledge crept into his eyes and she saw that and she looked down and began to eat her soup quickly. Her hand holding the spoon trembled.

He was embarrassed to the point of absurdity and he laughed. "Why, Ruth, what is the matter with you?"

"I suppose a woman always wants to be beautiful for the man she loves," she said, not looking up.

"But all these years we've been together," he urged. "We are so happy."

Her lips quivered. "It's ridiculous of me, but I'd trade them all, for this moment, just to hear you protest that I am really—quite beautiful."

"Doesn't it mean the same thing when I say I love your face, every line of it?"

She looked up quickly and down again. "Not quite," she said.

The honesty between them had been so absolute all these years that he could not now say what he wished he could, that she was quite beautiful. In some curious way the beautiful woman they had both seen had set a standard of beauty between them, and even had he been able to lie she would not have been deceived.

He did not know what to make of the predicament that had risen between them and out of nothing. The peace which had seemed so stable a part of his home was shattered and Ruth was a stranger. As a stranger he looked at her again, and saw a tall angular woman, middle-aged, whose chin receded slightly, and whose eyes were pale under her ash-gray hair. He could not bear to see her thus and his appetite was suddenly gone.

"I don't know what to say or do," he stammered. "I feel upset— we've never quarreled, Ruth."

"There is no reason to quarrel now," she said. "Nothing is changed. I've always looked like this."

"But you haven't," he said half childishly. "You look—quite different. I've never seen you look the way you do now."

"Perhaps you see me now as I really am," she said in her quiet voice.

The maid came in and took away the soup plates and served the roast beef and a salad and hot bread. Then she went out.

"Let's begin again," he said. "What made you feel like this? Just seeing that woman?"

"It was the woman who changed you, not me," she said. "I tell you, I've always been like this."

"You mean—" It was impossible to go on and say, "You've alway suffered because of your looks?"

"Always," she said as though he had gone on.

"Haven't you been happy with me?" he asked, putting down his knife and fork.

"With you, entirely. With myself, no."

She made an effort, visible to him, and went on. "Once Stuart said to me, when he was only five years old, 'Why aren't you pretty like other mamas?'"

He longed to comfort her. "You know how children are."

"Terribly truthful," she said ruthlessly.

He tried to eat again, unable to cry out his denial.

In a few minutes, both silent, she touched the bell for the fruit ice, and they ate it. Then he burst out at her.

"Look here, Ruth, I don't know what all this is about. You've never behaved like this before. I've heard other men talk about the trouble their wives gave them and I've always thanked heaven you weren't like any other woman. Now if you're jealous of a woman I never saw before, that I'm never going to see again, whom I don't want to see again— Good God, I suppose I'm surrounded by pretty women in the office—I don't know—I never look at them—but I've always been thankful for the peace in my home—"

She rose, half smiling, and leaned on the back of her chair. "Give me five minutes alone," she said.

"But if you're suffering something inside yourself—"

"Just five minutes," she begged, "and then we'll have coffee in

62

the living room, shall we? The fire is laid ready just to touch with a match."

She walked upstairs to her own room and locked the door. She went to the window and threw it open and breathed in the cold night air until her blood ran through her veins hotly. Then she closed the window and went to her dressing table and turned on all the lights and let them shine down on her.

"You fool," she said in her calm voice, "you unutterable fool! After all these years, to forget!"

She sat steadily staring at herself, holding her body still, her hands folded on her lap. When she was twelve years old she had acknowledged herself for what she was. She saw now in the mirror that little twelve-year-old girl, in the first intimation of her womanhood.

Nobody will love me, that child had thought. In the terror of lovelessness, the child had begun to weep soundlessly. But I must be loved—somebody must love me!

For three years the child had walked in lonely wretchedness and then she had grown fond of a teacher, a middle-aged plain woman.

"I love Miss Forbes," she had told herself one day. "Why do I love her when she is almost as ugly as I am? But she's so *pleasant!*"

The word had been her beacon. Love came sometimes for pleasantness. What struggle then in the soul of the fifteen-year-old girl! The rebellions of adolescence were crushed down, her quick temper was ruthlessly subdued, her natural eagerness trained. She learned never to allow herself the luxury of contradicting anybody. She taught herself to watch for the comfort of others in a sort of supreme selfishness, that they might learn to depend upon her for that comfort. She cultivated the grace of silence and listening.

And then when she was twenty-four, Roger had fallen in love with her, not quickly nor passionately, but slowly, half unwillingly. She had courted him with exquisite skill, never pursuing, always gently making herself indispensable to him. Not once had she reproached him for anything, even when in the first summer she had known him, he had turned away from her for a while to dally with a pretty cousin who had come to visit them. But Sally had been spoiled and willful, and she had always been there, a foil for Sally's tempers. He had returned to her in a huff of relief and asked her to marry him and she had accepted him and they had been married almost at once. And ever since then she had done nothing but build around him the enchantment of her pleasantness.

"You fool," she said to her face in the glass.

The face stared back at her in all its plainness. "You'll spoil everything yet," she said to it severely. "How I hate you!" she said after a moment. Then she sighed. "But I have to live with you."

Yes, there it was, the old inescapable fact of her life. And if she lost her enchantment, he would see her as she was. He nearly did tonight, she thought. She was not in the least jealous of the woman on the train—it was simply that she had been off her guard by seeing one so beautiful. She had forgotten what a perfectly beautiful woman could be and she had been thrown back into the old darkness of her girlhood.

The five minutes were gone. He would be coming upstairs in another few minutes to find her. She touched her lips with her handkerchief, she took off the pale green dress she wore and put on instead one of dull red velvet. It dealt tenderly with her height and her angles. She brushed back her hair freshly. Long ago she had decided never to use rouge or lipstick. Why call attention to her features?

She went downstairs quietly, her step firm and soft, and she entered the living room. He was by the fire waiting and she was frightened by his look. How nearly, how nearly the enchantment had broken!

She laughed, "You know? I think it was that green dress! I don't think I'll ever wear it again. I never liked it."

A look of relief passed over his face like a soothing hand and wiped away the tension. "Silly," he said. "Come and pour my coffee!"

With a Delicate Air

"And i say Setsue spoils him," Aline said firmly.

She sat at her dressing table, trying the effect of her gold earrings with her new black frock. Above her own handsome reflection she saw her husband's, no less handsome, she secretly conceded. The two of them together were a stunning combination. People had said so on their wedding day, and they still said so, although Ballard, their dear and only child, was now twenty-five years old and a married man. He had brought back a wife from Japan.

She decided against gold earrings and reached for her pearls. White with black was still the best, especially since her hair had silvered so nicely.

"Stephen, why don't you answer?" she said rather sharply.

He was tying his black tie, his chin outthrust. "I was thinking what to say." He gave the ends of his tie a sharp pull and then stood looking down at her in the mirror.

"Well?" she demanded. "Don't you agree with me?"

"No," he said, "no, I don't. I know what you mean. But I don't agree with you. . . . It's a different technique, that's all."

She lifted her clear blue gaze to meet his. It was ridiculous to

65

recognize again how much they looked like each other, especially now that they both had white hair above faces still young.

"Technique," she repeated blankly.

He laughed. "Don't be so naïve, woman! You all have techniques!"

"Stephen, you're repulsive!"

"Not more than I can help," he said. He put his hands on her shoulders. Still very pretty shoulders!

She shivered slightly. "Why are your hands always cold?"

"Sign of a warm heart." He took his hands away.

Instinctively she evaded talk. "We'll be late."

She rose, he took her fur cape from the chair where she had put it down, and held it for her.

"You look beautiful," he said. "Beautiful and stately."

"Thank you, dear," she said. "You aren't bad yourself, you know."

He smiled at her, and she turned her cheek. "I'm all made up."

"I know," he said and kissed her cheek. "You don't need to tell me. I know you better than you think."

She did not reply to this. They were really late. She swept into the hall, her furs wrapped about her. At the head of the stairs Setsue stood waiting, very pretty in her Japanese kimono. The kimono was a sign that she and Ballard were spending the evening at home. She smiled and gave the little involuntary bow which was her greeting, even though she had seen her husband's parents only a few minutes before.

"Please be careful," she said in her high soft voice.

Stephen laughed. "What do you think we are going to do?" he inquired playfully. "Throw ourselves down the stairs?"

"Mother's dress is long," Setsue said with touching anxiety. "So high stairs," she added.

She stepped back, waited for them to proceed and followed, three steps behind.

"You don't have to see us out, Setsue." Aline said. "We are quite capable."

"Oh, please," Setsue breathed. "It is my duty."

66

At the sound of their voices in the hall Ballard came from the living room, comfortable in old clothes and slippers. "You'll have to let her do it, Mother," he said cheerfully. "She's relentless. She enjoys it, you know."

Setsue laughed and hid her laughter behind her wide pink silk sleeve.

"What are you laughing at, pint-size?" Ballard inquired, taking his pipe out of his mouth.

"You," Setsue said.

"Why?"

"Because you are laughing at me."

"You see how silly she is, Mother," Ballard said fondly.

They were both laughing at Setsue now, Stephen and Ballard, and over her sleeve she looked from one to the other, her great eyes warm with adoration. Suddenly she was serious.

"Ballard, your father's coat on top," she exclaimed. "Quickly, to help him!"

She was pattering toward the closet, reaching for the coat. "Here, here," Stephen said above her head. "I'm not used to being waited on."

"No, no," she said. "Let me." Standing tiptoe she tugged in silence, she smoothed his collar, as unconscious as an eager helpful child of the amusement of the two men.

"I am not amused," Aline said suddenly, "and we are late." She went down the front steps, Stephen behind her, and settled herself in the car.

"I still insist that she spoils Ballard," she declared. "He doesn't even pick up his newspapers—just throws them on the floor—"

"That's not too serious," Stephen said, peering into the darkness. The car started with a jerk and he turned into the street.

"It's symbolic," she retorted.

"I still say it's part of her technique," he said, chuckling.

"If you see through it," she inquired with sudden spirit, "why do you stand goggling at her?"

"See here," he demanded. "You don't dislike your daughter-in-law, I hope? That *would* be serious."

"Why?"

"I don't want to see our son put in the position of having to choose between his two women."

"Then don't goggle at her," she cried.

"My God," Stephen said quietly. He stopped the car.

She was instantly ashamed of herself. "Go on. We haven't time for a fight. I'll behave myself."

"You'd better," he said between his teeth, and started the car again.

It was a trying evening for all that. A small dinner party at the Boscrafts', who were old friends, the guests only six in all, the conversation should have been general. The food was excellent and Helen Boscraft had made a pretty table arrangement, illuminated by tall silver candles. She made valiant efforts as hostess to keep men and women together in impersonal talk, and failed. The conversation drifted inevitably to Setsue, recently arrived.

"How does it feel to have a Japanese daughter-in-law?" Marian Tully asked boldly.

"Pretty nice, I should think," her husband chuckled. "And I mean *pretty* pretty."

Stephen answered cautiously. "Ballard seems happy with her."

"I'll say!" Henry Boscraft boomed from the end of the table. "He looks like a tomcat that's eaten a songbird."

"Henry!" Helen warned from the end of the table.

"Does she help with the housework, Aline?" Lilian Schelley inquired.

"Very nicely," Aline said.

"She wants to do everything," Stephen added.

"That can be trying at times," Aline said carelessly.

"I should think so," Helen agreed.

"Come, come, Steve," Tom Schelley said. "What's it like, really? Are Japanese women like ours?"

He leaned on the table, waiting for the answer.

"No," Stephen said quietly. "Not in the least."

"What's the difference, old boy?" Henry asked.

"I don't know," Stephen said. "I haven't defined it. Perhaps it's indefinable—very delicate. I haven't given it real thought."

Liar, Aline thought. He thought about Setsue incessantly. Why was she unique? Or was she unique? If not, why were Japanese women unique? Or were they not unique? Was it she, Aline Medhurst, who was unique? Or American women? These were the questions he had asked himself as she watched the slender young figure of her son's wife moving about her house in silent grace.

"Does she talk much?" Henry asked.

"No," Stephen said. "She's quiet. That is, she waits to hear what Ballard says—"

A roar of laughter burst from the three men.

"It's time for the ladies to go to the drawing room," Helen said abruptly.

"What are the men laughing at now, I wonder?" Marian inquired. They were sitting about the fire, in the drawing room, sipping their coffee and waiting.

"Can't you imagine?" Aline retorted. "They are talking about Setsue."

"Of course they are," Marian said. She held her narrow hands to the fire. "How clever you are, Aline! . . . I wonder why my hands are always cold."

"Do you take vitamins?" Helen asked.

"I did," Marian said. "Then I found they were turning my hair dark again, and it looked so odd with my new silver mink. So I stopped taking them."

The women laughed gently. They turned their heads to listen, and heard the echoes of male voices.

"If she has children," Marian said suddenly, "will they look like her?"

"She's pretty, Marian," Helen said. "In her own delicate way."

"Not pretty, actually," Aline said. "Her nose is too flat."

"She's not as pretty as almost any American girl," Marian said

69

with decision. "And she'll run to fat when she gets old. I know that pale, moon-faced type. Japan is full of them." Marian herself could never run to fat. Her lean frame, determinedly slender, was not young so much as ageless. Laid in her coffin, she would look as she did now, neither dead nor alive.

"I don't believe she thinks of herself," Aline said.

"What does she think of?" Marian inquired. She examined her silvered nails, scarcely paler than her narrow hands.

"I believe she quite honestly thinks of Ballard and of us because we are Ballard's parents."

"That won't last," Marian said dryly.

Remembering this conversation days later Aline had to confess that it had lasted. Setsue remained unchanged. She had fitted herself into the household in small imperceptible ways, until they were all depending upon her. It was easy to smile when Setsue bobbed up from her chair to fetch, to carry.

"Let me, please—"

"Thank you, Setsue—"

It became a formula—a formula, that is, until one day she chanced to see Stephen put his arms about Setsue when she stood on tiptoe to arrange his coat collar. It was in the hall, in the morning, which could have been any morning because she herself did not always come downstairs to breakfast with him. Thus to her shocked amazement she saw Stephen, her husband, stoop down from his height to kiss Setsue. And the diminutive creature, who was entirely woman, received his kiss as though she were accustomed to it. Would not Ballard protest? For Ballard stood there, too, his pipe carelessly in his mouth. He did not protest.

"I'll be at the office by noon at the latest," he said. She remembered then that Ballard had a doctor's appointment. He had been in an automobile accident in Japan, where lived the most reckless drivers in the world, he had explained, and it was while he was in the hospital that Setsue and he had met. She was not a nurse. Her father had been his surgeon, and he had brought her to visit his American patient. They had fallen in love almost at once.

Silent upon the stairs, Aline allowed her husband to leave the house without a morning greeting, and still silent in the shadows she watched her son put down his pipe and take his wife in his arms and kiss her passionately. Would Setsue respond? Could the child be a woman, the delicacy yield to abandon? There was no doubt of it. Setsue melted into his arms, she returned kiss for kiss.

And now Aline was ashamed to be the watcher.

Her son! He was a man, wholly separate from herself, belonging entirely to another woman, a woman strange to her. A painful heat burned in her breast. For what did that kiss of passion mean there at the foot of the stairs? What except that Ballard, the man, was jealous of Stephen, the man, and by the kiss reclaimed his wife? Silently she returned to her own room and stood by the window to gaze unseeing across the dewy lawn. What was going on in this peaceful house? What if she and Ballard were being deceived? No, but the deception was not Stephen's. He was too good, too unsuspecting. She had seen many women attracted by his looks, his natural kindness expressed in unconscious charm, and she had not suffered. She had merely been amused. Let them try, she had thought, amused. They had tried, pursuing until they met the wall of his invincible goodness. Against that wall they could only break their hearts. For once he comprehended their intent, his refusal, never put in words, was absolute. Their letters were unanswered, or replied to by his grim and elderly secretary.

Dr. Medhurst regrets—

Their telephone calls were never answered. And when she herself met them, it was to be infused by such genuine pity, all unspoken, that they shrank from her presence. But Setsue was here in the house, protected by her position as Ballard's wife. . . . None of them were safe! What catastrophe if—

She turned from the window and the dewy lawn and went downstairs swiftly to find her son.

"Yes, Mother?"

He was at the breakfast table, most fortunately alone.

"Sit down," he said. "Setsue is making some fresh coffee. . . . Breakfast?"

"Toast and coffee," she said, pouring a glass of orange juice from the pitcher. "I'm terribly lazy, letting Setsue get the breakfast every day."

"She loves it," he said cheerfully.

She sipped the juice. "Ballard, I want to talk with you alone," she said abruptly.

"Problem?" he inquired.

"Perhaps."

Setsue came in with the coffee. She put the pot down on the table and bowed deeply to her mother-in-law.

"Good morning, Mother," she said.

"Good morning, Setsue," she said.

She ignored the bow. On the third day of her son's return she had begged him privately to tell Setsue she did not like to be bowed to but Ballard had refused to carry the message. "She's only doing what she's been taught to do," he said. "She wouldn't feel happy not to do it. It's her way of showing love and respect. And I want her to be happy."

"Sweetheart," Ballard was saying, "your honorable mother-in-law wants to talk to me alone. Vamoose, pigeon!"

Setsue laughed, the dimple in her left cheek deepened, she bowed to him and trotted away, her sleeves flying.

"Why did you tell her?" Aline murmured and buttered her toast.

"One nice thing about the kid," Ballard said. "You can always tell her. She's without guile."

"She's not stupid," Aline argued.

"Certainly not," Ballard agreed. "But she's disciplined."

"I hope so."

He lifted his eyebrows at her. "Now why that tone of voice?"

She hesitated.

"Don't beat around the bush," he said.

"I won't," she said grimly. "Indeed I won't. Tell me—does your father kiss Setsue goodbye every morning?"

72

They stared at each other across the table.

"Why do you ask?"

"Because of what I saw this morning."

He put down his fork. "Very well, Mother. I may as well tell you. Setsue is worried. She doesn't want to offend him because he's my father. But she wants us to move away."

She dropped her face in her hands. "I thought so."

"I don't blame Dad," Ballard said.

She lifted her face. "Why not? Unless you blame Setsue."

"She is incapable of—of what you suggest," he said shortly.

"Your father is still a young man," she argued. "Barely fifty! Plenty of women—"

"Not Setsue."

"Then why—"

"He began this morning-kiss business in fun," Ballard said. "I'm not sure just when it stopped being fun. But Setsue knew."

"How could she know if she did not respond?"

"She's all woman."

"What does that mean?" she demanded.

"She knows what a man is thinking before he knows it himself," Ballard said.

He caught his mother's skeptic glance. "I know," he cried. "It sounds fatuous, but I assure you it's true. It happens with me. I imagine that I've kept my mood to myself, or I don't even know what my mood is beyond a vague depression. And she defines it for me by some word or touch, something that shows me that she knows."

"She spoils both of you." Her voice was suddenly hard. She drank her coffee to keep from the foolishness of tears.

"The strange thing is that it's not true," he said in wonder. "Oh, we accept the little services, I grant you. Slippers, and so forth. But that's not it. . . . She . . . she doesn't *use* us, as a means to something else."

"Now what on earth does that mean?"

He avoided her demanding gaze. He took up his fork and began

73

to eat his scrambled eggs as though he were in haste, his mouth too full to talk.

"You don't intend to tell me!"

He looked at her, exasperated. Then he shouted.

"Setsue!"

She came in immediately, her geta pattering upon the polished floor.

"Sit down," he commanded. She sat down, between them, half bowing in Aline's direction, and folded her hands in her lap.

"I've been telling our mother we want to move into a house of our own." He spread raspberry jam thickly upon a slice of toast.

"You'd better watch yourself," Aline said. "You'll be getting a potbelly. That's your third slice of toast."

He put down the toast. "There," he said. "That's what I mean. Setsue would never say that to me."

She shrugged her shoulders. "I'm only thinking of your own good. It's not my waistline."

Setsue intervened. "Please, Mother. You are thinking also my thoughts. When you are forty years old, Ballard, please remember what your mother says."

Ballard grinned. "I will," he promised and he bit deeply into the toast and jam.

"Now hear me, Setsue," he went on. "Mother thinks you don't enjoy my father's parting greeting. Express yourself. Say what you think, I've a notion you two women agree better than you think you do."

He waited, expectant. To his surprise his wife's face flushed a deep pink. Her large black eyes filled with tears. She rose from her chair with unusual decision.

"Excuse me," she said. "I cannot speak against your father. I will do whatever you say." She touched her eyes with the ends of her long sleeve and turned to leave. Ballard leaped from his chair and stopped her halfway to the door.

"Wait," he commanded. "I'll go. Don't be afraid of my mother. She's honest, too."

He dropped his napkin on the floor, kissed her, and went away. Setsue picked up the napkin, folded it neatly and put it on the table at his place. Then, hesitating, she slid into her chair and waited.

Thus confronted, what could Aline say? The round pretty face was that of a child. How could one accuse? And yet, this morning —ah, nothing but honesty would serve!

"Tell me how you have bewitched them both," she said. "Tell me how you do it."

The child was no child. "It is not that I bewitch them," she said. "It is that they are ready to be bewitched. This is their sadness— and yours."

Their eyes met, no barrier between. "Mine?" Aline inquired.

"Sad for you," Setsue repeated. She folded her hands together upon the edge of the table and looked at them. "So sad," she said again.

Aline lit a cigarette to give herself time. She drew a deep breath of smoke. "I can't, you know, go fetching slippers and picking up dropped table napkins and so on. That is, I can't do it as if it were the right and natural thing to do. Because I don't think it is. I don't believe in spoiling people just because they are males."

"Oh no," Setsue agreed, startled. "I also. These are small things, not necessary. I do such things because I am taught so. But you are American, not taught like this. You would be pretending only. For me it is not pretending—but also not important."

"Then what is important, pray tell? What's your secret, Setsue?"

"I have no secret."

"You have! Look here, Setsue—I saw Ballard's father this morn-ing—"

Setsue turned pink again. She put up her right hand. "Please— I don't like!"

"Then why did you—"

"I cannot hurt people. To hurt is never to help."

"So what do you propose to do?"

"To go away. Not to be here. I have asked Ballard this and he agrees to it. He knows how I feel."

"He isn't jealous?"

"He is not jealous. He trusts me. He understands me. Wonderful way!"

Aline crushed out her cigarette. "You are rather wonderful yourself. And rather wise. Thank you, my dear. It's decided."

She rose and restraining the impulse to kiss her daughter-in-law's cheek, she smiled and went outside to the terrace, glancing back. Left behind, she saw Setsue, as calmly as though she had not dealt with cataclysm, collect the dishes and take them to the kitchen. And in the morning sunshine, Aline inspected the daffodils about to bloom at the end of the terrace. Tonight, when Stephen came home, she would tell him.

. . . "I see no necessity for it," Stephen said violently. "This great house, empty, with only the two of us—"

"Two of us isn't enough?" she inquired and hearing the edge of bitterness in her own voice she regretted it. She should have waited until after dinner. But she could not wait. She had followed Stephen upstairs and seated here by the window she had announced the decision.

"Setsue wants to move," she said. Unfair, she knew, because Setsue would have been happy enough to have stayed, except that—

"I can't believe it," he exclaimed.

"You betray yourself," she said quietly. "You don't want her to go."

They faced each other.

"I saw you downstairs in the hall this morning."

"Ballard was there," he said, instantly defensive.

"It begins that way," she said. "It will go on to times when Ballard is not there."

He sat down suddenly on the edge of the bed. "What do you want me to do?"

"Nothing," she said. "Nothing at all."

"Then why bring it up?"

"I hope it is not too late. . . . Stephen, what is it about Setsue? Please, please be honest with me!"

"I don't know."

"Because you aren't the sort of man—"

"No."

"It's not mere youth—"

"No."

"Not her coaxing ways—"

"Part of it, perhaps—but no."

"Then what—"

"She makes me believe in myself."

"Stephen! As if you didn't always believe in yourself! The most assured and successful man! Look what you are—president of your own company—chairman of half a dozen important boards, respected citizen—"

He tapped his breast. "In here."

"What's in there?"

"A man—not at all sure of himself—or who he is."

"But how can she—"

"I don't know. But she does."

"You aren't in love with her?"

He considered this. "I don't think I am—honestly I don't think so. But she understands me—by instinct."

"Then you *are* in love with her."

"No . . ." He actually blushed. "That is to say—I don't want to kiss her except in Ballard's presence."

"You will!"

"I fervently hope not."

"So do I. . . . Oh Stephen, where have I failed?"

"You haven't failed, Aline. You're a wonderful wife—always have been. But—"

"But what?"

He looked at her helplessly. "I don't know."

"You won't tell me!"

"I wish I could."

77

There was nowhere to go from there. She saw that he could not tell her more. This intelligent charming man who was her husband could not tell her more even about himself. He looked puzzled, almost frightened, and suddenly she was sorry. She went to him and kissed him. "I shan't scold you," she said.

"Thank you," he said humbly. "It's kind of you, darling."

"You're good," she said. "You're really good. And I wish you would forgive me."

"For what? You've done nothing to hurt me."

"I wonder," she mused. "Oh, I wonder— But never mind." She touched his cheek with her palm and left him.

The dinner passed pleasantly that night. She realized as she had not before how much Setsue did to make such occasions pleasant. As usual, Setsue talked very little and what she said was not brilliant, not even very clever. She communicated by smiles, by looks, by thoughtful listening. When she spoke it was with understanding of each of them, interpreting one to the other.

"Setsue," she said suddenly, "let's leave the men to their apple pie and coffee. Let's go into the drawing room."

She rose as she spoke and took Setsue's hand in hers.

"But why?" Stephen demanded.

"Oh, I want some woman talk," she said, evading. "Setsue and I."

Still clinging to that hand, she drew Setsue away with her. "Your hands are always warm," she murmured.

"So coarse," Setsue sighed.

"Not coarse," Aline replied. "A very delicate hand, my dear, and still it's warm."

In the drawing room Setsue waited until her mother-in-law was seated.

"Withdrawing room," Aline said cheerfully. "Where ladies gather after dinner to tell each other secrets. And I have guessed yours, my dear."

"My secret?" Setsue echoed. "What is it, please?"

78

"You don't know—honestly? Tell me, what is it you want most for my son?"

"His happiness," Setsue replied at once.

"Nothing else?"

"What else can there be?" Setsue asked.

"And how can he be happy?" Aline asked.

"Just being himself," Setsue said.

"Is this your ambition?"

"What else?" Setsue asked again.

"Don't you want him to be successful—in his business, for example?"

"He will be successful if he is happy in himself," Setsue said.

"Or rich?"

"He will be rich," Setsue said. "If he likes."

"You don't want anything for yourself?"

"Oh certainly," Setsue said. "I also wish to be happy in myself."

"What is being happy in the self?"

Setsue considered, her head bent in thought above her rose kimono. The room was very quiet. "I think it means not to be used for something else," she said at last.

"Not to be used for something else," Aline repeated. These simple words, what did they mean?

Setsue lifted her head to look her in the eyes. "It is to say, I do not use Ballard—or his father—or any person—to get something else. Like that is to say, supposing I want to be rich, which I do not, only supposing—I must not use Ballard to get rich for me— or if I should wish to be famous, or wear fine clothes, or anything, I must not use him to gain such things for me. He belongs to himself—not to me."

From the faltering English words a pure light shone into Aline's mind and heart.

"Good heavens," she murmured. "I never knew—I didn't think."

How much had she used Stephen? Not consciously, oh, never consciously! But what had she really wanted out of life for herself —and made him her instrument? In small things, in many small things, mounting in the years to an entire direction, she had used him. She had made him the means. This house, for example, did he really want this house? What had been his dreams? What life would he lead now if he were free? She did not know because she did not know him.

"You are a babe," she said to Setsue, "and out of your mouth has come wisdom."

"My mother taught me," Setsue said modestly, "and her mother taught her."

The two men came in before Aline could reply.

"Ballard and I have been talking," Stephen said abruptly. "I agree with him. I quite understand that he should have his own house. In fact, I think it's a good idea."

"So do I," she said. "But I'm glad we've had these months together. Thank you, Setsue."

"I have done nothing," Setsue said. She made her little bow, first to Aline and then to Stephen. "I have done nothing at all," she repeated. Then with her usual delicate air she added a few more words.

"Just being myself. . . ."

Beyond Language

WHEN WU LIANG HEARD his general say, "Prepare to leave with me for America. We sail in six days," he saluted sharply and by main force kept his face severe and correct, as wheeling and clicking his heels together, he marched from the room. His German army instructor had taught him to do so, and he did. But once outside the door he exploded into joy and ran down the corridors and back to his quarters to shout to his fellow soldiers, "I am to go to America—the general is taking me as his aide to America!"

They had all crowded around him at once, shouting and thumping him on the back and moaning in envy. To go to America! Well, ever since it had been rumored that the general was going they had all wondered which of his aides he would take with him. Even the most hopeful of them did not dare to think that they would all go, not when it was to be remembered that the general was not exactly paying his own way. He was, so to speak, being given a vacation by the government, an honorable vacation, to be sure, but one which would take him away just before he planned another war of some sort. Or, to put it another way, he was being asked, if he preferred, to go on a mission to investigate social and economic conditions in the United States. The general was choleric and being of humble origin, had no great education, and he did not understand the modern government they were trying to make these days in China. "If I see a place to make war, I make it," he said stoutly. So he had gone and made war quite by himself, even against the Japanese, and though he lost and made a great deal of trouble for his government because they had to apologize for him and make reparations, still it made him intensely popular with the common people so that he could not be arrested and beheaded in the most natural and convenient way. Instead the president said, "Take a vacation or go on a mission to America, with all expenses paid, and do not come back for a year."

So there it was, and Wu Liang and his comrades had been in a fever for weeks. Secretly Liang had always had the certainty, almost sure, that he would go, because he was the general's English. The general, having so little education, indeed so little that he avoided signing so much as his name, kept quite a staff of aides, each one of whom spoke some language he did not, and for Chinese he had an old scholar. When anyone said, "Do you speak French?" he replied with dignity, "Certainly I do," and immediately he called for Li Chu-ren, who had been educated in the best schools of Paris and spoke the most delicately chiseled and elided Parisian. He came quietly in and stood beside his general, and then the general said triumphantly to his visitor, "Speak on in your French."

So it was with all the languages. The first question the general asked therefore when he heard he was to have a vacation in America was, "And what language do the Americans speak?" When he heard it was English he replied placidly, "Very well, I will go, then. I can speak English." And so he had sent for Wu Liang who spoke beautiful English, to learn which his father had sent him for years to a mission school, where he had been taught carefully by two elderly unmarried ladies from New England.

But when Liang told them at home about going to America it was not so joyful. He was an only son and he had not yet been married long enough to have a son of his own. His father looked very grave indeed. He blew the ash out of his water pipe and said, "I warned you long ago against being a soldier. I knew no good would come of it. And you only two months married and in five days you must be gone for a year!"

His mother, who was somewhat spoiled by her husband because in her youth she had been very beautiful so that he had not even complained against her because she had but the one son, now began at once to weep aloud. She reached for Liang's hand and clung to it and turned her weeping face toward her husband. "I am sure you could do something if you would!" she cried, letting her tears run down her cheeks unchecked. For years she had turned her beautiful weeping face to her husband with these words, and instantly he had always replied, "I will—I will—only cease weeping and spoiling your beautiful almond eyes."

Now however he only glanced at her and then squinted down the brass tube of his water pipe. "Something's wrong with it," he muttered to himself. He would not for an instant encourage the notion which had occurred to him during the later years, that his wife was not so beautiful weeping as once she had been, and that her eyes did not matter to him as much as they once had. However, he was a good husband and so he said, partly from habit, and partly to still her, "Well, lady, I'll see— But it is very hard to do anything with generals. They are like women—used to having their own way."

At this his lady made ready for a fresh outburst. "I'm sure—" Whereupon he said pacifically, "There—be silent—I will do what I can."

Then since he was a man of influence among generals, being a well-known banker in Tientsin, he put on his wine-red satin and sent for his best and newest motorcar and went away, trying to decide how much he would have to pay the general to leave his son behind. He came back at the end of three hours, shaking his head, somewhat puzzled, since he had never heard of a general who would not talk of any price. "He said," he told his wife, "that if

83

he did not take Liang along he would not be able to speak or understand English."

But what old Mr. Wu did not know, of course, was that his son had swung himself in great haste into a ricksha and had cut across the city through little alleyways and rushing into his general's presence had told him of his father's coming and had begged him not to be moved for any cause. He did not say what was the truth, "I have wanted all my life to go to America." He said instead, "I want to follow you and serve you and there is none among your aides who can speak the American language as I can, and you will be very uncomfortable, I fear, if you leave me behind. The Americans are a sharp people and they will take advantage of you as a stranger, of course. We do the same thing ourselves, and why would not they? It is scarcely to be supposed they are more stupid than most people are."

So the general shook his head indefatigably during all the three hours that Mr. Wu argued. The promise of gold was of course tempting, but then his young aide had said the Americans were sharp. No, no, he must understand the American language. He remained firm.

But it was only that night when for the first time Liang had opportunity to talk to his young wife that he wondered if he had been quite right about it. He scarcely knew her, since it was a marriage arranged for him in his childhood by his parents, and it had not occurred to him to try to speak to her during the day. Besides, she was difficult to talk to. She had been reared in an old country family, an excellent family but so old-fashioned that she might have been born and alive ten centuries ago instead of today, she obeyed so rigorously all the old-fashioned rules for women. If, for instance, he came into the room where his mother and father were, and she was there, she withdrew. She never spoke at all in his presence if they were not alone and so it was easy to forget her— Indeed, he had never yet quite realized that she was there at all or that she was his wife, except that he found all his things so neatly kept and when he wanted something to eat there it was at his elbow and

84

his tea was always hot in the pot, and his uniforms were brushed and beautifully clean and his puttees shone beyond belief and all those small things which he could never get the slaves to do exactly right were now done.

And even when they were alone at night she never spoke to him first. He had to ask her some question and he never knew what to ask her. He had to think up something like, "Did you have a good day?" or he would say, "Is there something you want that you have not?" To which she would say in a small soft voice without looking at him, "I had a very nice day with your mother," or she said invariably, "I could ask for nothing more, I thank you, than you have given me in your splendid house." So after a while he used just to ask her nothing, and so she said nothing.

But tonight to his astonishment she said something to him the moment he came into the room. He was very late and a little drunk, perhaps. His fellow aides had given him a dinner of congratulation and he had bet winecups with them and had lost rather heavily. There she was sitting on the edge of the bed, fully dressed, waiting for him. He looked at her astonished. In the dimness of the candlelight he saw her just the least bit out of focus. Her face was not quite clear. But her voice came very clear, filled with importunity.

"You are always asking me—you ask me over and over again —if I have all I want."

"And if I do?" he said, astonished.

"And I always say I have everything."

"And so you have," he said a little pompously. The wine was beginning to flush up into his cheeks. His head swam. He felt his heart grow large and generous toward himself and everyone. After all, he was an important man. The general could not do without him.

She went on. "Yes—but not if you go away. If you go away this house is empty for me. I shall have nothing left. I ask only this—do not leave me."

He was so astonished that for a brief instant his head steadied itself and he saw her face quite clearly there between the scarlet

85

bed curtains. It was pale and pleading, and the soft pale lips were parted a little. Under her smooth black hair her forehead looked high and childish, although the bangs she had worn of course as a girl were now pulled out because she was a married woman. She was as old-fashioned as that. And she was looking at him, her soft black eyes steadfast. He had never seen her quite so clearly before.

Then she was clouded again. He had a little difficulty finding a chair, his feet were so unsteady, and she sprang to guide him.

"I am perfectably able—" he began, and then he remembered what she had just asked. "It is absurd," he said with dignity, making his voice severe, trying to hold himself straight in his chair, "just as I am now realizing the ambitions of a lifetime."

"Yes, of course," he heard her voice murmuring, dejectedly. But he could not finish. He was suddenly very sleepy. It had been an exciting day—a long merry evening. He did not remember exactly what he had said or what he was going to say. His head fell forward upon his breast. He felt someone helping him to rise, to stumble to the bed. Someone straightened his crumpled limbs and covered him warmly and gently with the quilt.

In the morning he woke quite himself again and in a great haste to be up and getting ready. Four days and he must be all ready. He must get a new uniform—no, two new uniforms, at least. The American tailors would not know how to make Chinese uniforms, of course. And there would be feasts every day, the general's feasts in the day which he must attend, and his own which he must get in somehow, and the general's new uniforms. The general was ordering a dozen new uniforms with buttons of solid gold, and he was now so fat that it was a trying matter to fit him. It was impossible to contemplate that in four days they must sail. He gulped down the tea his wife stood holding for him on a tray and did not look at her. He remembered there had been some talk in the night, but he did not know about what and he had no time to think.

But the four days passed somehow and they were all very cross and tired. The general had threatened delay an infinite number of times, but each time he remembered that for every day of delay he had to forfeit some of the money that had been given him for expenses, and so he hastened himself nearly into an apoplexy, and at the end, the tailor having been unable to finish the dozen uniforms, he had uncompromisingly packed him along, ignoring the poor man's protests. He had thought for a moment, in his anger, of beheading the man, but then it had occurred to him that the uniforms could not perhaps be finished at all in such case. So at the set hour at last they were all on the ship, and the ship left immediately and the little tailor was already beginning to look green above his stitching as the ship rose and fell to the long sea waves.

And only then in the lull of the days did Liang have time to remember anything, and he remembered in the frenzy of his mother's weeping and in all the commands of his father not to eat American food and not to take American wines which were poisonous and not to pass any money until he had looked at it twice, and above all not to speak to any foreign women, did he remember that his little wife had touched his hand at parting and had whispered, "I am as one dead until you return to me." But even so there was no time to think what this could mean, since the general was instantly and continuously seasick, and required the presence of his aide day and night, and he could not be made to understand why the captain could not stop the ship until he felt better. So there was really no time to think.

And then almost immediately, or so it seemed, they were in America, and one thing after another happened and he had no time to remember anything. There were the newspaper reporters to whom the general must grant interviews and now Liang was very busy and he had to talk and hear for the general all day long, and at night he had to go to long dinner parties and he had to stand up beside the smiling general and make his speeches for him and interpret into Chinese for him everything that was said. Then there were railway tickets to be bought for all the huge party of the general's favorite wives whom he could not leave behind and their children whom they could not leave and the servant who took care of them and the tailor and the two secretaries and they went whirling across America and to New York. The general said, "I have been told about that New York where the houses are like the cliffs of T'ai and I must see it." So thither they all went, and everything began over again.

But then it was in New York that Liang met Josie Pang. The moment he met Josie Pang, America ceased whirling around in a mad huge noisy pageant which nobody could understand. It all stopped, focused in her, and suddenly life took on reality again.

For Josie Pang was very real. He met her, it is true, in a ridiculously unreal place, in the great garish gilt-ceiled ballroom of an enormous hotel. They were invited to a reception by the Canton Merchants' Association of New York City, because the general had put up a fight against the enemy, and the general and his ladies and the secretaries and Wu Liang had been pulled up twenty stories in a moment to the ballroom. The general closed his eyes in the elevator because he was always giddy, and he was giddy when he stepped out and he entered the ballroom still leaning upon Liang, his eyes tightly closed until he felt steady again. From under the general's huge arm Liang looked and saw the amused eyes of a young woman, very cool, sharp black eyes, and in that instant everything suddenly became sharply real.

She is laughing at me, he thought furiously, and he was for the first time really impatient with the general. "Stand still, sir," he said abruptly. "We are arrived." He pulled down the general's coat and tidied him and propelled him toward the reception committee. Then he turned toward the young woman and looked at her sternly.

"If you knew how funny you looked!" she said. And suddenly she laughed. He wanted to turn away from her, but he could not. She had the clearest, most impudent laugh he had ever heard in his life. He was not used to being laughed at, being the only son of a wealthy banker. But then he could not exactly tell her so. His uniform with the gold epaulets should have spoken for him. But doubtless she was too ignorant to understand what it meant.

"Who are you?" he asked loftily.

"I am Josie Pang," she replied simply. "My father is the head of the Canton Merchants' Association."

He looked at her. He wanted to say something clever and cold, something to show her she was only a woman after all. But he could not think what to say. She stood before him careless and assured, as he had never seen a woman stand. She wore a coral red dress, fitted closely to her slender body and then flaring out like rose petals. Her hair was cut close to her head, smooth shining black hair. Her face was pale and smooth as a fruit, and her lips were painted red, and her eyebrows were drawn black and fine above her sparkling malicious eyes. He could not think of anything to say at all.

"You—you—" he gasped, in hopeless anger, "you don't even look like a Chinese woman!"

There was nothing worse than that, surely, but then he thought of something worse and went on, "I might even think you were American except your face—you look like a Japanese, that is what you look like— A Japanese in a red American dress!"

She ought to have been crushed and silent. She should have turned away. If he had spoken to his little wife like that, or even to a slave, she would have had the knowledge and the grace to turn away, drooping and rebuked. But this girl went very red. "And you," she said, her voice so clear and cold that anyone could hear it, "you are certainly as rude as any Japanese could ever be!"

They stared at each other aghast, and then, as though it were mutually agreed upon, they turned and fled from each other.

But there was no getting away from Josie Pang anywhere they went. She was always at the dinners being given to them, and always managing something. People said continually if a confusion arose about the menu or if someone did not know where to sit, "Where's Josie? Ask Josie Pang—she made the arrangements." Yes, Liang grew very tired of Josie Pang everywhere, even though every time he saw her she had on a different dress.

There was a gold dress she wore one night at a great dinner in Chinatown where the general had to make a speech. It was made of some smooth supple foreign cloth, but cut high in the neck like a Chinese robe, and Liang liked it. He had disliked seeing her smooth young throat and bosom shown for any man to see when he looked at her. But then he would doubtless not have noticed what she wore anywhere if that had not been the night she came forward so shamelessly to interpret the general's speech. He had been put to shame in that matter. For it appeared that none of the Chinese in Chinatown could understand the general's speech, because they were from Canton and the general was from Shantung, where the people speak thick in their throats instead of spitting the words off the end of their tongues so that they pop like firecrackers as the Cantonese do. So there was a predicament, the general waiting to tell them how he fought the Japanese and they starving to hear and no language common between them. The general turned angrily to Liang: "Twist that tongue of yours, can't you?" he roared. But Liang could only say, "Sir, I am like you. My tongue is what my fathers gave me, and they were all of Shantung." So the general and the people could only stare at each other confounded, until someone shouted, "Josie—where is Josie Pang?" Then she came forward out of the crowd where Liang had already seen her sitting as golden as a star among them, although he pretended he had not.

"Let the general speak to you," she said composedly, "and I will hear your English, and put it into the people's tongue."

So the three of them stood together before the people, and the general shouted his fiery tale and showed the people how he had ambushed his men and how attacked the enemy from the rear, and how prevailed here and there, his tale growing from moment to moment, and Liang put what he said into English and Josie Pang caught the words so quickly from his tongue and slipped them so swiftly into the other language and with such vigor and wit that it seemed as though she became a voice for the general himself, and the people roared and clapped their hands, and the general laughed and sweated and redoubled his efforts and made it a great tale.

When it was over, and he had received their congratulations, he looked about him for Josie Pang. He whispered hoarsely to Liang, "Where is that young woman? She is the cleverest female I have ever seen. Find her for me. With all my women I have not one like her."

Now Liang had never cared what women the general had. They were nothing to him and never had been. But when the general said this he felt a curious blow in the heart. But no hand had touched him. It was something else. It was that he did not want the general to think about Josie Pang. The general said, "Bring her to me." He rose unwillingly and grumbled, "How do I know where she is?" The general stared at him astonished, never having heard such a tone before. "Go and find her," he said angrily, and stared at Liang sternly until he went out.

But Liang knew perfectly where Josie was. He had seen her go out, her gold dress glinting down the narrow hall. He followed and went into the door of the reception hall and there she sat alone, smoking a cigarette in a small gold holder.

"Hello," she said cheerfully.

Liang sat down. He should have said at once, "The general commands your presence." But he could not do it. Instead he said in a sullen voice, "How is it you speak two languages each exactly as though it were the one to which you were born?"

"I was," she replied, smiling. "My father is Chinese, and my mother, who died when I was a little girl, was American."

"I thought you did not look Chinese," he said rudely. He was glad, glad she was partly American. For that was why he did not really like her. No, no he did not really like her. She was so managing, she was so sure of herself, like the women he saw on the streets everywhere. He got up abruptly, without waiting for her to answer, and went back to the general. "I could not find her," he lied.

"Ah, well," the general sighed, "another time. An old man learns to wait."

Inside himself Liang said, "There will be no more times. I will tell her to stay at home."

But this Josie Pang was a constant misery to him. She would not listen to him. He had made an opportunity the very next day when he met her at a party. He had taken her aside. She said, "Why should I stay at home? I am amused by that fat old general." And how could he say to her plainly, "The general is a lecherous old man." One did not put such thoughts into a virtuous woman's head. He began pompously, as an older brother might speak to a young wayward sister. "The general might place you in a difficulty. He might begin negotiations with your father."

But Josie Pang laughed and laughed. "My father? He would not think of forcing me to anything I did not want. He knows I will only marry the man I love!"

She was as bold as that. He had never heard the word "love" upon any woman's tongue, but it rolled from her like any common word. "The man I love—" He could not bear the phrase. There could be no such man.

"Who is the man?" he demanded.

She looked at him, smiling, arch, assured, as no other woman had ever looked at him, her enchanting face alive with coquetry. His head began to whirl suddenly, and he turned decently and marched away, left—right, left—right, as his former instructor had taught him to do. When the general said peevishly, "Where is that young woman I remember from last night? I thought I saw her, but I am not sure since her dress is not the same today," Liang answered coldly, "I have not seen her. She is not here." But inside he was hot as flame.

Not until he was alone in the nights did Wu Liang ever remember his little old-fashioned wife. The days were so full, so mad, he was so fevered with his continual fear that Josie Pang would not be there to be seen and by his torment if she were there lest the general see her afresh, that he was dried and lean as a pine tree blown by winds. Even when the general forgot all about her she could make him miserable, for he never could know just where she was and what she was doing. He quarreled with her incessantly over all she did and said. She was too bold, or too gay, or her dress did not please him, or she put out her hand too freely to take a man's hand in the barbarous western handshaking, or she did not take his hand willingly enough when he put it out, and there it was. He hated her and could not be pleased with her, and he could not forget her, and at last he knew he loved her. All day long he thought only of her, and in the night when he remembered his old-fashioned wife, he made himself hard and cold and told himself, "I never chose her," and he said, "In these days and times I do not have to stay by my parents' wishes," and he put her out of his mind and waited for the day to come back.

How long he would have gone on so he could not have told, except that suddenly the general fell ill, and long before the year was out. It was the American smell, he said, that made him ill, the smell of meat and milk that reeked everywhere, or else it was the American water that was strange to him, or the American earth that did not suit his Chinese nature. And he could not buy anywhere his bread baked hard in a pan and his garlic-laden pork rolls, or any food fit to eat, and he patted his great stomach, which he said hung on him like an empty bag. He wanted to see no more, to hear no more. Even the magic music machine which had so pleased him and his wives at first so that they sat for hours turning one button and another to hear one squeak after another come out of the air, he now would not hear. "All the noises are the same," he said gloomily. "I am a man of war. I shall not be myself until I have a roll of pork and garlic in me and I can go and make a war somewhere. Why, I cannot even wear my sword nowadays, my belt is so slack on me!"

So nothing would do for him until Liang had bought the tickets for them all except the tailor, who had decided willfully against return, because only when he had left her did he know what a shrew his wife had been at home. "I'd rather stay an exile all my life in a barbarous land than return to her," he said. And he hired

93

a room and set up a shop in Chinatown and kept one of the general's uniforms in the window to show what he could do and draw trade to himself.

"I will look after him," said Josie Pang to Liang. "Let him be."

It was at that moment he realized that he was leaving Josie Pang behind.

"But who will look after you?" he cried. All the days and weeks he had been scolding her and looking after her, never telling her he loved her, but only looking after her. He began to stumble miserably, to stammer to her, "I—I have a wife, too. I wish I had never to go back—never, never."

"What do you want?" asked Josie Pang calmly.

"I do not want to leave you," he whispered.

"That's easy," said Josie Pang. "I'll let the tailor look after himself. I'll come with you."

The nearer Liang came to the shores of China, the more American Josie Pang looked. In America she had looked Chinese, and after he had fretfully decided he loved her, she looked very Chinese, or so it seemed to him as he glanced at the girls he saw on the streets in New York. Well, anyway, Josie's eyes were very black, and if she curled her hair he knew it was done with a machine and could be stopped.

But in Shanghai she looked oddly fair. It was true her eyes and hair were still black, as he could see, but her skin had a ruddiness that looked foreign when it was set beside the smooth paleness of a Chinese girl. And beside the exceeding slenderness of the Chinese girls, her straight figure had a squareness at the shoulders, a slight heaviness at the waist.

"Let your hair grow straight, can't you?" he said to her one day gloomily. "My mother won't like it."

Josie looked at him. There was a sudden glint in her eyes, but he did not see it. He was beginning to dread very much what he had to do. He had to go home and tell his old father and mother that he wanted Josie for his wife and not that little old-fashioned creature they had chosen for him. It had seemed easy enough to think of saying it when he was in New York. He would just go in very breezily and say, "I have decided—" Now, only three days from that staid home on the outskirts of Tientsin, it seemed a thing quite impossible to say.

"Your mother will have to learn that I do my hair as I please," said Josie, in a composed voice.

It seemed a very unreasonable speech, he thought, staring at her. She was leaning back in the modern upholstered chair in her uncle's house in Shanghai. She had, he found, several uncles in Shanghai, all rich and so good-humored when he met them as to seem casual. Josie had introduced him to them as casually as possible, too. "This is Wu Liang—I'm going to marry him." Considering the difficult time ahead of him, she had seemed abominably casual. For one thing, he was so helpless. Everybody knew at once his responsibility toward Josie, but no one knew he was already married—well, in a manner married. No one could say that old business was a marriage. Josie had swept it away again and again. "If you didn't know her how could you marry her?" And sometimes she said, "If you don't love her, and you do love me—" But still he was irritated when she made her casual announcements and he would like to have said stiffly, "That is, we shall be married if I can make the arrangements." But of course he could not say it.

He wondered sometimes if he were a little afraid of Josie. While she was lying back in that angular modern chair, her smoothly waved head against the black and white check of its upholstery, he found there were a number of things he had wanted to say to Josie at different times, and then he had not said them. He had a discomfort in him of accumulated repression to which he was not used. He had always said anything at home and they had all listened. He looked down at Josie gloomily, making up his mind he would say something now. He would say, "My wife must be Chinese because I am Chinese, and she must obey my mother because it is the Chinese custom." But before he could say it, she had burst out laughing.

"I don't care!" she said, laughing. "Don't be so solemn, boy! Anyway, I've been thinking maybe I'd look better with my hair straight —smooth and slick, you know. There's a girl I know in New York wears her hair that way, too."

She leaped to her feet and thrust her arm into his. "Come on, let's go to a movie!"

So there was no reason for his saying anything. Josie seemed to give up easily so often, just before he got angry, but he always had the feeling that she had not really given up—only just enough to keep him from saying anything this time. But he couldn't be sure about her, and now she was coaxing him, and he let himself be coaxed. She could be very sweet. He liked sitting in the darkness and watching a picture. Soon her hand would take his. And when Josie had kissed him that first time when he was holding her coat for her after a dance and they were alone together in the hall, she had said, laughing, "Look at the clinch in the movies next time, boy, and learn how to do it! Don't tell me you never kissed a girl before, and you looking like a Chinese Clark Gable!" He was ashamed to say he never had. And next time he had watched Clark Gable very closely to see how it was done. But he felt when he was kissing her as though he had gone into some foreign moment. Each time he was blushing and charmed, and his blood was hot and whirling, but it was not quite he who held Josie in his arms. It was really Clark Gable. Left to himself he never could have done it.

But he went to the movies with her, and he sat gravely watching the lover's technique, Josie's hand in his. And when the moment came for him to leave her and go home, he really loved her very much. He hated to leave her, because he dreaded what he had to do, and partly, too, because he was afraid Josie would have a good time while he was gone. There were so many pretty cousins in her uncles' houses, so many young men coming and going in smart western costumes. He held her hand at the station recklessly, regardless of the possible presence of someone in the general's suite loitering about, or even of the general himself popping his head out of the window of his private car.

"Goodbye—my—my darling," he stammered. "It is only ten days."

"Only ten days," Josie said cheerfully. She was looking very pretty in a soft gray cloth suit, with a huge Chinese chrysanthemum pinned, a froth of yellow, against her shoulder. Her eldest uncle was famous as a chrysanthemum connoisseur. He gazed at her as long as he could while the train drew out, and she still looked at him cheerfully as he lost the sight of her.

He went despondently down the aisle toward the general's car. She was going back to a gay party, he knew—one of the cousins was having a birthday. He forgot that she had run out of the merriment to go to the train with him. He thought instead of the smart young men and grew quite desperately determined. He would say to his parents—

But it was even harder to say than he had thought. His mother had burst into tears and wept steadily and so he and his father had gripped the matter hard between them, father and son. He had stood his ground. He had said, over and over again, "My mind is made up. I will marry her. I can leave my home and renounce my name, and I will do it for her."

His father was pacing back and forth, his soft old-fashioned velvet shoes thudding on the brick floor, his hands clasped behind him. Now he stopped and glanced at his son. "If I had another son I would let you do it," he said, "but you are all I have, cursed that I am!" He paced on again, calming himself. Liang could see his father, willing himself to quietness, repeating within himself the sayings of sages, the wise words from Lao-tse and Confucius. He waited. In other times this meant usually that he had what he wanted.

But this time it was not quite all he wanted. His father said, "Let us put it thus. Say nothing to my daughter-in-law, your wife. But we will invite the other one here. My gorge rises at the thought of a strange woman in this house, but let it be so. Let her stay,

97

say, not more nor less than twenty days. If at the end of that time you are both of the same mind, I will sorrowfully follow your desires."

At this his mother burst out afresh, upbraiding the old man. "I thought you would— Can't you even control your own son? Will you—"

But the old man put up his hand against her voice. "Be quiet," he said. "I always do what I can."

So Liang went back very triumphantly to Josie Pang. He found her looking much prettier than he had remembered. And he was in his gayest spirits, considering their difficulties entirely over. He could not keep from boasting a little. He stood before Josie Pang, in his best uniform, boasting, "I was perfectly courteous remembering he was my father, but perfectly firm. I said—"

But Josie Pang seemed not to hear him. She was looking at him steadily. She interrupted him. "He said I was to come and visit for twenty days?"

"Yes—and then he would let us do what we wish."

She repeated thoughtfully, "He will let us do what we wish—"

He was troubled by her tone, by her bright hard look. He was suddenly afraid of her, afraid she might ask him, "And what of that other woman?"

He began to talk very fast. "Yes, and it is just the same as consent because of course at the end of the twenty days we will wish—"

He bent over her in the Clark Gable fashion and kissed her. For he did not want her to ask him any questions. He did not want to have to tell her of that night when his little old-fashioned wife had waked him to sob, heartbroken, "You do not love me—you have not once loved me all these nights." He did not want to tell Josie Pang about that night. Perhaps he was just a little afraid of her.

But she did not ask him anything. She let him kiss her, and she said nothing. He straightened up and looked about him a little desperately. Now what could they do?

"Let us go to the movies!" he said heartily. It was an inspiration. "All right," said Josie Pang. But she said it listlessly, or so he thought.

How the thing might have turned out if the old general had not suddenly conceived a war, Liang could not have said. But it was spring, and the old general's blood was restless and he was tired of his women and the journey to foreign lands made the days in his courts seem dull and besides the government of the republic was not pleased at his early return and he was quarrelsome and fret himself and the upshot of it was he thought of a war to amuse him and take his mind off his troubles and ease his blood. But he had no money and he had to borrow a sum from a foreign bank on the pretext and security of making new roads, and to negotiate with the foreigners he needed his English, and so no sooner did Liang bring Josie Pang home than he had to leave her sometimes for two and three days at a time to talk English for the general and to soothe him when he gnashed his teeth because the foreigners were so cautious and distrustful of him that they delayed. And all the time Liang was distracted because Josie Pang was in his home he did not know at what odds with his father and mother.

But when he ran home between whiles for an hour or so while the general slept and rested himself to fret and clamor again, he was always surprised at the quietness of the house. Josie Pang would be reading in the court, or she would be pacing the peony terrace, or playing with some child of a servant. She had not changed a whit. That is, her hair was still waved, and she wore her American garments, and she could not understand anything, since none of them spoke Cantonese. But she was a little different, too. She did not once allow Liang to touch her. Even when they chanced to be alone, if he put out his hand she drew back, shaking her head, laughing, "No, no—it seems wrong here."

He did not press her, knowing that at any moment a slave or indeed his mother or father might come in, and the thing could not be explained.

99

So as the days passed she grew to be like a guest, but she was always amiable. When the lady, his mother, inquired how it was her hair was so waved, she explained the machinery to Liang for him to tell her. And she was most courteous to his father, although they could not speak to each other. Liang grew very hopeful when he saw the courtesy between them. He said to his father ardently, "Now you see why I love her."

His father did not answer at once. He smoked his water pipe the two whiffs, blew out the ash, and squinted down the pipe to see if it were clean. Then as he pressed in a fresh morsel of tobacco he said no more than this, "There is a woman in her, it is true."

But then he was used to his father never saying much.

But most strange of all was the friendship which Josie Pang had for the small old-fashioned creature, his wife. It began by Josie Pang's talking to him about her. She said one evening when he came home, "She is really very pretty."

"Who?" he asked. Josie was looking very pretty herself in a blue linen frock.

"Your little wife."

"Don't call her that," he said violently.

Josie smiled. "She looks like a little flower of some sort, the kind you don't notice—not much color, but very fragrant. I like her."

"I love only you," he said.

"How she waits on you!" said Josie Pang, quietly. "She runs back and forth keeping your tea hot before you come home. She is forever in the kitchen working over your dinner, or cleaning and folding your uniforms."

"A slave could do such things," he said stubbornly.

But she shook her head, still smiling.

Afterwards he thought, if he had only been more careful, he might have seen. But she seemed to be so eagerly awaiting the end of the twenty days, even as he was. He could scarcely wait—twelve days, fifteen, eighteen, nineteen.

"Tomorrow—tomorrow!" he said to her. He avoided his wife completely. But then he was so busy he could not have done otherwise. The old general was quite frantically promising roads and developments through all sorts of cities and towns he hoped to conquer.

Then suddenly the evening of the twentieth day was there. Liang went to the general and said very firmly, "I must go home for two hours." The general stared at him outraged, but Liang went on desperately, "If you do not allow it, I must resign from your service." Now Liang had the general by the nose, because the loan was about granted, so the general said grudgingly, "Well enough, but come back at the end of the time and no later."

So Liang went home and he found them all waiting—his father, his mother, and Josie Pang. But the old man had sent his little daughter-in-law away. "Go and visit a friend this evening," he said to her. "You look too grave and pale. Forget that son of mine for an hour or so, and be merry with other young wives."

So though she was unwilling, he coaxed her, and ordered his second best motor for her, and saw her driven away. When he turned to go back into the gate he saw Josie Pang standing watching, and though she had put on her most American frock and had waved her hair afresh and painted her face so that anything less like a decorous female he had never seen, when she smiled at him warmly, he smiled in return, a small quiet smile half hidden by his scanty beard, and went on. Within himself he thought, There is one woman to whom one need say nothing, and she understands. And going to find his old wife he said to her, "Have my man-servant bring the best car to the gate in an hour," and did not stay to answer her questions.

Thus they were all waiting, so quiet that Liang felt his heart, which had been beating hard, quiet itself, too, as he sat down. He had made himself very fine in a fresh white uniform and when he had turned to his parents and looked warmly at Josie Pang he sat down and began to speak quickly and loudly before he grew afraid again.

"Well, my father, the twentieth day is over."

"Yes, my son," said his father, reaching for his water pipe and tobacco pouch.

"And according to your promise we are to have what we desire."

"So you shall, my son," said the old man, making his pipe ready with great care.

"Well, then—" said Liang eagerly, but the old man nodded at Josie and interrupted him.

"Ask her what her desires are. Let her speak first."

Liang smiled confidently. "Her desires are mine," he said.

"Ask her," said the old man. "She is not one for whom a man can speak."

So to humor him Liang turned, laughing, to Josie Pang. She sat there quietly, upright in her foreign dress upon the old carved redwood chair.

"He wants to know your desire," Liang said in English. "As if I did not know!" He leaned toward her, gazing into her eyes, careless of the decorum of his parents. Let them see how unchanged—

But she was looking back at him steadily. She spoke very clearly and kindly, even with a sort of playfulness as though Liang might be a little child. "Your father is the wisest man I've ever known. Tell him, Liang."

Liang translated, astonished, and his father bowed his head a little, smiling.

"Tell him, Liang, that he knows my desire. It is that you shall live happily here with your little wife."

"No—no!" He leaped to his feet and ran to her, but she put out her hand and held him off.

"Yes, Liang—listen! I couldn't—why, I couldn't do for you what she does. I can't cook and sew and wash and do for you as she does."

"I told you any slave could—"

"Yes, but she wants to—I don't! Can't you see the difference?"

She was holding him off, her hand firm as iron against him. "I couldn't live here. I'd be so restless—so bored. I don't belong here. I'd make you all so unhappy—yes, I would—I'm bored already,

102

though I've stayed out the twenty days to be sure. No, no—we couldn't live anywhere else—and no slave could do for you what she does—it takes *love!*"

He drew back then, so that she did not need to push him away. Her hands dropped. He stared at her, hurt to the heart.

"You don't love me, after all," he said stiffly.

She looked around the room, at his parents, into the court, she saw all his familiar life. "Not enough," she said. Her voice was clear and gentle.

But he was really very hurt, and when he was hurt he was always very angry. "You are spoiled," he said, with violence.

"Very spoiled," she agreed.

"You are like all American women," he shouted at her. "You want men to wait on you and amuse you and take care of you and you want to do nothing."

"I am like all American women," she said, smiling a small bright smile. But she was not looking at him. She was looking at his father. His father was smoking. The smoke gurgled twice through the water and he stopped and blew out the ash and filled the pipe again in his old quiet routine. His mother was watching him placidly. They were not afraid at all. He stared at them all, taken aback. He would have said they had decided everything between them before he came, except he knew they could not speak the same language. But he did not enjoy not understanding things. Besides, he felt Josie Pang had made a fool of him.

"I suppose there is no more to be said," he said sulkily.

"Nothing more," said Josie Pang cheerfully.

"Then I must be getting back to my work," he said with dignity. "The general is waiting for me."

He turned to go, but she stopped him. "Just one thing," she said. "Remember this last thing I tell you. No one will ever love you as much as that little wife of yours. She is the best—"

But he broke in on her. "Thank you," he said, holding himself very stiff and straight. "I think I know how to appreciate my own wife." He turned and clicked his heels together and left the room

103

smartly as his German military instructor had taught him to do.

When he had gone the old man said to Josie Pang in the northern Chinese which she did not know, "The motor is waiting, ready to take you to the train. It is my best car."

And Josie Pang said, smiling most brilliantly, "I'll just go and get my hat."

Though she spoke in English, they understood each other perfectly.

Parable of Plain People

THOUGH WANG THE ELDEST of the Village of Wangs always spoke of himself as a poor man and one who knew nothing and of his life as bitter, he did not in reality consider himself poor or ignorant nor did he think his life was bitter. At least, he often told himself it would not have been bitter if his overlords could have been removed by some stroke of heaven. Without these overlords he could have managed very well. That is, he had five acres of flat, well-nurtured land, a thatched house with thick mud walls, his own threshing floor, a good well and several date trees for shade and fruit. Besides these trees he had a pear tree and a grapevine. He raised everything he and his family used except tea, and cotton cloth and on occasion fish or beef. Pigs and chickens and ducks he had and four geese, and he ground his own meal in a quern. At least, his wife and daughter-in-law did.

Perfectly satisfied he would have been with his life and his situation if it had not been for his overlords.

His two sons were good young men. The eldest was married to a girl from a neighboring village, the daughter of an old friend. When this friend was young, and he also, their marriages were within the same month, and within three months their wives were pregnant, and they vowed their children to each other, if they should be boy and girl. For himself Wang the Eldest vowed that he did not care whether his was boy or girl. Still, it had been a satisfaction to him all these years that the strong young man was his, and he used to joke with his friend often over their small cups of rice wine at a birthday feast or at New Year.

"I have the best of that bargain, Elder Brother! I won your first fruit!"

The girl was sober and quiet and not too pretty and she had twin boys.

And then he had betrothed his second son to a young girl from a village to the south. The marriage was to be a month later.

Thus the affairs of his house were arranged and the generations were proceeding in order. All would have gone well with Wang the Eldest's house had it not been for his overlords.

This second son was not as strong as the first. He had caught the smallpox when he was six and it had left him with a weakness which kept back his growth for a full year, and he was small and not able for hoe and plow. So Wang the Eldest had taken care to betroth him to the daughter of a silk weaver, having it in his mind that he would begin silk-making in his house and take his second son from the fields to be the master of the work. He had not seen the girl, but everyone in the village spoke well of her. They said,

"She has silk-weaving hands. When she tends the worms they eat and grow fat. She does not bruise them in moving them, and when they have spun, she winds off the silk from the cocoons like the Fairy of Silk-weaving herself."

He was pleased when he heard this and he made the betrothal complete. Only then did it occur to him to ask if the girl were good-looking. It was too late if she were not, but still he owed it to his second son to warn him if she were not. That is, he would call his second son to him and say while he stroked his beard,

"Son, beauty in a wife is useless. It does not cook the rice or spin the silk or light the lamp. On the other hand, it beguiles a man into wasting his time. He lies abed when he should be up and at work, and even while he works his thoughts go to bed again. Beauty in a wife is an evil thing."

Since they told him that the girl was very pretty, however, he said nothing to his younger son. The day for the marriage came and with it the bride, and the wedding went off with great merriment. He took care that everything was a little less good than it had been at the wedding of his elder son, and so there was no jealousy. And to offset the greater beauty of the bride, his elder son's wife gave birth to a third boy the very night of the wedding. No greater sign of luck could have befallen the house.

And within a few months all that had been told him about his second son's wife was true. She coaxed the finest of silk from the worms she reared and he planted a field of new mulberry trees, giving up for it the half of a wheat field. Silk would bring in more money.

All his affairs therefore were prosperous and he would have had no troubles had it not been for his overlords.

For this man Wang did not consider death a trouble nor the failure of a crop a trouble. In their time his parents had died and he had become the head of his house. He buried them and mourned them and burned incense before their tablets, but their death was not trouble. The end of any long life was death, and next to life, quiet death coming peacefully upon the old was good. And when his second son's wife's first child was born dead, though a boy, he still did not count it trouble. This soul, he argued, was mistakenly born into the body of his flesh, and perceiving it a mistake, had in courtesy withdrawn from his house. He urged this upon his son and daughter, and if they grieved it was not before his eyes. Within a year they had a living child, a little girl, and he was glad to have her, and laughed when his second son apologized to him that his first child was a girl.

"A house needs women, too," Wang the Eldest said, "and there are boys yet to come." As indeed there were, for between his two daughters-in-law three out of his next four grandchildren were boys.

He had no complaint therefore against heaven except there were still his overlords.

As for the famine that fifty-first year of his life, though it was one of the worst he had ever seen, it was not trouble, evil as it was. He felt its coming in the delay of spring because there was no rain when rain should have fallen. Leaves crept out small on the trees, and the seeds put out weak short stems and the fruit trees flowered meagerly. He had seen famine begin before in just such ways and he made ready for it, and the household weathered it as they had weathered other famine, generation after generation. They ate little and slept much and they all lived, and when it was over and he was harvesting again Wang the Eldest thanked heaven as usual. He said to his sons,

"Shall I curse heaven because in the midst of many good years there is here and there one evil? I do not measure heaven by a year but by my life, and my life is good."

There was, therefore, only one trouble that Wang the Eldest had and it was his overlords. Had he been able to live as a man without these overlords, he could have lived in peace and in plenty and he would have counted himself a man without sorrows. As it was, through no fault of his own, Wang's sorrows overfilled his life and all of them sprang from his overlords.

Who were these overlords?

First there was the man surnamed Li and named Yi Ching. Why was this man his overlord? Wang the Eldest did not know. But he was the chief of the gentry of that region and he owned much land and wanted always to buy more, so that in any famine year he sent out his agents to gather in the acres of starving men. Wang the Eldest feared this Li, for he was a rich and powerful man who lived from the rents of his land. He did not stay on the land as a man should but he lived in great cities and took the rent of his land. Once Wang the Eldest even heard of his going to foreign countries for pleasure. Against Wang the agent of this Li had an especial hatred because Wang would not sell him one foot of his land and the man was vexed and furious that he had no way of forcing him, because Wang the Eldest's land lay surrounded by Li's land and Li wanted his land in one great straightly flowing piece. For no other reason he found ways to outsell and undersell the grain and vegetables which Wang the Eldest had, and this was trouble.

Second, there was the magistrate of the county whom Wang had never seen in his life and who cared nothing for Wang, and yet he was one of the sore troubles of Wang's life. Now in the old days of the Emperor, it was often expected that a magistrate was evil, but if he were evil beyond what he was expected to be the people cried out and sent memorials to the throne and if they were angry enough the magistrate was sent away. But these times were new. There was no emperor, and if the people of any region were angry there was nobody to cry to and if a memorial was sent to the new government a body called a Bureau answered if there were an answer, and the magistrate stayed on, and wreaked his vengeance on those who had complained against him.

So after Wang the Eldest saw men put into jail and beaten for complaining he kept prudent silence, and he paid his taxes over and over again, until the government was ten years in his debt and he dared not complain. To his family when the doors were shut at night he did sometimes complain. He said,

"It seems that when Emperors were put away heaven also passed away with them. Nothing is now done according to the decree of heaven, and when a plain man cries out to heaven none hears, since now we have no emperor whose duty it was to hear the people when they cried." But outside he said nothing because he had heard a neighbor say in his despair, "In the old days we had only one magistrate's stomach to fill, but now under this republic there are nothing but magistrates and officials, all empty and demanding to be filled." For this the man was put in prison and died there after three years waiting for a trial that it was forgotten to give him.

There was yet another overlord, and this was a man who rebelled against the new government and took his plunder as a bandit and a war lord, marauding the countryside wherever he went and fighting with others like him, so that Wang the Eldest bought an old foreign gun which he did not know how to shoot, and he put iron plates on his gate and a new iron bar, and he built the earth wall around his house and courts two feet higher. This war lord was a restless, evil, idle man who loved strife and hated peace and imagined himself a mighty fellow, destined to save his people and be their king and head. Men like him followed him and flattered him, and he thought the earth was his.

These were Wang the Eldest's overlords and the overlords of all the plain people like him. In their hearts these people thought always of how to rid themselves of these accursed overlords, these governors who did not govern, these landlords who did not love the land, these men who allowed no peace because they themselves loved war. How could these overlords be driven from the earth so that men could live and enjoy their life?

"I have no troubles except these men," Wang the Eldest often said to his sons. "They have no blood of mine in them, I do not know them nor have I done them any hurt. Yet they take the harvests for which I labor, and they destroy all for which I live."

But he could do nothing. Each man in his house felt as he did but each could do nothing and nothing was done. Wang the Eldest continued to pay taxes far in advance of what he owed, and he entered into a long lawsuit against Li who claimed ten feet of his land at a boundary, and he saw his ripe wheat fired because he would not pay a sum to the bandit chief. He lived in misery because of these overlords whom he never saw, to whom he owed nothing.

"Of what use is any good I have, when these men are my overlords?" he cried.

But they were his overlords. I am helpless, he thought, looking about at his children. A good wife, good sons, good land, and all my labors are nothing because I am oppressed and robbed by those against whom I am helpless, the rich, the ruler, the war lord.

But after a long while he thought of a way to free himself. They thought he was mad. His sons and his neighbors cried out and his wife wept, thinking that his vexations had driven him mad. Wang

110

the Eldest let them think what they liked. For he knew how to free himself at last and he set about doing what he had planned as he lay awake night after night. He chopped down his trees, and he set fire to his own house and burned the furniture that was his. Then he put a torch to all the grain standing in his fields and when it was ruined he flooded the land from the canal nearby. It was a waste, and all he had was gone.

"Now," he said to his family, "now we are free. We are beggars, but we have beggared ourselves at least."

Who last heard of Wang the Eldest? Mad they called him, but he was not mad. He wandered the roads of the nation, thinking himself cursed above all men. But he was not more cursed than others like him, anywhere.

The Commander and the Commissar

THE COMMANDER STOOD in a curve of the Tibetan mountain and watched the long thin line of his battalion struggle up the narrow road of rock, their heads bent to the bitter wind. One thousand men in single file, each with a weapon! They were invincible, the best army in the world, so he believed, and he shouted to encourage them.

"Here we encamp for the night!"

They responded to him as they always did. They lifted their heads and smiled at him, and pride came hot to his heart. He leaped upon a boulder that they might see him the better and he stood there in the strong Tibetan sunlight, his arms folded, his legs astride, behind him the soaring peaks of the snow-covered mountains. He fixed his face in lofty gravity, repressing a smile of exultation. To smile was unbecoming to a leader of men, and such men as the Third Battalion. They were soldiers of the famous Second Field Army commanded by his hero, the One-Eyed Dragon, so-called because had lost his left eye in battle.

The mission was the reward the Commander had been given for years of devoted and loyal service, ever since as a youth of seventeen, now fifteen years ago, he had been seized in his village with his friend, Kao Li, and impressed into the Communist army. With them twenty-three other men had been seized, some young, some older, and among these had been a weak and sickly young man, Yang Fu-ping. Because of his frail looks, he had not been seized, but when he saw that he was not chosen, he begged to be taken.

"I am the only person in this village who can read and write. I have read the teachings of Marx, Lenin and our great Mao, and I can be useful to you."

The military officials, whose business it was to find new recruits, considered and when they had asked Yang some questions, which he answered very well, they took him, too, and placed him in a political school, in order that he could become a commissar. He was clever and he learned quickly. To his superiors he was suave and obedient but to his inferiors he was arrogant and a tyrant. Among his inferiors he always put first the other boys from his village and especially the one who was now the Commander of The Third Battalion, who had been the strongest and most handsome of all the boys in the village, the one who could win every race, the one to whom the Commissar's parents pointed, saying, "How is it that the gods did not give us a son like that, instead of this weakling we have now?" To this day the Commissar could not forget his parents' discontent with him, nor could he forgive the Commander for his strong healthy body and fine looks.

To others he said, "I have known this fellow from his birth—a good animal, but stupid. He must be watched. He is still able to be softhearted and sentimental, in spite of our teachings."

As for the Commander, it was true that he had a soft heart and loved people easily. He had wept aloud for his mother that day when he was taken from her but, after the first terror, he had enjoyed his life, especially as Kao Li, his childhood playmate, remained with him. They talked together secretly of the village and their parents, and though it was forbidden to have such deviating thoughts, they continued to hide them. The Commander had not

113

been ill-treated, and since he really was of simple mind, he accepted his new life, and the daily excitement of attack and retreat in the warfare with enemy forces had been exhilarating. He forgot his family after a year or two, his comrades took their place and Kao Li had been with him as a brother and was now his faithful aide. Since the Commander was strong, he had been sent to military school and, being zealous, had risen quickly. When he had been commended for zeal, he was told that his family was informed of his achievements, that they received extra comforts because of him. Once a year at New Year he wrote to them, and always a letter came back, saying that they were comfortable and happy and praising the new regime. In this way he felt he was still helping his family, although he no longer needed them. It occurred to him now, as he stood on the boulder, that he would write to his family of this mission as soon as it was over without waiting for the New Year. He did not doubt that he would be successful, and thus he would bring more honor not only to them but also to his village.

His orders for the mission had been clear. The General had said, "You are to proceed to the first military post to the west, conveying supplies and silver. It is a march of six days." The General had turned to a large map of Tibet behind him on the wall. "You are to proceed to this point." He put his forefinger on a spot on the map. "You yourself are to be responsible for the box of silver ingots. It is to pay the soldiers at the post to buy food and to hire local labor—"

The General had broken off here and had glanced behind him. "Ah, yes, the Commissar—he will accompany you. This will free you for military decisions."

Behind the General stood the Commissar, Yang Fu-ping. He was now a dark, thin, small man in a dirty uniform of gray cotton cloth, but the Commander recognized him. He was the arrogant enemy of his youth, the boy with bitter eyes and a scornful mouth. Eyes and mouth had not changed, and as the Commander stared at the Commissar he remembered the taunts and the jeering that had wounded him often in the village.

"You ox—out of my way! I am a scholar—"

"You turtle's egg—you are no son of your father—"

"Oaf, you will never learn to read and write, with that thick skull—"

The Commander spoke now. "How can this commissar endure the mountain paths, the cold wind, the poor food?"

"He is our best and most clever commissar," the General replied. "And you are to give him a horse to ride and his tent is to be put on the warm side of a rock. . . . You will need him when you face the savage Tibetans. He speaks their language and you do not."

The two exchanged a long look, the Commander and the Commissar, and the Commander turned away.

"What are the dangers I am to expect upon the way?" he asked.

"Not more than a few Tibetan bandits, hiding in the hills," the General had said carelessly. "They are armed only with bows and arrows."

When the Commander had repeated this to his men, however, as they set forth on the mission, he was surprised that those men, the famous "Wanderers of the Yangtze," seemed afraid. There was even some muttering among them.

"Who knows how many of those bandits are hiding in the hills?"

"Who knows whether they have guns?"

At this the Commissar had grown angry. "Do you believe our great Mao or do you not? The Tibetans have been slaves for hundreds of years and now we have freed them from the capitalist western animals. Hate us? They welcome us! They are working day and night to become good socialists under our great leader Mao."

The men had been silent for it was forbidden to answer the Commissar. But the Commander could not restrain himself.

"My men know very well what they should do. When they do not know, I will tell them."

To this the Commissar replied by spitting in the dust and rubbing the ball of spittle with his foot. The Commander remembered what he had forgotten—that this was the Commissar's reply when the village boys had made fun of his weak helpless body. I spit upon you, I rub you out—this was the meaning of it.

The Commissar continued. "The westerners try to bribe the Tibetans but their bribes are refused—except by a few ignorant persons. Moreover, all Tibetans are furious because the westerners have kidnaped their own leader, the Dalai Lama, and are holding him hostage in India. All Tibetans are waiting to be liberated."

In spite of this encouragement, the men had remained uneasy. Like children they complained privately to the Commander that the Tibetans they saw on the way were very tall and strong, and that they climbed the cliffs like yak instead of men. The Commander had laughed at them and scolded them as they moved their eyes constantly over the high cliffs above the narrow path along which they crawled. A few rebels, hiding in the crevices of the mountains—nothing to fear, he told them, especially as they had been given two Tibetan guides.

Nevertheless even these two guides troubled the Commander in ways that he could not explain, for at the border he had been warned by the Chinese officer in charge of the post there.

"You must be watchful of Tibetans," the officer had said. "They hide in the valleys and they are the color of the gray rock. You must shoot any Tibetan you see and shoot at sight. They are clever and cruel."

"I know our guerrilla tactics," the Commander had replied. "I have myself listened to our great leader Mao, and I know tactics he used during the war."

He had been watchful every step of the way as he marched ahead of his men. It would have been his right to ride one of the pack horses, but he did not allow himself the privilege. The only love he knew was the love he bore his men. For he had never loved a woman. There had been no time for such love. Now and again, overcome by lust, he had seized a woman after a battle somewhere, a stranger to him, and he had compelled her to his desire. Yet the exhaustion of war lessened such need and it had been months since he had thought of a woman. Thus the whole power of his hidden, loving nature could be expressed only toward his men. They were his children. He wanted them to be happy, and he could only make them happy by giving them promises.

"Take comfort," he called to them now. "We will eat and sleep. Be cheerful, my little brothers! Tomorrow we reach the pass. Our guides have a fire already burning."

He was not comforted by his own words. For the guides paid no heed to him nor to the men. They had made a fire of yak dung and upon the circle of stones they had set their small copper tea-kettle. Steam was coming from the bent spout. In a few minutes they would make tea, the thick tea of the Tibetans, and into it they would drop a lump of the rancid butter they carried with them—a vile dish, he thought, yet his mouth watered. He had not eaten since dawn, nor had his men.

"You will feed upon the countryside," the General had said as they parted.

"Certainly, comrade," the Commander had replied.

The trouble was that here in the Tibetan mountains there was no countryside, no village, no town, nothing but bleak cliffs and soaring snowy heights.

He bellowed at the guides. "You Tibetan dogs! You are always hungry! Weaklings!"

To this the guides made no answer. It was possible they did not even understand Chinese. Their dark, reddened faces, set in grim lines against wind and storm, did not change. They poured the hot tea into two copper bowls. Then, hands cupped about the bowls for warmth, they supped loudly. The Commander felt a snatch of hungry pain in his belly and he turned away.

Ah, his men! Standing above them on the boulder the Commander watched them struggle up the narrow path. They carried huge and heavy packs upon their backs, and as they drew near he saw that their faces were drawn in lines of deep weariness. His heart melted in tenderness, for it was his fault, in a way, that the packs were too heavy. He had tried to hire horses as well as yak at the border post to carry the supplies, but at first no horses were to be found, and few yak. Blank Tibetan faces and empty Tibetan eyes had stared at him when he demanded horses.

"Are there no horses in this whole cursed country?" he had cried loudly.

No one had answered. But the Commissar heard the curse and he put it down in his little book. That night he had accused the Commander.

"It is forbidden," he said, "to curse the proletariat. Our leader Mao wishes no great-Han talk. We are to treat the subject peoples as friends and younger brothers."

The Commander did not dare to answer the Commissar. He had grunted and kicked a busybody of a hen, scratching in the dust, and the fowl had flown away shrieking. Then he had shouted at his men.

"We need no horses! We are strong! We will carry the supplies ourselves!"

Nevertheless, before the next day began a few horses were found, and he had ordered them loaded and sent on ahead. Then he had divided among his men what supplies were left, and every man carried a load.

When all was ready for the march, at the last moment the Chinese officer had taken him aside once more into the small bare room, icy cold in spite of spring, and there on a board table he had unrolled maps.

"Here is your route," he had said, and he traced with a dirty forefinger a winding red line wavering up into the mountains. "This is the only pass in the whole range of these mountains," he said. "Do not lose your way."

At the end of this fifth day of the march, the Commander was troubled. To his words of encouragement now few of his men replied. They came near, one by one, loosened their packs and let them fall to the ground. Breathing the scanty air in great gasps, they threw themselves on the ground or lay down on rocks to rest. Soon, impelled by cold, they got to their feet and gathered the stones to make the usual fortification for the night. However

118

tired they were, however hungry, the Commander insisted upon the fortification, for only within these stone walls, he had been told, could they be safe against ambush. While the men worked, the two Tibetan guides sat by their fire and warmed themselves. A glimmer of mirth broke across the masks of their faces as they watched the men. Seeing this cruelty, the Commander snarled at them with obscene curses.

"You sons of turtles! You children of rabbits! You animals, born of incest!"

The Tibetans seemed not to hear and again he could only conclude that they did not understand Chinese. He would have liked to order his men to beat them, but he did not dare to do so. They were Khambas, well over six feet tall, and the fiercest men the Commander had ever seen. Moreover, he was dependent upon them and so he could only curse them. His men laughed at the curses he contrived and their laughter was his comfort. In a few hours they had eaten and were ready to sleep, he with the box of silver for his pillow. And so they prepared for the next day.

This sixth day was the final one. The dawn came up like a city burning on the horizon and within an hour they were on their way again. At noon, when they paused to eat the dried meat and bean curd which was their only fare, the Commander was approached by the Commissar. As far as possible the Commander ignored the Commissar, but it was impossible at this moment. The small, bitter-faced man stood in front of him, cupping his hands about his mouth so that the wind could not blow his words away.

"Comrade, I must have a horse!"

The Commander stared at him. "There is no horse."

"You must take part of the load from a horse and let me sit on the pack for I can walk no further."

The Commander would have liked to shout out a few words. "Then lie down and die!" But he did not dare. Nor did he dare to let the Commissar die, lest he be accused of murder. He could only order one of his men to prepare a horse.

Who could have thought that when the two Tibetan guides

saw what was being done for the Commissar, they, too, would demand horses? Yet this is what they did, and so stubbornly that they stood without moving for nearly an hour. In desperation, while the sun passed the zenith, the Commander had at last to yield. He ordered two more horses unloaded and the guides mounted. When his men began to climb the last steep miles to the pass, he walked behind the mounted Tibetans, anger burning inside the frozen frame of his body.

Through the short forenoon they climbed, until an hour or two before noon, they reached a small plateau. From this narrow level the mountain rose sharply into an inclined cliff, to which the path clung steep as a ladder, the rock cut into still more shallow steps. Then, before the Commander ordered a halt, his men gathered about him. He looked into the faces he knew so well, which were so inexpressibly dear to him. They were dark with fatigue, the lines cut deep, the eyes sunken. Should he cry a halt for the night or could they make the final miles to the pass? He fancied that their eyes pleaded with him to rest, but their voices did not speak. He was about to open his mouth when he heard a loud shout. It came from the two guides, who had mounted their horses again and were galloping across the plateau to the path. He could not, for pride's sake, allow his men to stop.

"Sons of Han!" he cried. "We must not fall behind these Tibetan dogs! We will make the pass before night."

The men replied as gallantly as ever. In silence they took up the march, and he led them. He was as weary as any of them, but he was sustained by their weariness. They depended upon him, they looked to him, they loved him. He would lead them over the pass and down the slope, and there they would rest.

What he did not count upon was the wind. He had heard of the winds of Tibet, those cruel gales, the icy breath of the mountains. Now, halfway up the path, in midafternoon, he heard a strange moaning roar. The sky, clear since morning, was suddenly black, and out from the dragon shapes of the whirling clouds there burst a wind so fierce, so frozen with needles of ice, that it fell

120

upon him and his men like a solid wave of searing cold. He saw his men fall to the ground, struggling under their packs, and he saved himself only by clinging to an arm of rock and hiding his face. Then, fearing to lose his guides, he lifted his head, and saw the two Tibetans riding ahead, their shawls across their faces, their fur hats pulled low. The Commissar rode behind, bent over the saddle.

"Up with you!" the Commander shouted to his men. "The wind will get worse until we are over the pass. Over the pass!"

The men tried to shout, they repeated his words, "Over the pass," but the wind tore their voices to broken echoes. Nevertheless, they struggled to their feet and began the last steep climb. And the Commander led on.

The howling wind now became a screeching devil. His face burned as though he had thrust his head into flames, and he held his right arm across his nose and mouth. He dared not turn his head to see how his men fared. He could only trust them to follow, as he himself followed the lead of the horses, the mountain-climbing Tibetan ponies whose narrow hooves fitted into the cracks and crevices of the rocks. Those moving hooves were all he could see. In the strange wild wailing of the wind he heard no human voice, and only the sharp crack of icy pinnacles, yielding to the force of the wind. He could not think. His whole mind, his entire being, was concentrated upon one step and then another. Each breath burned his lungs with agony, but he struggled on.

At last he reached the pass. There, his back to the rock, he waited for his men. He dared not count them, less than a thousand now surely. Had the missing ones fallen down the precipices? He could not inquire. With what he had he must press on. The wind was the enemy. To camp here on the pass was impossible. They must escape the wind. He turned again to follow the guides through the pass. He had one comfort. They could only go down. There would be no more crawling up the rocks.

In an hour, long as eternity, the guides did indeed lead them down a steep slope, the way still very narrow, no more than a gully between the cliffs on either side, but at least the wind was gone. They had escaped it, they had come down out of it. In the sudden quiet the Commander felt giddy with exhaustion. His men were as giddy as he, staggering, collapsing, retching, vomiting blood. He roused himself to walk toward them as they came out of the wind and fell to the ground at his feet.

Then he saw the Commissar. He, too, lay on the ground, gasping for breath. The Commander stopped.

"Comrade, where is your horse?" he demanded.

"He ran—after the—guides," the Commissar gasped. "I fell—and the beast ran—"

"We must follow the guides without delay," the Commander said angrily.

"Impossible," the Commissar groaned. "I cannot move. We must make camp."

The Commander was about to retort that he must think of his men and their safety. Then it occurred to him that if the Commissar made the decision to halt and encamp, the blame would not be upon him, the Commander. He shrugged.

"For me, it would be better to push on and reach our post. But if you say—"

Before he could finish they heard a great noise from the mountain behind them, the shout of many voices. The Commander looked up and saw mounted men, Tibetans, ten, twenty, thirty, descending the sloping cliffs, their horses sliding over the moraine of broken rock and ice. They held their swords upright before them, and the sun glinted upon the polished metal.

"Take care!" the Commander cried to his men but it was too late. The Tibetans had already fallen upon them. They seized the loaded yak that brought up the rear behind the few horses and rode up the wind-swept pass, pulling the yak after them. The Commander was speechless. They were in a trap. The guides were nowhere to be seen. Had they joined the robbers? He searched the mountains on either side of the narrow pass. The canyon where they stood gave no cover and on the steep slopes he saw, his eyes long trained for ambush, here the glint of a rifle barrel and there the half-hidden movement of a fur-hatted figure. A hundred Tibetans in such ambush could destroy the entire column of his men.

"You two company captains," he ordered, "come aside with me."

Two young men followed him a few steps down the path, and leaning against the cold wet rock of the cliff, he faced them with Kao Li, his faithful aide, at his side.

"Let us estimate the situation," he said. "Thus far we have fulfilled our mission. By tomorrow night we should be at the outpost. We cannot allow ourselves to be stopped by a few Tibetan dogs."

He waited, but they said nothing. Accustomed only to obedience and exhausted now by cold and weariness, they looked at him with dull eyes.

"Have you nothing to say?" he asked.

Kao Li replied, "Comrade, you speak, we will obey."

The Commander considered. He felt a shameful wish to weep, to argue with these young men, to plead that this fearful moment was not his fault. He refused his own longings and turned away from his private terror. These were his sons, his children. He roused himself to think. If he could encourage his men to retreat through the pass—but he could not. The winds would scatter them, blind them, make them the helpless prey of the mounted Tibetans. Those Tibetans could slaughter all his men and seize the precious supplies, for which thousands of other men waited. . . . Or suppose he divided the men into two parts, each to storm the cliff on either side of where they stood and thus drive the Tibetans out of ambush? Folly, when the Tibetans could shoot them from the crevices where they hid, and seize the supplies! He looked again at the cliffs. If his men could collect enough stones to build a fort, here in the pathway—but there were no stones, no earth, not a handful. The ageless wind had blown away every particle of dust. There remained nothing except to use their mortars in concerted action and blast the Tibetans out of their hiding places. But can solid rock be blasted? He gave up this dream also as he stared up at the gray cliffs. Seeming empty and lifeless, he knew they hid the enemy. The enemy? He had been told that the Tibetans loved the Chinese,

123

welcomed them, waited for them. Who had told such lies? The Commissar! He looked at the Commissar. That fellow, the enemy of his childhood, was lying on the ground, rolled in his blanket.

The Commander began again: "Our orders are to get every man and all the supplies safely to the post. If we fail, it will mean death to our brothers waiting there. We are their only hope. Therefore we must save both men and supplies. Yet if we force the men to fight, they will die of exhaustion. These Tibetan bandits will do anything for money. Therefore let us negotiate. They will ask a big price, but at least not everything will be lost."

The Commissar now came to life. He got up from the rock where he lay, he tightened his belt and thrust out his lower lip. Then he folded his arms and strode to face the Commander. "And after we have paid this high price, how can we keep those bandits from attacking us? And taking everything?"

The Commander answered in a sturdy voice. "I shall buy their weapons."

"And with what?" the Commissar asked.

"With the silver," the Commander said.

At this the Commissar went into his usual action. He strode five steps this way and took five steps back, casting black looks at the Commander from under his frowning brows. Then he stopped so close that his foul breath stank in the Commander's nostrils.

"Is is your silver? Do you dare to use silver belonging to the people of our country?"

The Commander understood very well that the Commissar was declaiming for the men to hear, and by so doing he was excusing himself at some future time when the Commander would be tried for failure. Under his padded uniform the Commander felt rills of sweat burst from his skin and run down his body. The Commissar was his superior in rank. He must save himself here in these wild mountains, for he could not save himself in that inner chamber, where sat those few in whose hands all destiny lay. There the Commissar was privileged.

124

He began to argue, in order to save himself. "Would the people choose to have our men lost with the supplies, not to say the men waiting at the post? Time is what we need—time for our men to escape with what we have left. As for the silver, we can take most of it from the box and put gravel in its place, keeping only enough silver to cover."

The Commissar spat into the dust. "A child's plan!" he sneered.

"Have you a better?" the Commander demanded. When the Commissar did not reply, he went on.

"Find me a piece of wrapping paper from the supplies," he told Kao Li. "I will write an offer to the bandits and you must mount a horse and take it to them. Put down your gun, so they see you come in peace."

Kao Li obeyed in silence, and upon the paper the Commander wrote in simple clear letters these words:

Our Tibetan Brothers! We should not war against each other. Let us meet for mutual understanding. He gave the paper to Kao Li, who went away holding it high like a flag, and he carried no weapon.

The Commander watched. No sooner had Kao Li reached the base of the cliff than a burst of strong fire from machine guns split the icy air. From the sound of the fire the Commander knew that they were Russian machine guns, and this could only mean that they had been captured from Chinese forces. Kao Li fell from his horse, dead!

The Commissar was also watching. "These bandits are well armed," he said grimly.

The Commander could not speak. What had he done! Why had he allowed Kao Li to carry the message? Straining his eyes into the twilight, he now saw a Tibetan horseman come sliding down the slope, his sword held upright before him. He paused beside the dead man, dismounted and cut off Kao Li's head with the sword. Then he took the sheet of paper and went back again into the mountain, leading with him the horse upon which Kao Li had ridden.

The Commander forgot where he was. He saw only Kao Li's headless body. He ran up the path and with his foot he caught the head as it rolled down the sloping cliff. Kao Li's face looked up at him, the eyes startled in sudden death, and he gazed down at this face caught by his foot. The Commander remembered Kao Li as a child in his village, his faithful follower from the days when they had flown kites together until this day. To Kao Li he had been always a hero. He felt a deep pain in his breast and the pain rose into his throat and swelled into a sob.

Yet there was no time to mourn even for his friend. A Tibetan horseman came riding out of the rocks, holding in his hand a sword, upon the point of which was the paper. He came near, and lowered his sword, so that the Commander could take the paper. Then he galloped away. It was the same paper which Kao Li had delivered, and upon the back of it were a few Chinese words, brushed in classic strokes.

We agree to meet. Let the meeting take place behind the third pinnacle to the west an hour from now.

The Commander hastened back to his men and gave his orders. The Commissar and the two captains must accompany him to the trysting place. Meanwhile he ate some dried bean curd while he considered how to speak to the Tibetans. The hour was soon gone, and he and the Commissar and the two captains climbed to the third western pinnacle. There they found a little valley almost free of snow, in the center of which was a small deep lake, dull silver in the light of the moon, which now rode high over the mountains. Opposite the path by which they had come the Commander saw the flickering lights of lanterns and he slowed his pace lest he reach the trysting spot too soon and appear as the inferior. Timing his approach, he arrived at the same moment with the Tibetans as they came toward the lake. There were three of them, all on horseback. The leader was a tall man and very broad across the shoulders. He wore a long, wine-red robe, edged with fur and opened at the collar to show the fur lining. He carried his fur hat

126

under his arm, and his head was shaven. Black brows and a handsome face the Commander saw, and then he saw that this face was not brutish or stupid, but intelligent and alive. It was the face of a priest, a lama, and not of a soldier. He waited for the Tibetans to dismount, but they did not. They sat their horses easily and in their turn they waited.

The Commander, seeing this, gave his gun to one of the captains and stepping forward, he folded his arms and began.

"Our Tibetan brothers, greetings! We are not come to make war but to bring peace. Our peoples have been neighbors from ancient times, and we are one family—"

The Commander made his words clear and simple and he spoke slowly, supposing that the Tibetans did not understand Chinese. To his surprise, the lama replied in excellent Chinese, very learned.

"You are not our brothers. You are invaders. You have destroyed our towns. You kill our true brothers."

The Commander was taken aback, not only by these words but also by the way in which they were spoken. This was a man more learned than he himself was and in Chinese. He glanced sidewise at the Commissar. Upon that lean and scornful face he discerned a cold fury. The Commissar stepped forward, stretched out his right hand and pointed his little finger at the Tibetan and shouted. "We men of Han have saved you from slavery to the western imperialists! Deny it and you will die!"

"Oh fool!" the Commander hissed under his breath, but the Commissar did not hear him.

He shrieked as loudly as he could at the Tibetans.

"Your ancestors were our vassals! Your land is our land! We will allow you to live upon it, by the mercy of our great Mao Tse-tung, but not until we have driven away the imperialists of the West! For this you should only be grateful! You should welcome us!"

The lama refused an answering anger. He spoke steadily and in patience. "It is true that half a hundred years ago a band of western men invaded our land. They were armed with such weapons as we

127

had never seen and we were compelled to yield to them. Yet all they wanted of us was trade. True again, we did not want their trade, because they took more than they gave. But they went away and left us as we were. Few of them have ever returned. I have traveled far in our country and I have not seen a man of the West. We were never slaves to them."

"You lie!" the Commissar shouted.

The lama proceeded as though he had not stopped speaking. "Whereas you and your people," he went on, "have forced your way into our country. You have come here, more than one hundred thousand of you. You have taken our government. You have seized our best land, and we have become poor and few. You even steal our children and teach them your lies so that they fear you and your masters. Our food you rob for your soldiers and our young men labor like convicts for you. And worst of all, you try to destroy that which we hold most dear—the religion of our forefathers, so that even our Dalai Lama is driven into exile. Is this not slavery? Is this not death?"

Into the clear cold air of the approaching night the Tibetan's calm voice poured forth these words in purest Chinese. The Commander found himself listening against his will.

The Commissar turned to him in fury. "Do you stand there silent? Are you a deviate?"

The Commander made an effort. "It is for your own good," he told the Tibetan. "We offer you a full share in our glorious future."

"You offer nothing—you only take," the lama said. "Therefore we do not trust you. But you cannot destroy us. We are fighting for more than life. We are fighting for our own way of life. You will fail, even though you kill us all."

"Ah ha," the Commissar exclaimed. "Now it is you who are wrong! Our great leader, Mao, says that all peoples are to keep their own religion. Can you doubt his word?"

"If he means what he says," the lama replied, "then why are you here?"

128

"Come, come," the Commander said. "Let us cease this useless talk. Why am I here? I am here to buy your firearms—that is why I am here. I have a thousand armed men, and I do not need your arms, mind you—but instead of seizing your weapons, I will allow you to sell them to us. This is mercy."

The lama suddenly laughed. It was joyous laughter, as though he had heard a fine joke. "Why should we sell our arms? We need them to drive your men from our land."

"You will die tonight!" the Commissar bellowed.

"Not tonight," the lama said gently. "We know how many men you have—not one thousand. And they are exhausted. They cannot breathe in this thin air. But we can. It is our air." His voice suddenly changed. It was low and fierce as he went on. "We can see in the dark. We know every rock and stone in these mountains. They are our mountains. We can smell you wherever you hide. It is you who die tonight."

The Commander felt the sweat run down his body again and he knew he was afraid. But why was the lama not afraid?

As for the Commissar, he gave a false roar. "One hundred of you against our hundreds—"

The lama leaned down from his horse. "If you could have understood what I have told you—even you might have been spared."

With these words he spurred his horse into a gallop and disappeared into the mountains, his two men following. The Commissar turned on the Commander. "Do you stand there idle?"

The Commander, thus harried, pulled his pistol from its holster to fire after the lama. His hand dropped. It was useless. He and his men were covered by rifles hidden in every fold of the mountain. He turned and went back to his waiting men. They received him in silence. He knew now why the lama was not afraid. He too had once fought like that, he and his men, upon their own soil, for their own lives, against an alien enemy, the armies of Japan. But now he was the enemy—he and his men. . . . Suddenly in the darkness he heard the strange low wailing of men who are lost

129

in battle, the hopeless ones, for whom when the night falls there can be no dawn.

"Aie, my mother—my mother—my mother—"

These grown men were wailing like children for their lost mothers. One by one they took up the moaning cry, until only the Commissar and he were silent.

At this moment the Commissar lifted his head and shouted once more. "We are the People's Liberating Army, one thousand strong! How can one hundred Tibetan bandits defeat us?"

The Commander seized him by the neck and shook him.

"Be silent, you fool!" he hissed between his teeth. Then he saw that face between his fists.

"Fool—fool! Had you been silent, I might have saved us all. You and your lies!"

He could not restrain himself. All the anger of his childhood welled up in him, all the anger of his manhood denied. His hands tightened on the scrawny throat, he watched the eyes bulge. The Commissar struggled, but he was too weak and in a moment he was still. The Commander loosed him then and lifting the living body he threw it over the cliff. Then he looked toward the mountains around him. The wailing of his men had ceased. They were moving away from him, they were separating themselves, they were creeping into lonely hiding places. They were deserting him, in terror each for himself. He tried to call them, but his voice died away. He remembered the brave words he had been taught.

"Plant the red flag—liberate every mind—"

"Production is the heart of socialism—labor is its breath—"

"Be positive—not negative—"

"Serve the people so the people can care for you—"

None of these fine words seemed useful at this moment. The silver moon was sinking behind the mountains. Soon the night would be all darkness.

"Aie, my mother," he cried, and his voice rose to a wail. "My mother—my mother!"

130

And now he heard the voices of his men answering him again, like echoes from whence they hid. "My mother—my mother—"

He ran to join his men. They were all lost. They were lost, far from home in the cold mountains of a strange and enemy country. The Commander was no longer alone.

Begin to Live

THE TRAIN WENT SWINGING around the curve and out of the window he saw the town. The wild gaiety on his face froze.

"What's the matter, Tim?" Bob asked him.

He stood up and began pulling down his bags from the rack. "I'm home," he cried.

He kept on grinning to hide the way he felt, because the men were staring at him. In a few minutes he'd tell them all goodbye and maybe never see them again. He had not thought of this until now. He had only been thinking of seeing his folks again, and the town. All during the crowded trip over he had borne with daily small grievances because he saw this moment so clearly ahead, the moment when the train would round the curve of Piper's Hill, and he would see his town, there by the river, waiting. Now the grievances seemed precious for a moment, Bob's untidiness which even army discipline had not changed, boots on the bed, clothes anywhere, Hank's incessant snicker, the senseless obscenity of some of the men. He had borne it because he saw the end of it all, and in bearing had learned to keep up the eternal kidding that was only a vent for overstrained men.

132

"Well, Tim—write once in a while, will you?" Bob said.

"Sure," he said. He felt his face still frozen in the silly grin, and he drew down his mouth to get rid of it. He hoped his mother wouldn't cry when she saw him. He was so much more lucky than some of the other wounded. He was already used to doing without his arm. His work was done, his fifty missions completed. All he had to do now was to begin where he had left off two years ago. And it had happened on the last flight.

The men watched him and showed their envy through laughter and through silence. He was the first one to get home. He felt them wondering about him, seeing themselves in him. Their eyes were doubtful. For the first time he felt them wondering if it was going to be easy to get home. For the first time he wondered, too.

The train ground into the station and he leaped up, his bags over his right shoulder. The men yelled at him and crowded to the windows. Hank whistled through his fingers. A sigh swept over them. "Boy, look at the blonde!" That was Kit.

Then he saw her. She stood surrounded by his family, like a madonna in a frame. He leaped to the platform, dropped his bags and put him arm about her tight. The train tore on, but he stood there, his face buried in her neck, her hair against his cheek. He felt her tremble, she laughed and pushed him a little, and he saw her eyes were wet. "Tim, here's your mother—your dad—and Mary—"

But he had let himself go so much that he could hardly pull himself together. He was almost faint, not just because it was Kit, but because he was still alive. Now he really knew it was all over. He would never have to feel the bomber lift him into the night and go out wondering if he would come back. He was back to stay.

"Tim, son—" his mother was murmuring. He felt her soft cheek wet under his lips.

"Well, Tim," his father said and coughed and gripped his hand.

Mary put her arms around his neck. "Grown, haven't you, kid?" he said unsteadily.

133

"Oh, Tim," she said, "I want you to meet my fiancé." She pulled forward a tall thin boy whose face went white and then red.

"You aren't old enough—" He tried to tease Mary and then found his mirth dried in him at the sight of the boy's eyes.

"I hope to get into the air myself," the boy said, pumping his hand up and down. His bony young hand was strong.

"Swell," Tim said, and saw the boy lifting into the night, wondering if he would ever come back. He'd have to tell him—what? How could you tell another living soul what it was like?

Everybody was trying to get to him at once. He saw more than half the town was there—just as he had known they would be. They had come to see him off and now they were here to welcome him home. It was all just as he had imagined. He'd forget those two years, rip them out of his life, burn them up and scatter the ashes.

They were walking along the board platform. The day was gorgeous, September, silent and golden, grape-scented. The sunlight was as clear as English ale.

"We're a little shabby," his father said. "There hasn't been any chance to paint and repair during the war."

"Looks swell to me," he replied.

The air was so still that he felt all motion stopped. Even when they were walking along the platform, and even when they were climbing into the car, he felt transfixed in the stillness.

"It's because I have been rushing so much all these months—always under orders to go somewhere, to do something," he told himself. Aloud he said, "Nothing looks changed, Dad."

"No, we don't change," his father replied, and started the car slowly. "Have to be careful of tires these days."

"So I heard," Tim said. He sat between his mother and Kit in the back seat, and he held Kit's hand tightly.

The house was just as he remembered it. But he saw it as he had never seen it before because he had seen so many in Tennessee, in Georgia, in Arizona, in England, in Normandy, and the roofs of houses in Germany under his bomber. This house was at once

134

familiar and strange, his own and yet separate. They went in and he looked around while they watched him.

"God, but it's good to be home," he said. But he was still dazed with the silence and he sat down in the brown leather chair by the fireplace. They all sat down and looked at him and he looked at them. He wanted to tell them—what? Everything he wanted to tell them was shut off by this feeling of being stopped.

He laughed. "I feel the way I used to feel when I got out of the roller coaster at the fair."

They laughed, too. Here they were, this was the moment to which they had all looked forward, and none of them knew what to do with it.

His mother got up. "I'll go and see about the dinner—we'll have plenty of time to talk—I have everything you like, Tim."

She went over to him, put her hand on his shoulder. "It's you— you're real—" The tears came into her eyes, and he knew she was thinking about his arm. He could not speak, even to tell her he was lucky to be alive.

"Now, Mother," his father said gently.

"Oh, I know," she said under her breath, "but I can't get used to him—after everything—"

She hurried away, and he stared through the window. Did they have to get used to him, too?

"I'll be going along," the tall boy said. "So long, Mary."

"So long, Frank," Mary said, but she got up, too.

The tall boy went over to him and put out his hand. "Goodbye, Tim. I hope you don't mind my calling you that. I hope sometime when you've—you've rested I can come and talk to you about the air force. I'm supposed to join up next month—I'll be eighteen, then."

"Sure," he replied. "I'll be glad to tell you anything I can— though you'll be told, well enough, what you have to do."

"I guess so," the boy said, and went out with Mary, their young hands gripped together at the door.

"They're awfully young," he said staring after them.

"Too young," his father said, "but we figured that if he's old enough to join the army he's old enough—for anything else. Of course they won't be married right away. He has his training ahead of him. After all, your mother and I—we got engaged like that, in the last war. My parents objected. We never forgot it, and I guess when Mary and Frank came to us we couldn't refuse them what they wanted, never having forgotten . . ."

His father's voice trailed off. It came over him that he was a third in the room where Tim and Kit might be alone. He smiled shyly and got to his feet. "Reckon Mother needs some help," he said and walked softly out of the room.

Then Kit came over to him and knelt before him and put her arms around his waist, and lifted her lovely tender face. He stared down into it and did not move. "You're tired," she said.

He put his hand slowly into the hair over her ear. It was wonderful stuff. He had dreamed about it, how soft it was, how alive. He felt her little left ear, flat under his palm, and then he tipped her head upward and looked down into her sweet blue eyes.

"This is when I'd like my hand back," he said unsteadily. "One isn't enough to love you with."

"I'm only thankful," she whispered, "so *thankful.*"

Then he wanted to tell her everything, in one word, in one moment, and have it over with so he could forget it. But how could he tell her about what he had been through? He did not know how to begin, or even how to put it into words. It was all feeling. That was the strange thing. It wasn't important what he had done or even what had happened. It seemed to him now that what had happened in these two years was mechanical and meaningless, but all his feelings were important—the way he felt, for example, when he was in the sky. Being in the sky so much made a man solitary. The earth rounded under him, separate and distant. He left the world and entered the universe. And the moment when out of the sky the enemy bullet had pierced his flesh—the unexpectedness of it, nothing in sight, no one, and yet death was hiding in the clouds! But how could he tell such things to Kit, in a moment? He bent and kissed her lips. Better not to talk, better simply to kiss!

. . . "Dinner's ready," his mother called. They laughed and Kit jumped to her feet. "We've been here almost an hour," she cried.

"It's been only a minute," he said.

The dining room was fragrant with food as they went in and they sat down in a stir of cheer. His mother was a good cook and when she put a meal on the table she thought of nothing else.

"Sit down everybody," she commanded. Until everything was tasted and proved, she could not tolerate conversation. "Now, Father, put the gravy on the mashed potatoes before you pass the plates back. Tim, you're letting your biscuit get cold without buttering it. Mary, the olive oil—" She tossed the salad expertly, "Goodness, Tim, it was a relief when we beat Italy and could get olive oil again!"

Italy! His best friend had been killed at Anzio Beachhead. He thought of it and decided not to tell it. Anzio Beachhead had nothing to do with the sun-filled dining room and the tableful of good food.

"This roast," his mother was saying, "I've been saving points for it for weeks, Tim, in your honor—"

His father carved well because his mother had taught him how. He laid the pink-tinged slices upon one another and his mother watched.

"Tim likes it rare, Father," she reminded him.

He started to speak and did not. He liked his meat well done now. But how could he say that without explaining what he did not even want to think about? He had to forget the way raw red flesh looked, bombed flesh, torn muscles, splintered bones.

"Thanks, Dad," he said, and took his plate and covered the meat with mustard.

But it was a fine dinner, especially the pumpkin pie. "One thing they couldn't make right in the army was pumpkin pie," he said.

"Well, now, you're back to home cooking," his mother said to

137

comfort him. "Kit's been learning how to cook while you were away. I've been teaching her all your favorite dishes."

They were good to him after dinner. "You're sleepy," Mary said.

"Goodness, the boy's tired out," his mother cried. "You go on up to your room, Tim, and stretch out while we clear up."

He looked apologetically at Kit and she smiled. "I'm going to help wash up and then go home." She lived in the next block. "When you wake up you can give me a ring."

"You're swell," he murmured, "you're all swell. I don't know why I'm so tired."

"You're let down," his father said kindly. "I know how it is."

He looked at his father with an instant's wonder. Did he know?

"I came back once from a war too, you know," his father said half-shyly.

"Of course," he said. But he had forgotten there had ever been another war.

He had come upstairs for a moment to wash up as soon as they reached home, and had opened the door of his room and looked in. Everything was the same. Now when he came in he saw only the bed. It was a big double bed, for he had been the sort of little boy who fell out of bed regularly. "We'll have to get him a bed so big he can't fall out," his mother had declared, and had given him the spare room bed when she put in twin beds. They called it the guest room after that.

He opened the drawer of the bureau, found an old pair of pajamas and put them on. He got into the bed, savoring every second of it, and lay there, his eyes wide open. That last night he had slept here—how different he was then—a boy! He was not a boy now. He knew everything, life and death, but especially death. He did not know how to begin living again. Even with Kit—he couldn't simply make love to Kit all day. They had to begin to live. But how? In the army somebody always told you. He sighed and fell asleep.

. . . When he woke he heard laughter and voices. The house

was full of people. He lay still, listening. God, I don't want to get up again, ever, he thought. But in a moment the door opened softly and he saw his mother's face and he called to her. "Yes, I'm awake —what's going on downstairs?"

"Some of the folks have come in," she said. "Do you feel like coming down?"

"Sure," he lied, "sure, I'll be right down."

He got up slowly when the door closed. Well, what should he put on, his uniform or one of his old suits? He opened the closet door and saw his three suits hanging there, all carefully pressed, and he took the dark blue coat from a hanger and slipped it on. It was too tight. "Gosh, I've grown, actually," he muttered.

Then he was glad he had put on his uniform. He was used to it and he felt more himself in it. But of course he had to get some other clothes. Tomorrow maybe he and Kit would go downtown together.

He pinned on his medal and flicked a towel over his shoes and smiled at himself in the glass. He looked just the way he always did before he took off. The fellows had laughed at him sometimes for brushing his hair the last thing. Well, it made him feel better before he went into a fight. Only there were no more fights! He stood, pulling at his lip, forgetting himself. It was exactly as though you had trained yourself hard to run a race forward and then found there was no race. Your muscles urged you on and then your mind told you something else. But what?

"Coming, Tim?" His mother's voice floated up the stairs and he hurried down. They were all gathered in the big living room at the foot of the stairs, and they looked up as he came down. He saw them, watching, admiring, friendly, and he waved his hand over his head, and was conscious for a moment of his empty left sleeve.

"Hi, everybody," he shouted, and made himself go on. But it was like taking a nose dive. It was all right, though. In a minute they were around him, patting his back, shaking his hand, clinging to him. He knew they did not know what to say. He knew they had all been warned to ask no questions. On the train he had read an article in a magazine telling people how to treat the boys when they came home and there had been great stress on not asking them any questions. But he could feel them wanting to know, just the same. Of course they wanted to know. He had been through something vicariously for them. They had worked and bought bonds and prayed in churches for him because through him they were fighting. If he could have sat down and said to them quietly, "Look, I'll tell you just how it was—"

But he could not, and the feeling of being stopped came over him again. He had lost it for a moment when they were all shouting to one another. They were the same but he was not. He knew now that this was the trouble. He went on laughing and talking, asking them a hundred questions, because they could not ask him one. But he knew that he would never be the same again. It was not his arm—it was everything he had been through, good and bad.

He would tell Kit so that night. If he could tell her, he thought, maybe she could help find out how he was changed, and what it was he had changed into, and if they knew that then everything would be clear.

He went over to her house after supper, and the family left them alone. Everything was perfect, the quiet comfortable room, the wood fire, the stillness. They sat crowded together in the big armchair, and her head was on his breast. She lay there silent so long that he lifted her chin.

"Asleep?" he asked.

She shook her head and he saw her eyes were full of tears.

"What is it?" he asked, and was frightened. Did she feel the change in him?

But she answered simply and truthfully. "I am only happy."

He pressed her head back again. There was no reason why he should not say now what he knew she expected him to say, "We will be married now, right away, Kit. We've waited so long." They had planned to be married on his first furlough and then the furlough had been canceled and he had been sent straight over, as

140

a few of them had been, to meet a sudden crisis of which he did not even now know the meaning. But he did not feel it was fair to her to say such a thing until he had found out for himself and for her, what sort of a man he was now. He could describe some of the changes. He could say, for example, that he was a harsher man than he had been, more given to impatience and abruptness and ill temper. He swore easily, and his blood tingled quickly. Would he ever break the habit of physical violence? Maybe he would be the sort of man who would thrash his children—maybe even beat his wife. How did he know? And if he didn't know, how could she?

He put his lips into Kit's soft hair and sealed them.

. . . "I suppose my job is the first thing," he said to his father the next morning at breakfast.

Mary was not down yet and his mother had been called to the telephone and he and his father were alone for the moment.

"You're counting on your old job?" his father asked.

"I suppose I ought not to count on anything," he replied.

He and his father had never been especially close. His father was a quiet man, hardworking, a partner in a law firm, at home pleasantly submissive to the family. He had never thought much about his father. Now he was embarrassed by a look of yearning in his father's gray eyes.

"I don't seem to have a special desire for anything," he went on.

"You wouldn't have wanted to go on with flying?" his father asked.

"God, no!" he replied violently, although he had not thought of it until this moment. Could he ever have taken a plane up without remembering the times he had gone up on his missions of death? "Just now I feel I never want to step into a plane again," he said.

"I can understand that," his father replied. "Well, why don't you go and see Mr. Gedsoe and find out how things are?" So that was what he did after breakfast, still wearing his uniform. He still felt more assured wearing it.

141

But Mr. Gedsoe was wholly kind. He sent for him to come in without any waiting, which was unusual in itself, and he got up and shook hands when Tim came in.

"Been expecting you," he said. "I thought your job would be the first thing you'd be coming back for, what with Kit waiting for you." He gave his dry click of laughter. "I've seen all the old bachelors in town try to get Kit while you were away, and she's been as faithful as an old wife—more faithful than some of the wives, I can tell you."

"Is my job still here?" he asked.

"I've had a fellow holding it down, but I'm going to move him into the selling end, so that you can have it back, unless you want the selling end yourself. I notice the fellows coming back are sort of restless. I'd give you a raise in any event."

Gedsoe and Billings was an electrical manufacturing house.

"I don't want to travel," Tim said.

"In that case," Mr. Gedsoe said, "you can begin when you like."

Tim met his eyes and caught the glint of curiosity in them. Mr. Gedsoe looked away. "We're glad to have you home, Tim," he said. "And I want to tell you, I've always looked on your job as simply one in a series of steps up. You're one of the men I'm looking to for the future, when Billings and I get old."

"Thank you, sir," Tim said. But did he want to sit in this office behind Mr. Gedsoe's desk? He did not know. Then for some reason he felt impelled to speak of his arm. "I ought to say I don't think my arm will hold me up on the job, Mr. Gedsoe—lucky I have my right one."

Mr. Gedsoe averted his eyes. "Of course not," he said quickly. But he had been thinking of it. There was guilt in his face.

I can feel people, Tim thought in astonishment. I know what they're thinking.

But he felt no less remote for this new sensitivity. On the contrary, he was ashamed to have seen into Mr. Gedsoe and he bade him goodbye somewhat formally. Then he went out again into the sunshine and walked slowly homeward. Every few minutes someone called to him and he answered gaily. Gaiety, he had found in the army, could become a habit, meaningless but useful for a screen.

There was no reason why he should not just begin to live, he now told himself. Kit had been faithful and his job was waiting. When the men used to talk together in one of their rare sessions of gravity, that was all they wanted—that their girls should be faithful and their jobs waiting. But he still felt stopped and motionless.

Maybe if I get off this damned uniform, he thought suddenly, I'd get out of this rut.

He heard running footsteps behind him and turned and saw Frank loping along. He came up panting.

"You passed right by our house," he gasped, "and I was coming to get Mary— We're going to look at some furniture."

"Already?" Tim smiled.

"Of course we're not getting married just yet," the boy said earnestly. "That's something I wanted to ask your advice about. My mother and Dad want us to wait. Mother says—"

"If you want my advice," Tim broke in, "I'd say, don't wait. Get married before you go over."

The boy's eager face turned pink. "I'm awfully—I'm very glad to hear you say that," he stammered. "It's hard on a fellow. I mean, Mary says she'd rather—she says it would give her something—but of course there's my mother—"

"It'll be easier for you, too, when you come back," Tim said. "It will give you something to go on—something ready that you have to do. You'll have your orders, so to speak. That makes everything easier."

He longed for Mary's sake to pour out on this young creature some of the things he had learned. But what had he learned? Except how to hit a target with a bomb? It had been no easier to go up the fiftieth time than it had been the first. You didn't really learn anything in war. It got worse, not better. That's why so many of the fellows took to getting half-drunk—but you couldn't drink if you were going up in the air. You had to face death cold sober.

143

Yet it wasn't his own death he had found the hardest to face. It was having to let death loose on a lot of other human beings. Of course you couldn't think. Some of them were able not to think. But he had not been one of these. He had all his life been cursed with imagination. Every time he came back he had imagined what he had done. But he had to do it next time all the same.

This boy who was going to be his brother had an imagination, too. You could see it in the lines of his head and in the look of his eyes. He'd be changed when he came back.

They walked along side by side, and the boy's hands were thrust into his pockets. As though he felt Tim's thoughts, he said after a moment, "I want to ask you—was it as hard as you thought it was going to be?"

Ah, the imagination was already working! "It was pretty bad," Tim said gravely. "But of course you have to do what you're told. That takes the responsibility off—some, at least."

"I suppose so," the boy replied.

That was all he could say, after all. They parted at the door, and Tim went up to his room and shut the door softly and sat down in the barrel chair by the window. He ought to call Kit, but he did not feel he wanted to do anything. But after a while his mother tapped at the door.

"Kit's on the telephone, dear," she called.

"All right," he said, and went to the phone.

"Are you coming over, Tim?" Kit asked.

"Sure," he said, "Right away. Want to go downtown and help me buy some clothes?"

"That would be fun," she said.

. . . It was fun, but in the new clothes he felt more strange than ever, and when he laid the uniform away into a drawer it was as though he were burying something. They had been gay enough all morning, but he had not told Kit that Mr. Gedsoe said his job was waiting and he did not know why he had not told her.

144

His father came home for lunch today, because it was his first day home, and the family praised the new suit of brown tweed.

"You're so much better built than you were," his mother said fondly. "I believe the war did you some good, after all, Tim, now that you're safely home." She could look at him now without seeing his arm.

He smiled. It was much easier to smile than to answer. He had found that out already. But he was grateful when a moment later his father saved him another answer.

"Did Mr. Gedsoe keep your job, Tim?" his mother asked.

His father broke in. "Of course Gedsoe kept the job, Sally, but Tim may have other things in mind."

In this house his mother's rule was habitual, but when his father spoke in that tone of voice, his mother was silent. He caught his father's eyes, and for the first time the stoppage in him eased a little. Could it be possible his father understood?

"What are you doing this afternoon, Tim?" his father asked.

"Nothing until four, sir," he replied. At four he and Kit were going together to a party some of her friends were giving for him.

"Come around to the office, will you?" his father said. "I want to talk over a little business with you."

"I'll be there," Tim said.

But he could not think what business his father might have with him. Long ago the matter had come up of his being a lawyer and joining his father's firm and he had rebelled against it. He had always loved machinery and especially electrical stuff. He had had ideas about using electricity in ways not yet known. That was before the war—and it was part of the stoppage that he had not in all these three years given his inventions a thought. But war demanded incessant activity. Even the periods of idleness were only waiting to be active again. He had lost the habit of long ruminative patient thought.

His father's office was just as it had always been, the shelves packed with gray-backed books, the desk piled neatly with papers.

"Come in," his father said, looking at him over his spectacles.

145

He came in and sat down on the chair across the desk where his father's clients always sat and told him their troubles.

His father put his brief into a drawer. "I wanted to have a talk with you, Tim, before you went back to Gedsoe. You remember you once wanted to make a new model of an electrical typewriter? It was a good idea, if I remember."

"I haven't thought about it since," Tim said.

"Gedsoe is interested in it, though," his father said, "and I daresay you'll be wanting to take it up again. What I wanted to say is that I don't think you should be satisfied with Gedsoe's terms. He retains the patents, and complete rights. Now I think you should participate in the rights and I'd like to have Blair of our firm represent you, if you're willing. No reason why you should let Gedsoe—"

Outside the window a branch of red maple waved like a flag. Last month in France a girl had leaned out of her window and waved a flag at the Americans as they went marching by. He heard the feet of marching men drumming along a road. He had been ahead, in a jeep, and they had swept into the town. The next night he had bombed a town in Germany from a base in France.

"You aren't listening, Tim," his father said gently.

He started and flushed. "How did you know?" he mumbled. He met his father's eyes gazing at him across the desk.

"You feel stopped," his father said. "Nothing is real to you."

"How do you know?" he whispered. It had never occurred to him in his life that his father had understood him or had even given him much thought. The image of his father when it appeared at all, was of a tall stooped man, a gray figure in a gray suit, gray hair, gray eyes, kind enough, always busy.

"You don't know whether you want to go back to your job, you don't even know whether you want to marry Kit. You can't go backward, you don't want to go backward, and yet you don't know how to take the next step," his father went on.

"That's about it," Tim mumbled. "But how did you know?"

"The greatest problem that war leaves, in a man, is how to

146

recapture reality," his father said thoughtfully. "That's because war is unreal."

"It seemed horribly real," Tim said.

"Only life is real," his father returned. "You have to get back into life."

"I don't know how," Tim said in a low voice. "I can't seem to feel."

"You lose the habit of feeling, in war," his father said.

"I'd have said you feel so much in war that other feelings seem tame," Tim retorted.

His father smiled. "When I came back from war I didn't want to marry your mother," he said.

Tim said, "I'd forgotten that you were in that war."

"I fought in France in 1918," his father said tranquilly. "Nothing fancy like your bombing—just plain hand-to-hand stuff, bayoneting when I had to—" A strange look of torture went over his face and was quickly gone. "But I got the habit—as all men do in war— of direct violent physical action."

It was hard to think of his father as being direct or violent or physical. This quiet gray man, in his silent office!

"How did you tell Mother?" Tim asked suddenly. "I haven't been able to tell Kit."

"Good," his father said. "You mustn't. That is—if she is still the girl you want to marry."

"I don't even seem to want to marry," Tim said. He felt strangely naked before this man, as though for this moment he was not his father.

"That is simply because of the unreality." His father leaned back in his chair. "I had to go through with that, too. And I had to come into this office which was my father's then, and it seemed to me the most silent place in the world. My ears were full of drums and marching feet, and I had grown used to orders. Every moment of the day in the army I was under orders. I didn't have to think at all. I had grown out of the habit of thinking. Somebody said,

147

'Do this,' and I did it. It was all so easy. I didn't like the bayoneting
—that was all."

Tim held his breath. He did not like the bombing—that was
all. Yes, the rest was easy.

"How did you get yourself going again?" he asked.

"I was twenty-four," his father said. "Luckily I had finished
college—just as you have. My father handed me the briefs of a
case and told me to study them and report to him. I had to report,
because a man's life was in question. Even that didn't seem real.
I remember asking myself why I should spend hours trying to
save one man's life when I had taken God knows how many other
lives."

"You didn't tell—Mother—any of it?" Tim asked.

It was hard to say "Mother." He saw a young girl with tender
eyes, a girl like Kit.

His father leaned across the desk. "You must not tell anybody,"
he said sternly. "That is what I found out. Every time I tried to
tell anybody, it simply cut off the lines of communication between
us. It's only the people who have been through it that know. I
tried to tell my father, but he had never been through it. He—
he simply thought I was being nasty—I don't think he ever felt
the same to me again." He saw a slight sweat break out on his
father's forehead. "You can't tell people, Tim," he said. "You have
to keep it to yourself—and simply begin to live."

"Begin to live?" Tim echoed.

"Just begin," his father said firmly. "Begin to work, begin to
love. It doesn't matter how you feel. You begin to act, and then after
a while—maybe a long while—feeling comes. And then things grow
real again."

The two men leaned on the desk, gazing at each other.

His father spoke. "Remember how the first time you had to
attack you thought you couldn't?"

Tim remembered. His first mission had been to bomb a munitions
factory just inside the borders of Germany. He had been nervous
and his aim was not as good as it was later. He saw the fire burst

148

out of the houses near the factory and the people ran out like ants and he had been sick at what he had done.

"But you did it that time and again and again," his father said. He nodded.

"That's what you have to do now," his father said. "The first time you think you can't but you do it—and then again and again, and so after a while, you begin to live."

"I think you're right," Tim said slowly. "I know you're right." He rose. "I'll take you up on that business with Gedsoe."

"Very well," his father said and leaned back. The room snapped back to itself. His father turned gray again before his eyes.

"Thanks, Dad," he forced himself to say.

His father opened the drawer and took out the brief he had put away.

"Don't mention it," he said absently, already reading.

He went out into the sunny street again and drew a deep breath. It was still early to meet Kit but never mind. Why shouldn't he go and find her? She'd be at home. He swung on a passing street-car, and swung off again eight blocks down, and turned a corner and walked into the house, as he used to do.

"Kit!" he called.

He heard her running footsteps and he saw her looking down the bannisters. Her yellow hair fell softly beside her cheeks.

"Anybody home?"

"No—Mother's gone to a club meeting."

"Come downstairs, Kit."

She came downstairs half-timidly, "I was just going to put on my things—I'm a sight, Tim—I've been helping Mother and I haven't changed—"

She had on blue slacks and an old sweater and there was a smudge around her eyes.

"You've been crying," he declared.

She shook her head violently. "I rubbed my eyes, that's all. They got full of dust. We did the attic."

But he knew she had been crying. He knew it and his heart did

149

not stir. He had seen so many women cry over their dead children, over their ruined homes. What were the orders? "Begin to live," his father had said.

"Kit, I don't want to wait." His lips were dry as he spoke and he put out his arm and drew her against him. "I've been so dazed since I came back—I haven't even asked you. Kit, when are we going to be married?"

"Oh—" He heard her cry into his breast and felt her body grow limp against him. "I thought you were never going to ask me— I thought maybe you didn't want me any more."

That was what she had been crying about.

"Let's get married right away, Kit—"

"When, Tim?"

"Today—tomorrow—you set the day and the hour, Kit, a certain time, that I'll know is fixed and won't be changed."

She lifted her head. "Tim, you're sure?"

"Sure," he said steadily.

"Today a week, Tim—I can get ready—I have everything except a dress—and oh, Tim, let's just move into our own place and have our honeymoon there. We can find a little house, maybe we can in a week. I want to begin to live. I've waited so long."

"Today a week, we'll begin," he said.

She put her head against his shoulder again, sighed and closed her eyes.

But he did not speak. He stood holding her hand, his cheek pressing her hair. In the silence, while they stood together, while he waited, he felt something begin to beat in his breast, faintly, uncertainly. Was it his heart?

The Engagement

"I DON'T KNOW WHY," Miss Barclay said in a broken voice, "I don't know why I have to cry, but I do. It is so wonderful to see something happy again in this awful world!"

She was only a fitter in a shop, one of the best shops, of course, but still just a shop, and she did not often cry. Her mouth was ful of pins as usual, and before she dared to sob she took them out one by one and laid them in a little row on the floor.

Isabel smiled down upon the dingy gray head. A nice old thing, she thought, and it would have been simply too unkind if she had not come here for her wedding gown, although she would rather have gone to Bergdorf's. Still, Miss Barclay had always fitted her frocks for as long as she could remember and she had called up as soon as the engagement was announced.

"I've just read the news," Miss Barclay had trilled, "the wonderful, wonderful news! I know it's terrible of me, it isn't any of my business, but I just had to tell you how happy I am, and we all think it is just perfect, an ideal couple if there ever was one!"

Isabel had answered the phone, she answered every time it rang because it might be Lew.

"Oh, thank you!" She had smiled—even though Miss Barclay could not see her. It was sweet to hear people say that over and over. "My dear, you and Lew are simply made for each other—an ideal couple."

"You'll let me fit your wedding gown, won't you, dear?" Miss Barclay had pleaded.

"Oh, of course," Isabel had promised.

"I can't wait," Miss Barclay had breathed into the receiver at her ear. "When is it to be, dear?"

"In June."

"A June bride," Miss Barclay had gushed. "Perfect, dear, and I wish you all the happiness."

"Thank you," Isabel had said again. She expected all the happiness, she took it for granted, she had always had everything, and so now why not all the happiness?

Even Lew had enjoyed the fact that they were an ideal couple. He had proposed in the knowledge. Their families had always been friends, not quite neighbors, but near enough so that during school holidays when they were children they had met as a matter of course. Somewhere during their early teens Lew had not pursued the childish friendship. He had invited one girl or another to the Christmas dances, until suddenly last summer he had fallen in love with her, and a year from the day she had now set for her wedding day, the twenty-first of June, he had proposed to her. The distance between childhood and the proposal was long enough. They had found it exciting that they who remembered each other as quarrelsome wholesome children should now be quite different, two tall young creatures, one male, one female, both blond, both speaking, as they said, the same language.

"I never thought I'd want to marry you," Lew had said half humorously, by way of proposal, "but damn it, darling, I do."

"Why didn't you want to?" she had inquired, fending off what she saw in his threatening blue eyes.

"Because my parents have hinted for years that it would be so nice if—Oh, you know!"

152

"How hateful of them," she had observed. "I hope you told them what I have always told my mother."

"What?" he demanded.

"That you were absolutely the last person I would ever marry.

Lew had looked slightly shocked. "Well," he had said at last, "we were of one mind, anyway. So now will you marry me in spite of the cloying wishes of our beloved parents?"

She had wavered, moved by many impulses. That June day was made in the heavens, a day of gentle blue sky and rolling white clouds, they were in Lew's little open car parked on a hill, sitting side by side most conveniently. But this was only environment. Within herself were the impulses, the yearning desire, the beauty of possible love, so often dreamed of and never yet received or bestowed, the necessity, the urgent flow of her blood to her heart, the wish, the longing to begin her woman's life. And Lew was so easy to love, so handsome, so good-natured, and not at all stupid. They were well matched, two wealthy families, there would be no advantage either way, they could trust each other's love, they stood equally side by side, one did not give more than the other. Money was not important, perhaps, except that it was, in spite of what well-bred parents might say. She had made up her mind long ago not to marry a poor man, whom she could never trust. That was the word—she could *trust* Lew with all her heart.

"Thinking, thinking," Lew had scolded her tenderly, "and so do you love me, or don't you?"

Behind the habitual playfulness she saw his new anxiety, and that moved her suddenly to recognize what was quivering in her heart.

"I believe I do," she said, "only isn't it dangerous when we know each other so well? We won't have anything to tell each other."

"Oh yes, we will," he said. He had reached for her and pulled her against him. "All the little things maybe we have told—but none of the big things, darling, my darling—none of the lovely things about love!"

They kissed each other then as they had never kissed before.

153

Plenty of kisses they had given in the years since they were children, play kisses, good-night kisses when he left her after a dance, teasing kisses until suddenly they had not wanted to kiss each other at all. Now they did want to kiss each other, and most profoundly, most utterly.

"There," Lew had said at last. "Do you feel that to the soles of your feet?"

"Yes!" she had whispered. "Yes, I do."

And even at the end of that day, which they had spent in sheer exuberant speed, she clinging to him, her head against his shoulder, and he racing over the country roads, too happy to be sensible, even then Lew had said when at last they drew up before her house, "You know, kid, one of the nice things about all this, not the nicest, but nice, is that our swell folks are going to be happy about it. I wouldn't marry you to please them, darn you, but since I'm going to marry you anyway, it's pleasant to know they'll act like it's Christmas as soon as we tell them."

Well, it had been nice and it was still nice. Standing in the fitting room, trying to be patient while Miss Barclay mumbled over her pins, which she had stuffed into her mouth again as soon as she stopped crying, Isabel felt that if she were going to tell Lew, which she was not, she had rather tell him than tell her family, or his. They should never have announced the engagement to the families immediately, that she now knew. She and Lew should have got used to it first in secret. They should have tried it out thoroughly alone, knowing they were engaged for maybe only a month or even two until she was sure. Then she could quite easily have said to him, "Lew, I think I was swept off my feet or whatever it's called. I don't really want to be married, at least not to you. I'm terribly sorry, but that is the truth about me. I want you to find someone else right away quick. We'll go back to being what we've always been."

It was all her fault. It was always the girl's fault, her mother had taught her long ago. The girl decides, her mother had said. "Re-

member that, and then you will have only one person to blame—
yourself. It's much easier." That was what her mother had said.

Oh, it would be so pitiful for the families if she broke the
engagement now! She and Lew were the only children, and her
parents were so fond of his. They had always been friends, but
since the engagement it had been almost as though the two older
couples had already drawn themselves into one family. She was
sure that the mothers had talked about grandchildren, she had
caught them at it one day, dividing the matters of family names.
"The first boy of course must be named after Lew's father, but
perhaps the first girl—"

"After you, Elizabeth, of course," her mother had said sweetly
to Lew's mother. "I can wait. I do hope they will have four
children."

"I always wanted four," Lew's mother said.

She had interrupted the dream. "What is this—a seance?"

They had both looked at her with such guilty eyes that she had
laughed.

As a matter of fact, she and Lew had never talked about children.
She had hated being an only child and in her heart long ago she
had made up her mind that she would have a lot of children, not
just four, but for some reason she had never wanted to talk about
that when she was with Lew. They talked very little when they
were alone. He wanted to take her at once into his arms and that
was what she wanted, too. She could always trust him not to go too
far, he had breeding enough for that and they agreed without
words as to what too far was. They knew themselves as well as
each other. They were too modern to confuse their bodies and
their minds.

Sometimes she wondered if they had known each other less, if
she had not seen behind him the generations of his good family,
embodied in his two dignified and delightful parents, whether she
would have stopped it before now. And she supposed Lew, for
that matter, saw her family behind her, although he had never
said so. He was less conventional, or perhaps only less tender-

155

hearted than she was. He would have told her plainly if he had wanted to break the engagement. No, he loved her, she did not doubt it.

"There," Miss Barclay said, painfully rising from her arthritic knees. "I've got that train right at last. It hangs beautiful. I'm so glad you chose a pinkish-ivory satin instead of a yellowish one. Pink brings out your color so lovely. I'll help you out of it, dearie."

Isabel looked at her watch. "Lew said he was coming by."

Miss Barclay was shocked. "He oughtn't to see your gown before the wedding, dearie, it's bad luck."

Isabel laughed and two dimples sprang into her cheeks. "He says he doesn't want to be overcome by shock at the ceremony. He wants to be used to me beforehand."

Miss Barclay laughed, too. "Ain't he a card! Well, I can pick up the pins. Don't sit down."

They had not long to wait, not more than a minute or two, certainly not more than five. She heard Lew's footsteps, she heard his loud cheerful voice wanting to know where Miss Starr was, she heard the ripple of admiration among the women clerks. That was Lew Arnold, who was going to marry Isabel Starr—didn't you see it in the papers?

She opened the door and put her head out. "Lew, here I am. You're late. I was just about to give you up."

"I'm not in the least late. Good God, what a vision!"

"This is Miss Barclay."

"Miss Barclay, how do you do and have I you to thank for turning a tomboy, a hoyden, a mere kid, into this dream girl?"

Miss Barclay blushed crimson. "She's so easy to fit," she quavered, "a perfect fourteen, anything I put on her she wears beautiful— such style, Mr. Arnold." Her eyes filled again. It was so beautiful to see them.

The young man has a lot of style himself, she was thinking. Look at those shoulders, he don't need no padding, all the same he has a good tailor somewhere. Handsome as a god, as they say, and it's lucky the girl is so good-looking or she'd have a hard time holding her own, the way women are today. She could talk, because twenty-five years ago she'd lost her own fellow to a prettier girl, and her own best friend. He had simply come to her one day and told her straight out, "Bessie, it's too bad, but I've fallen for Louise." Well, there was nothing to do about it, although she had cried for days, and had cried easy ever since.

"Turn around," Lew was saying. Isabel turned slowly, smiling like an angel, Miss Barclay thought, with wet eyes, and he looked at the beautiful girl as if he could eat her up. Love was so wonderful, even if it was only for somebody else. She wiped her eyes with the corner of the pin cushion strapped on her left arm.

"Satisfied?" Isabel asked, lifting her long, golden lashes at Lew.

"I'd be a cur if I weren't," he said with violent decision.

Isabel kept on smiling. "Then I'm satisfied," she said. "Take it off, please, Miss Barclay. Mother and Dad are meeting me at Tiffany's. Mother is having her pearls reset for me."

Lucky girl, Miss Barclay thought, taking pins out of soft satin. Not only this young man madly in love with her, but pearls besides!

"If you'll just step outside a minute, please," she said to Lew.

He leaped for the door. "Excuse me," he said loudly.

Isabel laughed. He was sweet, Lew was, and she was such a fool. If she could just survive the wedding, once she was married hard and fast— Only, were marriages hard and fast these days?

"Thank you, Miss Barclay. It's lovely." She bent and kissed Miss Barclay's rouged cheek.

"Thank you, dear," Miss Barclay choked. "I've loved it."

Lew slid his hand along her arm and grasped her gloved fingers. "I'm glad you let me come and see your wedding gown," he said in a strange earnest voice, a little strained, she thought, glancing up at him. He was looking ahead, down the crowded sidewalk. It was noon, and people were out enjoying the sun in their lunch hour.

"Why?" she asked.

"Because now I know we really are going to be married," he said in the same earnest voice.

"Hadn't you believed it?"

"Not exactly," he confessed, "not all the time, that is. Now I know it's true. Invitations are out, wedding ring is engraved, gown is finished."

She took it up. "Flowers are ordered, cake is designed, if not baked, minister is promised."

"It is to be," he said resolutely.

They stopped at the door of Tiffany's. "Sure you can't lunch with me?" he suggested.

"I cannot," she said brightly. "Not today."

"Shall I come over tonight?"

"Why do you ask?" she replied. "Don't you always?"

"But do you want me to come?"

"Of course I do, silly."

"Sure?"

"Idiot!"

He put her hand to his lips and lifted his hat. She went into the great doors, wondering why she was such a fool as to ask one question of her heart. She did not know another young man who could or would kiss her hand so naturally, without self-consciousness, as Lew had done. There was really nobody like him, and their parents were entirely right and so was Miss Barclay. They were the ideal young couple, made to love each other.

Eugenically correct, she thought, remembering her biology professor in college, and laughing at herself inside. Then she saw her parents waiting for her patiently at the counter full of glittering gems.

Lew walked up the street in his usual high-headed fashion, unconscious of the girls who passed, their eyes stealing toward him. He was disgusted with himself. No, that was too mild a word for it. He was completely furious with himself. He had asked Isabel to marry him, it was his fault, and he had to go through with it.

If she had been another kind of a girl, if their families had not been so close, if there were not every reason in the world why it was so suitable, so right that they should love each other, he could simply have said to her, "Look here, kid, I'm awfuly sorry, I seem to have slipped up on myself. The old heart betrayed me. I just don't think we'd better go through with it. No, there isn't another girl—it's me, my fault."

It was impossible to say such words to Isabel. Behind her he saw not only her parents, waiting at the gem counter, but his own, his mother so delighted to think of Isabel as his wife.

"Darling, I have always loved her, I have always hoped—"

And his father gripping his hand in the most approved paternal blessing: "I can't think of a girl I'd rather have belong to us, son."

Belong was the word. He and Isabel belonged together, by every event of their lives. It was not as though he were in love with anyone else. He did not even consider any girl he knew half as beautiful as Isabel. But suddenly he was quite able to enjoy the superlative quality of her shining blond hair, her clear blue eyes, the lovely cast of her features, without any more wanting to kiss her.

Just when he had stopped wanting to kiss her was, as the King of Siam had said on Broadway, a puzzlement. He was grateful for the word. There were so many puzzlements in life, but this was the greatest, why he no longed wanted to kiss Isabel. She had at first been irresistible. He had wanted to kiss her that day on the hill as he had never wanted to kiss anybody before. She had grown up so beautifully; the long-legged skinny child with the sallow cheeks had bloomed so exquisitely. Her skin was transparently fair, the detail of her face so perfect, that he had been stunned by it when he perceived it when he came home finally from college. He had fallen in love with her immediately and violently and, he had supposed, permanently. It had been delightful to love someone who made everybody happy. He had wanted to announce his engagement the very day he proposed. He wanted to see the joy in their parents' eyes, it was all part of the perfection. There was no reason to keep it secret.

For months then he had enjoyed kissing her. There was not a great deal to talk about, they knew each other's lives thoroughly, they went to the same place in summer, they went to the same parties and night clubs, although he quite agreed that Isabel must not be seen too often at night clubs, her parents did not wish her to belong to that set, nor did he wish her to, either, and she had seemed quite content to spend evenings with him in the music room at her house, beginning with music, at which they were both good, but ending somehow always in the same way, with her in his arms, in silence.

There was not even a house to talk about. Since he was in his father's law offices, they had to live in town, and his parents had found a delightful apartment for them on the East River, which they were furnishing as a wedding present, and he and Isabel only went about docilely agreeing, or disagreeing if they wished, about carpets and draperies. It was to be a conservatively modern sort of place, conservative because in the best modern tradition, he was essentially conservative. All his best friends were conservative. It was hopelessly old-fashioned nowadays to be anything else. Only middle-aged people were liberals, and leftists were too absurd. Because he was a convinced conservative and not merely so by inheritance, he was the more angry with himself that he did not now want to marry Isabel. It was the sort of shifty thing a damned leftist would do, ask a girl to marry him and then change his mind about it.

When was it he had stopped wanting to kiss her? He did not know. There was no exact moment, no instant of repulsion. Indeed, there was no repulsion at all. She was still delightfully sweet to the senses, her lips so fresh, so skillfully touched with lipstick that there was not even the embarrassment of wondering whether it had come off on his mouth. That was a small thing, but it had put him off two or three girls. Isabel was too well brought up not to know what to do. She would always be too well brought up not to know what to do. She would be a skillful wife, a good wife, sophisticated in the best sense. There was every reason why theirs would be a happy marriage—except that he was a fool. When he kissed her now it was pleasant, but not necessary. There it was—pleasant but not necessary. That sort of thing might come after years of marriage, but it ought not, he felt, to come now. Then it would be too late, but now it was not.

He despised himself for five minutes, then remembered that he had eaten nothing since breakfast and was immensely hungry. He turned into the door of a favorite restaurant and sat down at a side table, and heard his name.

"Hello, Lew."

He looked up and saw his uncle at the next small table, an elderly bachelor who had enough money to do nothing and who therefore did nothing, a man about town, who occasionally put money into a play as his only serious diversion.

"Hello, Philip," Lew said. He had been forbidden the title of uncle.

"The shad roe is excellent," his uncle said.

"Thanks," Lew said. "I feel like a beefsteak."

He gave his order, and sat back.

"How are you?" he asked.

"Quite well," his uncle replied. "I am thinking of going to Paris very soon. Your mother wants me to wait until after the wedding."

"Don't bother," Lew said.

His uncle looked startled. "No wedding?"

"Oh, I don't mean that," Lew said hastily. "I mean don't let my plans interfere with yours."

"I never have," his uncle said calmly. He was a lean tall dried-up man, older than Lew's father. There were years when they saw very little of him, and then one day suddenly he would appear and they might see him quite often for a few weeks, coming home to discover him in the library reading, or simply sitting in the living room, looking reflective and absent-minded.

"There's a play I want to see in Paris," his uncle was saying. "I don't suppose a matter of a fortnight would matter. It's a hit, and I might bring it over next autumn, a musical comedy."

161

"Isabel and I would quite understand if you couldn't be at the wedding," Lew said.

"Though I have a flickering family feeling that I'd like to see my only nephew happily married," his uncle said, not looking up from his plate where the brown shad roe was lying, partially eaten. He picked at it delicately with his fork. "Suitable marriages are rare enough," he went on. "I'd like to see one."

Lew was suddenly moved to ask advice, not openly, not revealing very much. He trusted his uncle without loving him. It was impossible for anyone to love this tailored figure. But the mind within was dry and clear, even though the heart was withered or perhaps dead. It was not heart that Lew wanted at the moment.

"It's odd," he began.

"What's odd?" his uncle asked when he paused.

"Now that the wedding day is actually near—I've even seen Isabel in her wedding gown, and looking frightfully beautiful, too—I have a funny feeling that perhaps I don't want to go through with it."

He waited, not looking at his uncle, expecting he knew not what.

"Not odd," his uncle murmured.

"I really want to go on with it," Lew said quickly. "It is the sort of marriage I want to make. Besides, how could our families bear up? One can't think only of one's self."

"Have you any reason to think that Isabel is also reluctant?" his uncle asked in the same bland voice. He motioned to the head-waiter. "Bring me the wine list," he told the man. "This roe is tasteless. It wants a good wine."

The man was concerned. "Would you like to have something else, sir?"

"No, no," Philip said, "just the wine."

Lew's beefsteak came upon a platter, smoky brown, dripping pink juice and butter. He was ravenous, he cut a big mouthful and began to eat.

"I thought you said the roe was good," he said, his mouth full.

"It is," his uncle said. "It went tasteless while you were talking.

162

If it were only you and Isabel—You say she wants to go on with it?"

"I have seen no reason to think she does not," Lew said. He could not describe to his uncle Isabel's eyes, glowing above her wedding gown. He felt it a pitiful memory, he would always remember them if he allowed himself to be cruel to her and tell her.

The wine came, a mild white liquid imported from a vineyard of France, and the waiter poured it slowly and unctuously into the glass. His uncle sipped it.

"I suppose I might as well tell you," he said. "I don't suppose your parents will have told you. It raised a frightful scandal at the time. I deserted my betrothed at the altar. She was Agnes Van Pelter."

"No!" Lew exclaimed. Everyone knew Miss Van Pelter, the sister of the Wall Street money magnate who died years ago and left her his fortune. She had never married, but she had set up and managed two of the great charities in the city. During the first World War she had built orphanages and hospitals in Europe. Today she was an eagle of a woman, tall and handsome, her magnificent eyes black under her snow-white hair.

"I tried early to suggest my change of heart," his uncle was saying in his cool reflective voice, sipping his wine between words.

"Did you—dislike her?" Lew inquired. "That is the trouble with me. I don't in the least dislike Isabel. I've simply gone back to liking her as I always did."

"Ah," his uncle said. "Agnes was very different from Isabel. There was a touch of something else in her—Spanish, perhaps. I saw she would eat me alive. I got out of it to save myself." He shook his head. "I escaped, though I can't say I've ever recovered. I have never wanted to marry anyone else."

"Nor has she," Lew said.

"No," his uncle agreed. "Well, here we are letting this delicious food be ruined. That is a mistake, at any rate."

They fell to eating again, Lew very thoughtful.

His uncle was choosing a French pastry before he spoke again.

"If I have any advice," he said, selecting an inverted peach decorated with a frill of encircling whipped cream, "it is not to follow my example. Go through with it if you can, and I must say that a good many young men have confided to me over the years that there is a moment when any man doubts. Once that is over, they get on, I am told. I don't know. I only know that I don't regret what I did, though it put me out of society for a bit. Such things aren't as important as they were in my time. People forget easily nowadays. I'm glad of it."

"Make it concrete," Lew said.

"Don't wait until the altar," his uncle said with sudden force. "Do it now, or forever hold your peace!"

In the afternoon the advice seemed not so concrete. He worked with his father upon a case which had interested him until now, a man suing another man for alienation of the affections of his wife. His father had not wanted to take the case. It was distasteful, he had declared, to bring to the public view so private a humiliation. "The cold fact of the matter is," his father had declared, "the fellow had already lost his wife before the other man appeared. A woman who is in love with her husband doesn't fall in love with someone else."

Lew had persuaded him that nothing was private nowadays, that there was a case as well as a large fee. This afternoon, however, he, too, felt the whole thing distasteful. But now his father had become engrossed in the situation. Had a man the right to approach a woman who legally belonged to another man? If not, should he not be punished by law?

Lew consulted his papers. "She declares that she never loved her husband, that her parents more or less compelled her to marry him for his money, his position and so forth—family consideration, she calls them."

"Nonsense," his father retorted with legal vigor. "A woman cannot be compelled in this day and age, nor a man, either."

The afternoon was waning, the slanting sun fell across the mahogany desk between them and upon his father's lined and kindly face.

Suppose I tell him now, Lew thought. It was quite true that times were changed, the old conventional compulsions no longer held, his friends would forget, Isabel was so attractive a girl that soon enough there would be another man. And yet, he thought as he looked at his father, it was not a matter of convention. There was something beneath the old human conventions, they were the sound fruit of human experience. One sacrificed himself for the many. This was what it amounted to, one was unhappy so that several other people could be happy, and the living foundations were preserved.

No, he could not tell his father, for then his mother must know and Isabel's mother and father. And what of Isabel herself? Even if he sacrificed the parents, was she to be sacrificed? She loved him.

The wedding gown was finished, it arrived in its big box. When Isabel opened it a fragrance rose from the lace bosom, filled with soft tissue paper. Miss Barclay had tucked into the lace a tiny sachet, a morsel of blue satin soaked with the scent of roses. It was like her to think of such a gift, a small thing, but conveying, as Isabel knew, sentiment and tenderness. That was the trouble with people, they persisted in having feelings and tenderness, and they shared everything with her.

The door opened and her mother came in, her soft pink face all tender excitement. "Darling, a lovely wedding gift has just come in from Lew's grandmother. It looks like her silver tea set, the one that came from England with her ancestors. Oh, your wedding gown! Why didn't you tell me, so we could open it together?"

"I didn't think of it, Mother," Isabel said literally.

Her mother lifted the fragrant mass from its box. "What is that delicious scent? Miss Barclay would do something like that. Where will we hang this? In the guest room closet, of course, in the plastic bag. Or should we leave it in the box?"

"Hang it up," Isabel said. But there it was, her mother living again her own wedding day.

"I wonder if you can possibly know," her mother was saying. "Of course you can't. It's too soon."

"What?" Isabel asked.

"How I feel to know that I can be sure you are going to be happy. It means so much to me. I've worried ever since you were born. It's so terrible if a woman marries the wrong man, it's so wonderful if she marries the right one."

Now is the moment, Isabel thought. Now I must say it, I must say that I have found out that Lew is the wrong one, in spite of all that seems so right.

"Darling," her mother whispered. "I am so happy."

How could she speak a word? Her mother's eyes were actually wet.

The extraordinary hateful truth was that she was beginning to dislike Lew because she could not tell anybody that she did not love him. This was undignified and unjust, for was he different from what he had ever been? He was not. He was exactly the same man she had been in love with, she thought. Only a few weeks ago it had still been pleasant to have him kiss her. Now it was disgusting, or it would have been except that he was always so beautifully clean.

She came downstairs one evening to meet him, the last evening actually that they would have entirely to themselves before the wedding. Parties and dinners had accumulated for the days ahead. She had accepted everything, wanting to fill the time. It was easier to be engaged to Lew when they were at a party together. The girls were admiring and jealous, she was conscious of the appearance they made together, both so tall, so brightly blond, so suited to each other in the flesh. But it was the flesh that rebelled. That was the odd incomprehensible thing. Their minds were attuned. She and Lew had always understood each other's minds. They had always agreed on important matters, even on religion and politics.

They liked the same sort of clothes, the same colors. They would never have petty quarrels. She earnestly wished to love him with her whole being. Then why did the flesh deny him? She might go to a psychiatrist and ask him why, only there was no time. Perhaps nobody could know anyway.

The door opened and Lew came in, looking as he always did, freshly bathed and shaved and well dressed.

"Not late, am I?"

"No, I was early, I think."

He sat down as usual on the couch where she had been waiting and suddenly she could not bear it and got up.

"Lew, would you mind if we took a ride? I feel restless tonight."

"Not scared, are you?"

"Not of you, silly."

"Then what?"

He was looking at her strangely, she thought, almost as if he guessed.

"I don't know—nothing and everything. Perhaps I am tired. I've done nothing but stand for fittings, it seems to me."

He got up abruptly. "Let's go."

She was sure now that he guessed. He had not even kissed her. She wondered if she should offer herself for the kiss, and then did not. Indeed she could not. Instead she made the pretense of fetching a wrap, though the night was warm. She went upstairs and fetched her thin red wool coat, and stopped to glance into the mirror— White as a ghost, she was!

He was standing at the front door, looking grave, and now she was sure that he knew. She was sorry and glad at once, glad for it would be easier, sorry because he already knew the pain of the blow. But she would wait until they were away somewhere on a quiet road, under the moonless sky. Then she would tell him, and she would tell him that she could not imagine why suddenly love had simply left her. She felt cold and empty without love and she wished passionately that it would come back, that she could bring it back, and she would bring it back if she only knew how, for she wanted to marry him for every other reason. Once it was said, she could like him again, and she longed to like him, the old comfortable liking they had always had for each other. Perhaps that was even enough.

"Do you care which way we go?" he asked as he started the motor.

"No, only to get out of the city."

They drove in silence, and neither put out a hand to the other. He drove north under the black and starlit sky, and the night wind blew soft and warm upon their faces. It lifted the heavy curls of her hair and fluttered the thin white silk of her frock. It made disturbance enough so that it gave excuse for no talk between them in the open car, but that was no excuse for his not putting out his arm to draw her close. So he knew and it only remained to tell him now, at any minute. Her mouth went dry and her heart began to beat too hard, she kept putting off the instant when she could and must say, "Lew, stop the car here for a little while. I have something to say to you."

And while she was waiting she was surprised to hear him say the words, or almost the very words, she was thinking.

"Isabel, I'm going to stop the car here for a bit. There is something I must say to you before it is too late."

He stopped the car at the side of the road, under a huge tree. Above them were the stars, and all around them were the twinkling lights of little towns and suburbs, clinging to the city.

"Yes, Lew?" But she was quite dazed.

"I don't know how to say it." He was fumbling for cigarettes and found them. "Have one?"

"No, thanks."

"Do take one, Isabel—it will make it easier for me."

She took one and he lit it and she saw in the flickering of the flame that his big hand was trembling.

"I should have said this weeks ago," he went on, his voice suddenly hoarse. "Since I didn't, I've got to say it now, as much for you as for me. I can't go on, Isabel."

168

The sword was his, not hers, it was he who struck the blow. She felt it fall, strange that it was agony when it fell! She sat in stunned silence. And why not cry out immediately, "Oh, Lew, do you feel so, too? Because I was just trying to get up my own courage—"

But she cried not a word, she could not speak. She was raging with anger at him. Let him suffer, as she was suffering.

"I am simply bewildered," he was saying in the same heartbroken voice. "I hate myself. I know, I can even feel, that you are the same sweet and lovely girl I really do want for my wife. Everything about you is what I like. I am proud of you— It would be glorious to have a wife who looks the way you do, intelligent and interesting besides. But the glory has gone out of me, I guess. I don't know myself."

She spoke then. "It is very cruel of you not to have told me the very first moment you knew."

"It was beastly," he muttered, "but I didn't see it that way. I thought I'd get over it. I'd heard that most fellows get moods before marriage, I thought mine would pass. I suppose it's only within the last week or so—"

"The day you saw me in my wedding gown," Isabel said.

He hesitated. "Gosh, that's right! I believe that was the moment I faced myself."

"When you saw me as a bride," she suggested.

"I hate myself," he said humbly. "I take all the blame. I'll tell everybody."

"No, you can't," she said quickly.

Of course he couldn't, he saw at once that at least he must give her the advantage of him. He must let her be the one to break the engagement. But would she?

"I'll do whatever you say," he told her.

"Please take me home," she said.

He turned the car and drove at a swift speed back over the silent road. And in silence they sat side by side, he in sorrow and she in hidden anger. Why, oh, why had she not spoken quickly and fended off this blow? For it would always be a blow, she could never forget that it was she who had somehow lost his love, and when love came again, she would always take it uneasily, fearful of some lack in herself because Lew had ceased to love her. True, she did not love him, but that was not the same. It was not at all the same when a woman refused a man. It did him no harm, at least not for long. But as long as a woman lived she could not forget. Forever there could be no friendship between Lew and her, because when she saw him she would always remember and the wound would bleed, not for love but for pride.

"I shall always hate myself," he muttered in the darkness.

Still she did not reply. Let him hate himself. Let him always remember that he had done a hateful deed. Oh, he had the right to do it, they weren't living in yesterday, but it was strange how the old conventions held. There had been justice as well as mercy in the idea that a man must never be the one to break the bond of betrothal. He must contrive as a gentleman to let her do it. He must save her whole, because she had so little else except love and pride. The rest of the world was his, and was still his, she thought passionately, in spite of this most modern year.

The miles sped by, the hour passed, and they were at the door of the house. The upper windows were still dark. Her parents had come home from the theater and gone to bed and she could go upstairs to sleep and so postpone the wicked news.

"Shall I come in, Isabel?" Lew asked in his sad humility.

"No, thank you, Lew," she said.

"I can't somehow let you go," he argued.

"But you have let me go, haven't you? Just going into the house doesn't matter. Good night, Lew."

"Isabel!"

"Lew, I'll try to understand. Let me out."

But he did not open the door. He held it, forbidding her to go away alone. "I wish there was something I could do. I'm so fond of you, Isabel, I really am. I like you better than anybody in the world. I don't want you to hate me. Actually I can't bear it if you do. We have to talk or something. I've been friends with you all my life. I can't lose you. It would hurt me too much. And if we are not friends somehow, Isabel, how can our families be friends? We can't smash up everybody, can we?"

He was so earnest, so yearning, so wanting to be right, that she almost loved him. But not quite, never quite love!

She sat very still, looking ahead of her into the lighted street, struggling with her own passionately angry heart. Lew was right. They could not let everybody be smashed up. If she let him go on thinking that it was all his fault, then she must maintain the fiction for the rest of her life. Even if she sweetly forgave him and declared that everything must be as it had been since they were born, that the broken engagement must not change anything, still everything would be changed for everybody. Her parents would not want to see Lew any more or his family, and that was not what she wanted. She wanted to have everything as it had been before the engagement. Then the only way to have it so was to tell him the whole truth. She must not want to punish him for pride's sake. It was old pride, anyway, the pride of women dead and gone, it did not belong to her. It was an heirloom she did not want and she would simply throw it away.

"Lew," she said suddenly. "I'm hateful, too, in a way. I was just going to tell you the same thing—that I wanted to give it all up."

He let this soak into his mind. "Goddam!" he suddenly shouted. "Why didn't you say so before I did? I was sweating blood."

"It was hateful of me," she agreed. "But you took me by surprise. I had no idea that you—"

"Stop there," he commanded. "Don't say anything about love. I like you, I tell you! I can't afford to lose someone I like so much."

"I don't want to lose you, either," she said. "We'll have to tell them that we decided together, and Lew—"

"Yes?"

"We'll have to keep going together just like we always have, until the engagement, I mean, and make our families keep together, for a while anyway. And when we really get married, you to some other girl—"

"I feel that will be a long way off," he declared, and he pulled out his handkerchief and wiped his forehead.

"Silly," she said. She laughed for the first time in days, and went on, "and me to another man, then we'll all be friends for another generation. Oh, Lew, I'm so fond of you, too!"

She leaned toward him and their lips met in a pleasant kiss. Then he opened the door and got out and together they walked up the steps. He rang the bell and in an instant the heavy door swung open to receive them, as it always had, as long as he could remember. He used to wait like this on the threshold when he came to Isabel's birthday parties. The door was always shut like the gate of a fortress but it opened to him and he went in because he was welcome.

"Come in," Isabel said. "You don't have to hurry away just because we aren't going to be married."

"Hush," he said softly. "They might hear you."

"Who?" she demanded.

"Your family."

"Well," she said, "they'll have to know. Won't they?"

"Will they?" he asked uncertainly.

He stood there under the crystal chandelier, and she stared at him with surprise. "What's the matter with you, Lew?"

"I don't know," he said, "I feel queer."

"How?"

He did look queer. He was suddenly ash white.

"What have we been talking about this last hour, Isabel?" he inquired.

"About not getting married," she said promptly.

"I know, but why did we want to get married in the first place?"

"You must know," she said. "You asked me to marry you."

"It was for a lot of reasons," he said. He stopped and then went on again with sudden and inexplicable energy. "Look here, Isabel, they were good reasons and they still are. Our families, the way

172

you and I know each other—Damn it, Isabel, I don't want to marry a strange woman— I want to marry somebody I know, and I know you better than anybody in the world!"

She turned her head away.

"Strangers," Lew muttered, "in strange houses—I wouldn't like it."

"I don't want to marry a stranger, either," she said.

"There's a lot to be considered," Lew went on, as though he were arguing with her, "I have an advantage. If a man marries a woman he doesn't know beforehand he has to get to know her afterwards before they can really call it a marriage. Doesn't he?"

"You must know," she said stubbornly.

"I do know," he said violently. "Coming to the door, as I have hundreds of times, and seeing it swing open for me—it means something. This hall, this old chandelier, you standing here! We begin years ahead of other couples, don't we?"

He was touching, she thought, or he would have been except that he was too big, too much in earnest, plowing his way through his thoughts the way he always did, frowning like an ogre. She looked at him, not all at once but slowly, at first sidewise and then fully and then with a smile, beginning very small and growing in her eyes like a light. Then she laughed aloud, she could not help it.

"Oh, Lew," she cried, "am I a fool or are you?"

He grinned at her. "Both, I reckon."

That was what he said, but what he suddenly felt was that he did want to kiss her again, not the way he had kissed her before, but the way a man kisses the woman he knows better than any woman in the world, when their world is the same one. What was love anyway but sharing the same world?

"Look here," he said, but there was no use going on. He would simply let her know by kissing her.

In the middle of time somewhere they heard footsteps on the stairs. Her mother was there in her dressing gown, ruffles of lace falling from throat to hem.

"You look beautiful under that chandelier," she cried, her voice

173

all tears and soft laughter, "I don't want to interrupt the wonderful moment, my dears, but don't you think—"

"Certainly, Mrs. Starr," Lew said. "I was just saying good night."

"Ah well," he mother said, "there'll be other nights—a thousand and one, at least!"

"So good night, Lew," Isabel said.

"Good night, Isabel," he said. "I'll be over in the morning as usual."

"As usual," she agreed.

Melissa

"WILL YOU BE ALL RIGHT NOW?" her aunt asked.

"Yes," Melissa said. "I'll be all right."

Her aunt lingered. "I'd stay if I could, and if you're not all right—"

"But I am, Aunt Mary," Melissa said. "It isn't as if it was my first show."

Her aunt leaned in the twilight darkness of the theater and kissed her. "You know your lines perfectly—I told the director."

"They're easy. And I think he's nice. I'm glad he's young."

"It's his first Broadway show. I hope it's a success. Mind you, Lissa, I don't want you to think I shall spend any of the money you earn. It'll go into the fund for your education."

"I know, Aunt Mary."

Her aunt lingered anxiously. "You look so small sitting here in this big empty theater all by yourself. Don't you want to move up to the front? You'll be nearer the stage."

"I like it here, Aunt Mary."

Her aunt sighed. "Well, all right then, child. I'll be back for you at seven o'clock. Here's your lunch. Peanut butter sandwich with jelly. You can ask the stage manager to buy you a coke when he goes out for their coffee. Have you your two nickels?"

"In my purse."

"Goodbye then, child."

"Goodbye."

Her aunt tiptoed down the aisle, and Melissa settled herself in the seat. She was ten years old, small for her age and thin. Her hair was brown but since the play called for a child with blond curls her aunt had given her a silver platinum rinse, and she felt different, as if she were the girl in the play, the fairy child whose name was Melody. She liked the part, and she had learned the lines quickly.

> Are you in love, Mother? Is that why you're so happy?
> No, Melody. I'm not in love and that's why I am happy.
> But I thought love made people happy.
> It only makes me sad.

She could not remember her own mother, and Aunt Mary would not talk about her. Aunt Mary was her mother's younger sister, and her father was dead, but not long ago, and she remembered him, a tall slim man like the director up there on the stage, dark eyes, dark hair, a soft voice. He was walking about now, measuring off spaces and putting down chalk marks, the stage manager following. They were talking, but she could not hear what they said. The stage manager was an old man, and he had not spoken to her. She would not ask him to buy a coke for her except that she had promised Aunt Mary she would never go out on the street alone, or with anybody. She was left in the theater and here she must stay until she was fetched again.

The stage was bare under the white glitter of the unshaded lights above. Around here the darkness spread over the empty seats and up into the vaulted ceiling. Last year she had played in this same theater and she had been afraid then that one of the great chandeliers hanging up there in the dark might fall down and crush her under splinters of broken glass. But last year she had been small, only nine, much younger than she was now. Nevertheless she glanced upward and saw that she sat directly under the massive central chandelier and she got up and moved forward to the third row.

The young director turned around. "Hi there, early bird," he said.

"Good morning, Mr. Kean," she said.

He went back to work and she felt suddenly lonely in the silence. She wished he would speak again but she knew, of course, that an actor must not bother the director. Only the star could do that. She sat quietly, watching him. Now that she was close, she saw his ears, pointed and standing out just the least bit from his head. He finished his chalking and stood up and dusted his hands. Then he jumped down from the stage lightly and sat down beside her. She smiled up at him.

"Do you know you're quite lovely?" he asked.

"I think you're lovely, too," she replied.

"Thank you," he said, as though she were grown up.

"Do you have any children, Mr. Kean?" she asked.

"Not yet," he said. "In fact, I'm not even married."

"Oh," she said politely, "I was wishing you had some children. They might come here to watch the rehearsals and we could play —very quietly, of course."

He laughed. "You're an old-fashioned little thing, aren't you?"

"I don't know," she said. "Does that mean you don't like me for the part?"

"I like you enormously," he said. "And you were fabulous yesterday, simply fabulous. I knew you were the right girl the moment I saw you."

"Thank you," she said.

He laughed again as though she had said something funny and then he looked at her curiously. "Is that your mother who brings you and comes for you?"

"No, my Aunt Mary."

"No mother?"

"She went away somewhere when I was a baby."

"No father?"

"He died."

"When you were a baby?"

"No. I remember him."

She considered whether she would say that he reminded her of that young father, so tall and slim and gentle, and then felt too shy.

"You come here by yourself and stay all day?" he went on.

"I'm used to it." She smoothed down her short skirt. "I've been acting for three years. Do you like my dress?"

"It's very pretty," he said. "The skirt is like the whorl of flower petals. You're rather like a flower, you know, a flower with a pale little face, set in a flare of silver. Don't you ever play out in the sun?"

"Not when I'm working," she said. "I have to sleep late. My aunt won't let me get up until time for rehearsal even if I wake up. I do my lessons in between."

"Does your aunt have other children?"

"She hasn't even a husband. She works."

"Doing what?"

"She's a secretary."

"And why aren't you a secretary?"

She looked at him to see if he were joking and decided he was. She laughed.

"I'm an actress, so why should I want to be a secretary?"

"Sensible, but why an actress?"

"My mother was an actress. She sang and danced. She was a star."

"Was?"

"She got married to somebody in England."

"And you never see her?"

She hesitated.

"I think maybe she's dead," she said at last.

"I see." He got up abruptly. "Well, the rest of the cast is sauntering in. We'll talk again."

He vaulted up to the stage and she sat quietly, feeling a strange sweet comfort stealing through her veins. She had a friend here perhaps? It was always the question, would she find friends in the play? They were wonderful to her, of course, in every play. They gave her candy and chewing gum which she took home and gave to the other children in the apartment house, because she had to think of her figure. She mustn't get the habit of eating sweet things. It would be hard to stop when she got bigger and actresses could never be fat, not if they wanted to be beautiful. But being wonderful didn't mean being a friend. She had learned that in her very first play. She had loved everybody then, especially the beautiful star, and the star had hugged and kissed her and she thought it was real. But it wasn't. She knew that now. Every play was the same. They began acting like friends almost at once and soon they began to believe they were friends, and some of them got in love with each other, and nearly always the female star was in love with the male star or else with the director. A play was exciting and everybody was excited into loving somebody until by opening night everybody loved everybody. After that it all changed. Even if the play was a hit it changed. If it was a flop you might think the very next day that they had never seen one another. Her first play had been a flop, and the next day they didn't speak to her, not even the star. She went up to hug her after the first act, and the star had pushed her off.

"Run away, Melissa—don't be a pest."

She couldn't believe what she heard except that the beautiful face was angry, the face that she had never seen without a smile. Now she knew what her father felt when her mother had gone away. Her Aunt Mary had told her often enough. "He was struck down like a young tree in the forest under lightning. And I said to myself, 'I'll never let myself in for love—never!'"

The new star was coming in now, the star of this play, and the others made way for her, pretending that they didn't, of course. This star was beautiful, too, a movie star and it was her first Broadway show after ten years in Hollywood and everybody watched her because she was trying to make a comeback. She had yellow hair and big black eyes. The hair was not real, but it was a pretty color just the same, and she had a figure, her breasts round and full.

Melissa felt her own breasts anxiously. They were still quite flat, but they would change, her aunt said they would. They had talked about it only yesterday when her aunt was rubbing her dry after her bath. After rehearsal she was sleepy and so her aunt always helped her hurry to bed.

"Why am I so flat here, Aunt Mary?" she had asked, touching the two little buttons on her bosom.

"Good grief, child, you'll begin to swell out soon enough," her aunt had said.

"When did you swell?"

"Oh, when I was twelve or so—"

Her aunt was on her knees and wearing just her slip. She had taken off her dress so it wouldn't get wet. Her two little breasts, quite full and round, were plainly to be seen.

"You're swelled nicely now," Melissa said.

Her aunt had blushed. "Oh, good grief," she said and got up and handed Melissa the towel. "Here—finish yourself off."

The star's dress was cut very low and she did not care who saw her. She came close to the director and pretended she wanted to ask him something but Melissa knew by now that stars were only pretending when they wanted to ask something. They asked something so that the men could see how pretty they were, how long their eyelashes, and how low-cut their dresses. The director moved away but the star followed him.

I hate her, Melissa thought.

"Attention, cast," the director was saying. He stood in front of the group of seven people. Then he turned and stared down into the darkness of the empty theater.

"Melissa!" he called, "Why are you not here with the others?"

"Oh, did you want me, too?" she cried breathlessly and ran to his side. He waited for her and took her hand and she stood there beside him, feeling her hand warm and safe in his big one. Sudden love flowed out of her toward him. She looked at the star, a blonde, and she distrusted blondes, even the real ones. Her aunt's hair was a soft reddish-brown and her eyes were darker, almost black, not a glittery black, but dusky and gentle.

"Let us consider the play," the director was saying. "It is a comedy in the classical sense. That is to say, we find tragedy but not murder, death or violence. It is a subtle play—"

"Please, Mr. Kean," Melissa said, "what does subtle mean?"

He looked down at her and then at the others.

"Will anyone define the word for this young actress?"

No one spoke. They all waited for him to do it. They had to be told.

"To be subtle," he said at last, "is to know how to create an atmosphere, whatever lines you are given. True, the words are not yours, but what you do with them is entirely your responsibility."

"I can understand that," Melissa said.

The beautiful star was pouting. "I don't think any woman would say what the author has written in the second scene of Act Two. By this time she's in love with the man, or ought to be, and she would make it perfectly clear to him."

The director looked at her in silence. She let her long lashes flutter and fall.

"Let us decide this matter when we reach that point," he said. "One never knows where love will lead. Not all women behave in the same way when they are in love. We will see how this woman behaves."

The star lifted her long lashes again.

"Of course you know best," she said.

"The star is already making up love to him, Aunt Mary," Melissa said that evening at the supper table.

"Making," her aunt corrected. "Not making up."

"Making up is what I mean," Melissa insisted. "It's play love."

Her aunt set down the butter dish. "I wonder if I am doing right by letting you stay by yourself all day with those people."

"But I'm an actress, Aunt Mary."

"You're a little girl, only ten years old."

Her aunt sighed and sat down and mixed the salad. "I shall take a day off tomorrow and stay with you, anyway in the morning, and see for myself what sort they are."

Melissa opened her mouth to protest and then closed it again. Once in a while her aunt got worried and spent the day in the theater. It made her feel small and humiliated. Actresses could take care of themselves. They didn't need relatives sitting around, watching. Besides, she was almost sure now that the director was her friend. Then it occurred to her that the director would see her aunt and he might say to her, I am Melissa's friend. And her aunt would say thank you, and won't you come around some evening and have supper with us, and then they all would be friends.

"I wish you would come, Aunt Mary," Melissa said. "I do get afraid sometimes in that big theater."

"What are you afraid of?" her aunt asked.

Melissa looked plaintive and helpless. "I'm afraid the chandelier will fall on me and kill me."

"Stop acting," her aunt said. "You're not afraid of anything and you know it."

Tears welled into Melissa's great eyes, violet eyes, black-lashed. Tears were at her command.

"And stop looking like your mother," her aunt said sharply. "She could cry, too, whenever she wanted to, and it didn't mean a thing."

"Yes, Aunt Mary," she whispered, and wiped her eyes dry on her napkin.

She bent her head submissively and waited. If she waited long enough, her aunt would be sorry for being cross.

"I wish I knew how to bring you up," her aunt said. "You're so uncanny sharp, with all your play-acting. I don't know when you're yourself and when you're somebody else in your own mind."

182

"I don't know, either," Melissa said softly. She lifted her violet eyes to her aunt's anxious face. "Maybe Mr. Kean understands me. He's had so many experiences with actresses."

Her aunt laughed. "Oh, go on with you, you little owl," she said.

The next morning her aunt did not leave her in the theater. She lingered, looking about and sat down beside her in the third row from the front. Mr. Kean had come in with the stage manager and the two of them were talking as usual in low tones, up there on the stage, measuring and chalking and gauging where the set would go.

"Good morning, Melissa," he called down into the shadows of the empty theater.

"Good morning, Mr. Kean," she answered. "I'd like you to meet my aunt."

"Oh, for heaven's sake, Lissa," her aunt muttered. "As if he had the time!"

But Mr. Kean was already leaping down from the stage and walking toward them between the empty rows. He looked young and happy and excited about the play, and he shook hands with her aunt and smiled and her aunt smiled back.

"I don't want to take your time," her aunt said.

"Plenty of time," Mr. Kean said, and sat down between them. "So you're Melissa's aunt," he went on, "and why, Melissa my child, didn't you tell me how pretty your aunt is?"

"I wanted you to see for yourself, sir," Melissa said.

He laughed. "Perfect stage manners! Who taught Melissa, Miss—"

"Brown," Melissa said. "Mary Brown."

"Nobody taught that child," her aunt said. "She was born the way she is. Of course her mother was a great actress—at least that's what people said. You may remember Faye Delaney, Mr. Kean? That was my sister's stage name."

"Of course," Mr. Kean said. "Who doesn't?"

"She was my sister," her aunt said, "and how that happened I'll

183

never know. I think I am miscalled. She was the Mary and I am the Martha."

"What's become of her?" Mr. Kean asked.

"We don't hear from her any more."

Mr. Kean turned to Melissa. "Run away, child, I want to talk to your aunt."

She skipped away at that and danced, all by herself, up and down the empty aisles, dreaming that she was her mother, when her mother was a little girl and danced in the aisles alone, dreaming that she was— Who did her mother dream she was? So many questions and never any answers, never any answers!

. . . "Melody!"

Mr. Kean was calling her.

The dreams flew away like thistledown before the wind and she danced up to the stage.

"Take your place, please," Mr. Kean said. "We will begin rehearsal."

Sometime during the morning she glanced down into the empty pit. There in the dusk she saw her aunt sitting alone in the middle of the third row. She felt a warm comfort. Wouldn't it be wonderful if it were her mother sitting there— Not the mother who ran away from her but an Aunt Mary sort of mother, the sort that other stage children had, a mother who waited and had lunch with her and waited again and scolded the stage manager if the theater was too cold or the director if he was working the child too hard and telling him that Equity would not allow the child to work overtime, wouldn't it be wonderful—wonderful—

"Melody!" Mr. Kean said sharply. "We are waiting for you to read your lines now."

She spoke them at once. The others were still reading but she knew her lines by heart because she was Melody.

I am looking for my father. Has he been here?

Please tell me, sir, are you my father? Because my mother is waiting for someone. Is it you she is waiting for?

"Good," Mr. Kean said. "You're in the part already, my child."

"You're right about Mr. Kean," her aunt said that night. "He knows you very well. I suppose you're all alike, you theater people. . . . He has nice manners."

"Do you think he's handsome, Aunt Mary?" Melissa asked. She was tired and not hungry and if she kept talking perhaps her aunt would not notice that she could not eat.

"Well, yes, I suppose so," her aunt said. "But then I like that slim dark type. Not that it matters. Still, it's pleasant to meet a man with such manners after working in an office where the men bark at you all day."

"Mr. Kean is polite to everybody," Melissa said. "Even when the star argues with him he listens politely."

"That blonde!" her aunt said. "I don't like her looks. She's thirty-five if she's a day."

"Maybe forty," Melissa said. "I think she's disgusting."

Her aunt laughed. "Oh you funny little thing—why do you say that?"

"She thinks about herself all the time and not about the part," Melissa said. "A real actress doesn't think about herself."

"Now how do you know that?" her aunt asked. "Did Mr. Kean tell you?"

"Nobody told me," she said.

Her aunt looked at her for a long instant. "I have a mind to tell you what he said to me about you, but I hope it won't make you vain. He said . . ."

She paused and Melissa waited, pretending to eat.

"He said," her aunt went on, "that you were destined—that's the word he used—destined to be a great actress, much greater than your mother. He said just what you say, that you don't think about yourself—only about what you're supposed to be in the play, and it means you have the real gift. He told me I must be careful of you—because you're a rare treasure."

"Then why are you crying, Aunt Mary?" she asked in simple wonder.

"Oh because"—her aunt wiped her eyes and swallowed and then went on—"I'm not fit to bring you up alone, child, and that's the truth. I saw your mother ruined by the family because we didn't know what to make of her. We thought she was silly and heedless and half mad and because of us not understanding she did things she shouldn't have. She destroyed herself, in a way, and I wonder if she's happy, married to that Englishman! Anyway she left us. And when I told Mr. Kean about her he said that destructiveness only comes when life isn't lived. People who can live their lives don't destroy themselves. And I see that's true, Melissa. I've been thinking it all day. And it explains me to myself, too. For in a manner of speaking, I destroy myself. Here I am, twenty-five and not married yet, and not able to marry anybody that asks me, though Jim Erwin is a nice fellow and why I don't want him, I'll never know—a steady job and sure to rise in the company. And I come home and I'm cross to you and that's destroying you—"

"You're not cross to me, Aunt Mary," Melissa said.

Her aunt hugged her wildly. "Yes, I am! And I would be crosser if I didn't hold myself in. When you come home all happy and dreamy from the theater it makes me want to—to—beat you!"

Melissa opened her enormous eyes. "Aunt Mary!" Her voice was a whisper of fear.

"Oh, I wouldn't beat you," her aunt said, "and don't look at me like that, darling. It's just that I—don't know what to do with myself tonight. . . ."

She looked at her aunt's pretty face, flushed with tears. "You know what I think?" she said slowly.

"What, angel?" her aunt said, wiping her eyes.

"I think you're falling in love with Mr. Kean."

Her aunt pretended to slap her. "Oh go on with you," she said. "You and your actress ways!"

. . . Ah, but she knew, she knew very well after that. She had watched too many stars on the stage, making love to the leading

186

men, to the young directors. She knew that all one had to do with a young and pretty woman and a young and handsome man was to bring them together in a theater, especially an empty theater, where you could sit in the dark alone and watch a love story shape before your eyes into a play. Young as she was she knew, and the next morning she clung to her aunt's hand.

"I don't feel so well," she murmured. "Please come with me just one more day."

"And what about my job?" her aunt said.

"Please don't work," Melissa whispered. "Couldn't you just pretend you are my mother? The mothers don't work. They help the theater children. And we can live on what I earn, can't we? Maybe somebody even pays the mothers for taking care of the children."

"I hadn't thought of that," her aunt said. "I could ask your Mr. Kean."

"He isn't mine," Melissa said.

Her aunt laughed. "And he certainly isn't mine!"

"Maybe he belongs to both of us," Melissa said.

"Now how can you be so sharp?" her aunt said. "And I wonder if it's true you don't feel well."

"I won't go on with the play if you don't come with me," Melissa said.

"Well, one more day . . ."

. . . "And I wonder, Mary," Mr. Kean said when they got to the theater, "if you could manage to stay at rehearsals with Melissa? She performs with much more ease and security if you are here. The difference is remarkable. Remember what I said to you yesterday— She is one of the rare talents—and worth every sacrifice."

"It's no sacrifice, Mr. Kean, but—"

"Barney, please."

"I couldn't possibly—in such a short time as I've known you and not being a theater person."

"I've always known you, Mary—"

The lines were right, of course, and Melissa heard them and slipped between the empty seats and danced into the long dim aisle without being noticed. The lines were perfect and the play was going into rehearsal, not the play on the stage, but the real play, the love story, and the star was her aunt and Mr. Kean was the leading man.

When her aunt took her to lunch that day, and it was a lunch at the restaurant next door, not a sandwich out of a paper bag, they ate in silence. Once or twice she spoke to her aunt and her aunt forgot to answer. She sat eating and smiling and saying nothing and that was all right. It was only the end of the first act. But when there was a good first act, there would certainly be a play. Everyone knows that.

"Melissa," her aunt said that night, "you'll be shocked, but I've decided to quit my job. Barney—Mr. Kean, that is—thinks I owe it to you."

"Oh thank you, Aunt Mary," she said.

"And why do you thank me?"

"Because—really and truly, I am afraid in that big theater all by myself."

"You're not by yourself and you know it," her aunt said. "There's all the people on the stage."

"But when I'm not on the stage I'm afraid, and I don't come on at all in the second act and only at the very end in the third act. In between I am afraid."

"Don't say it's that chandelier," her aunt said.

Melissa hesitated. "It's not the chandelier exactly . . ."

"What then?"

"It's—not having my mother there in the third row, waiting for me."

Her aunt stretched out her arms. "Oh, you poor baby—why didn't you tell me the truth before?"

"I don't know," Melissa whispered. And suddenly she began to cry real tears.

"My God," her aunt whispered. "And I never knew!"

That of course was the beginning of the second act. She knew it the next morning. It was a long act, and it lasted for so many days that she began to wonder if there was something wrong with the play. There was usually something wrong with plays. They had to be rewritten and who was to rewrite this one? Mr. Kean took her aside one day on the stage where no one could hear.

"Melissa, will you help me?"

"Yes, I will," she said.

"I want to marry your Aunt Mary."

She threw her arms around his neck. "Oh thank you, Mr. Kean!"

"Will you call me Barney?"

She shook her head. "I'd rather not."

"Uncle Barney?"

She shook her head again. "I have a name for you but I don't want to speak it yet."

"When?"

She felt suddenly shy, a new feeling. "In the third act—maybe."

"We're working on the third act now."

"I don't mean this play," she said.

He waited but she only shook her head and he sighed. "Well, I respect your silence, Melissa, and some day you will tell me what you mean. . . . Now, here's my problem. Your aunt won't let me propose to her."

"Won't let you?"

"She says we haven't known each other long enough. But that's just excuse. The fact of it is I suspect that she doesn't trust me. She doesn't trust anybody in the theater. She thinks we are all play-acting people. Are we, Melissa?"

"We are and we aren't," she said.

"Will you stop playing the sphinx and tell me what you mean, my child?"

"Please don't call me your child," she said. "Not quite yet," she added.

"Certainly," he said. "Not until you say so."

"And what I mean," she said, "is just that we do mean what we are playing—while we are playing. Of course when the play is over—it's ended. There's nothing left. That's what she's afraid of.

189

She doesn't want to be somebody with nothing left in a play. She wants to be real."

"I see," he said gravely. "Thank you for explaining it to me."

And this, she decided, was the end of the second act. There was nothing to do except wait for the third act to begin. And in the intermission she danced in the empty aisles, as light upon her feet as a hummingbird upon its wings.

"Oh, I shall be sad, sad, sad when the play opens," she told her aunt that night.

"And why?" her aunt asked.

They were eating chicken stew and hot biscuits, her favorite food. Her aunt was a fine cook and now that she didn't go to her job she took time to make the dishes they both liked.

"Because I shall have to say goodbye to Mr. Kean. And my life with him will be ended. Maybe I'll never see him again and that breaks my heart."

"Don't play-act," her aunt said sharply.

"I'm not," Melissa said. "I've fallen in love with him."

"And don't be silly," her aunt said severely.

"I'm not," Melissa said again. "I've fallen in love with him as a father, Aunt Mary. Not as a lover."

"Oh for mercy's sake," her aunt said. "Will you please remember that you're just a little girl? Lover!"

"But I said—"

"Be quiet!"

She was quiet then, but she let tears slide down her cheeks slowly and her aunt saw them.

"What are you crying for now?"

"You're being cross with me," Melissa sobbed.

"I'm not cross with you," her aunt said. "I'm just—cross."

"Why, Aunt Mary?"

"Because I can't make up my mind."

"You mean about Mr. Kean?"

"What do you know about that, pray tell?"

"You're in love with him, Aunt Mary. Not play love—real love."

"Oh no, I'm not! I've sworn to myself I will not marry a theater man, not after your mother and your father and all their goings-on. I'd as soon marry a reed shaking in the wind."

"But you love the theater, Aunt Mary."

Her aunt put down her fork. "Now how did you ever know that?" she whispered.

"Because you've never been in love before," she said. "Have you, Aunt Mary?"

"Never," her aunt said. "And I've always said I hated the theater."

They looked at each other and a strange tenderness crept into Melissa's heart, an old sort of tenderness, a deep understanding of the woman her aunt was, and the man that Mr. Kean was, and of what the love between them was. She had seen the image of love again and again, played upon a stage, an image of something true. And here was the truth.

She got up from her chair and went around the table and put her arms about her aunt's neck.

"Please, Aunt Mary," she said. "Please do marry him. I love him so much, too. As a father, I mean. . . . The way I love you . . . as a mother."

Her aunt's arms went around her tight and warm.

"Oh, you little owl," her aunt said. "You darling little owl!"

Gift of Laughter

I‍T WAS THE DAWN of Christmas day, the day Mrs. Barton had been dreading. She woke and saw her room, its familiar lines dim in the early morning. She shut her eyes quickly and lay in her bed, quite motionless. It was here, the day she had been trying not to think about. That was the trouble with Christmas—it could not be put off. It came down upon one like the day of death itself, inevitable and sure.

For Mrs. Barton was afraid of Christmas. She had first realized this when she went shopping for Ranny's Christmas box, which, she had been told at the Red Cross headquarters, should be mailed not a minute later than the first of November in order to reach wherever Ranny was. She did not know where he was, but she had the name of his regiment, and somebody at the Red Cross had found out for her in general—enough, at least, so she could send his Christmas box in time.

That day she went shopping she had been able to keep hidden the fact she was afraid of Christmas by telling all the pleasant sales-girls that she was buying things for her son, "my only son," she had said with quiet pride, "who is near a front somewhere."

What made this war so much harder than the last one was that in this war there were so many fronts. The last time, when Ranny's father had been away at the front, it had meant, of course, somewhere in Europe and she had been to Europe so many times in her girlhood that she had been able to follow Ranald easily on the map she kept on the library wall. When he fell in the Sommes—well, she knew where he was. But this war! The thought of his being in places which she had never seen dimmed her fine gray eyes often. What if he fell as his father did, and she could not even get to his grave?

The pretty salesgirl, seeing that dimming, had smiled encouragingly.

"What's the color of his eyes?" she asked.

Mrs. Barton's face cleared. "Blue," she said, "the bluest eyes you ever saw."

"Then this is the sweater for him," she said and added, "I always did like a blue-eyed man."

"So do I," Mrs. Barton said. "His father had blue eyes, too."

Of course she was very busy getting the package off. There were no such things as Christmas seals and wrappings in the stores yet, but she had found a box of things left over from last year. The things really looked lovely when she had them all tied up. And she had bought candies and nuts in tins, guaranteed to keep in the hottest climates—but Ranny was not in a hot climate! There was a fruitcake, too. The size of the package finally had worried her a good deal. Suppose they said it was too big—no, they would not even tell her—they would, perhaps, just not send it. The idea terrified her and hastily she divided all the things and made three packages. By this time she had everyone in the house helping her, old Henry the butler, and Anne, his wife, and Dicken the chauffeur. Dicken was young enough for the draft and would be gone before Christmas.

"I shall send you a box, too, Dicken," she had told him.

He had touched his cap. "Thank you, Madame."

When he went away she put up the cars until Ranny came home.

It was the least an old lady could do these days, to save gasoline and rubber. When he went two weeks before Christmas she had said to him,

"Mind you remember your job is here waiting for you, Dicken."

He touched his cap again and said, "Thank you, Madame."

Her heart ached a little. He looked young and simple. It had occurred to her then that she did not know anything at all about him.

"Are you married, Dicken?" she inquired.

"No, Madame," he said, flushing suddenly and deeply.

"Have you parents?" she asked gently.

"Yes, Madame," he said again.

Silence had fallen between them like a wall, and since they were both shy, neither could surmount it.

"Well, goodbye, Dicken," she said and put out her hand. "I shall think of you and wish you luck."

"Thank you, Madame," he said and took his hand hastily away. It had felt large and young and heavy in her long thin one.

On this Christmas morning there were actually only old Henry and old Anne in the house. "And old me," she added with a sad solitary sort of humor. She smiled sadly, without opening her eyes.

It was now that she acknowledged that she was afraid of this Christmas day. If she did not make very definite plans today against this fear, it would be too much for her at last. For she was always aware in her secret sensitive soul that there might come, one day, a moment when looking about on her life she would decide it was not worth while. Did she inherit the light hold on life which had always been hers? Or was it only since Ranald's death? Her father, just before he was sixty, for no reason that anyone could discern had suddenly ended his life. It had seemed incomprehensible when she was young, but she understood increasingly as time went on why he had done it. It did not need a catastrophe to make life not worth the effort. The simple accumulation of disappointments might become too heavy. There was a point of time, merely, when the balance went over to the other side. It was only Ranny who

194

had made life worth while. All her life had been in Ranny since the day he was born, and now he had been taken from her. Ah, war was most cruel of all to a mother, like her, who had only her one son!

She thought of her friends and shrank from each of them. There were three or four like herself. If I were really kind, she thought, I would invite poor old Marnie Lewis and the others here for Christmas Day. But she knew she would not do it. There was no use in merely adding the loneliness of others to her own loneliness. It would be easier to cope only with herself. She would get up late and go to church and then come home and write to Ranny and tell him how lonely she was.

Now her fear narrowed down to one point—what would she do today when she had come home from church, had eaten her dinner, and had written her letter to Ranny? What positively would she do then? She felt tears come smarting up under her eyelids and she quivered. Then she got up slowly and put on her quilted robe and her slippers and went to the bathroom and washed herself and brushed her hair. On her way back to bed she stopped at the window and looked out. The day was clear and cold. There was no snow. Ranny when he was little had always prayed for snow at Christmas, and indeed even when he was grown had prayed for it a little, not formally, but only by hopes and wishes and loud protests of pain when there was no snow on Christmas morning. She smiled, and old Anne bringing in the breakfast tray a moment later caught the faint trace of her remembering smile and smiled back.

"Merry Christmas, Madame," she said. She had put a bit of holly on the tray. The two great hollies by the front door were very fine this year with berries. They had been planted the year Ranny was born, twenty-seven years ago.

"I was thinking how angry Ranny would be with no snow this morning," Mrs. Barton said gently.

"Wouldn't he just," old Anne agreed.

She spread the pale yellow satin cover over the great bed, and put the tray down.

"How pretty the holly is," Mrs. Barton said.

"Cheerful-like," old Anne said.

"It is indeed," Mrs. Barton said.

Old Anne went away then, pleased with herself, and Mrs. Barton began eating her breakfast. She had little appetite but she paid no heed to that. She ate on dutifully, chewing everything very fine, eating very slowly. It was of course barely possible that Ranny might send her a message today. But he had told her in his last letter that she must not be worried if she did not hear from him for a long time. He was quite safe—only she must not think he wasn't if for a long time, "A very long time, maybe, you won't hear from me, Mother." Since she had had a card two weeks ago, she must not of course expect anything today.

She lay thinking over the half-empty tray—for, after all she had not been able to eat much—of how Ranny always filled the house with his friends on Christmas Day. She had always devoted herself to him. Why had he never married? But of course she was glad he had not. "Nobody's good enough after you, Mother," he always said. That was nonsense, but after all perhaps a little true? They had been always so close, and he knew that after his father was killed in France there had been nobody else but himself. She had indignantly refused an offer of marriage when Ranny was thirteen, made her by Topham Stokes, who had been Ranald's friend and business partner. She had told Ranny all about it. To her astonishment and secret hurt he had been rather sorry.

"I like old Toppy," Ranny had said.

"I couldn't, Ranny," she had said coldly. "You don't understand. Besides, I have you. If I should put someone in your father's place it seems to me it would be an insult to you."

"It wouldn't be in Dad's place, exactly," Ranny had said. "Toppy's only Toppy."

"We won't talk about it," she had said.

Certainly she could not reproach herself that Ranny had not married. She had always told herself that of course a young man ought to marry and when the time came she would be brave. And she would be unselfish, too, and not expect all of Ranny's time and devotion. She had tried delicately to make it clear to him that at any time, especially after he was twenty-five, she would have quite understood if—

"Really, I would welcome a pretty daughter-in-law," she had said smiling. "Someone, say, like Alicia?" Alicia was the daughter of an old friend, a pale fair exquisite creature.

He had shaken his blond head and laughed. "Sorry, I can't seem to fall in love with Alicia, Mother," he had said.

Ranny was doing so well in the business by then, that Topham Stokes, now senior partner, told her that he had all of Ranald's brilliance at law. He was enormously popular, besides. But it seemed quite true that he simply did not fall in love.

She glanced at the clock. If she got up now and dressed slowly she would be just about in time for church. So she got up, taking the bit of holly from the tray and putting it under Ranny's picture on her dressing table. He looked back at her, his handsome face good-natured and gay under the officer's cap. He was such a good boy, she thought, always so good—the sort one could trust, wherever he was. She bit her lip. Ranald had been like that, too; Ranald who never came back. Goodness never *saved* anybody! And who would take care of her if Ranny never came back? Simply having money wasn't enough. She had always been a very feminine sort of woman —Ranald had said he loved her dependence on him. And Ranny had somehow come to take his father's place. How could she manage without him—if he, too, never came back?

She leaned for a moment on the table, all her soul in her eyes as she gazed at her son's face, and then she pulled herself together. No, she had no feeling that Ranny was dead. When—that is, if— he were killed she would know it instantly—Or would she?

"But I feel you are alive, Ranny," she whispered. She imagined— of course it was only imagination—that his eyes grew bright with life.

"Help me," she whispered. "Help me—when I come home alone today!"

But after all it was only a picture. She turned away from it, knowing that it was nothing more.

. . . The moment she entered the house after church she knew that something was wrong. That is, she felt there was a stranger in the house. Old Henry had let her in the door, looking upset.

"What's the matter, Henry?" she asked.

"There's a young person in the liberry, Madame," he said.

"A young person?" she repeated.

"You'll see, Madame," he said.

"But why did you let her in?" she demanded.

He held out a bit of paper that had been crumpled in his hand. She saw Ranny's handwriting.

Old Henry—admit this one, for Tigger's sake.

"Tigger!" she repeated. Tigger had been the name Ranny had called himself when he was small. It was a mispronunciation of Tiger learned when he was beginning to read. He had pounced upon old Henry one day from the upper balustrade.

"I'm a tigger!" he had screamed, and had felled old Henry to the floor. After that it had been a game for years for old Henry to pretend that he was desperately afraid of the Tigger. But no one outside the house had known of the game.

"Yes, Madame," he now said gravely. He met her clear gray-blue eyes. "Shall I stand by, Madame? While you see her, I mean?"

"No," she said. "No, I—I am quite able to—Henry, what is she like?"

"She's sort of like—like—almost anybody, if you know what I mean, Madame. One sees a lot like her—young girls, I mean. She might be—anything."

"I see," she said slowly. She gave him her furs and her coat but she did not take off her hat. It was a pale blue toque, very becoming to her white hair but it made her look stern.

198

She opened the door to the library and saw the young person sitting there in one of the high-backed oaken chairs.

"Yes?" she said in her clear clipped voice. "Did you want to speak to me?"

The young girl rose quickly and clutched her little bag. "Are you Tigger's mother?" she asked faintly.

"Tigger?" Mrs. Barton repeated.

"Are you Mrs. Barton?" the young girl asked.

"I am," she replied, and did not sit down. She was a good deal taller than the girl, who, she perceived, was sinfully young, surely not twenty, very small and soft and dark, and now obviously trembling. She was not even understandably pretty. Her little features were childish and only her eyes, large and black, were noticeable.

"Tigger—that is, Ranald—sent me," the girl faltered.

"My son?" Mrs. Barton said. She felt suddenly cold. "Sit down," she said to the girl, "Why do you say my son sent you? He is far away."

The young girl's pale face flushed a delicate pink. Then she gathered her courage. Mrs. Barton saw her lift her head and bite her lips. "Ranny told me exactly what I was to do before he went away. He said I was to come to you on Christmas Day."

Mrs. Barton listened without bending. "Why should I believe you?" she asked coldly.

For answer the girl put her hand to her round little bosom and drew out a thick envelope. "This is his last letter," she said and tore off a first sheet and handed it to Mrs. Barton.

"Little Tiggeress," the letter began. "I am writing this with my feet in a bucket of hot water. The splashes you see aren't tears— though I could shed them, you sweet and silly child, when I read your—"

Mrs. Barton handed the sheet back to the girl. She fixed her eyes upon the girl, defying her to know what was going on in her heart. Ranny—what had Ranny to do with this girl? Ranny had told her nothing. All the time she thought she had Ranny she didn't have him at all. She had been alone all the time, quite alone, but it remained to this Christmas Day at last to know it! Pride rose up and sealed her lips. She would ask nothing of this girl that her son had not wanted to tell her. Let them keep their secrets! She felt the tearing of her inner flesh. Now she really was alone.

The girl put the letter back under the little white satin vest of her brown wool dress.

"Aren't you going to ask me—who I am?" she said.

"No," Mrs. Barton said. "No, I shan't ask."

"But—but he told me to come today—Christmas," the girl faltered. "He told me to—to—"

"Why?" Mrs. Barton asked swiftly, "why on Christmas of all days?" She paused and then said what she meant. "Christmas is hard enough—anyway."

The girl leaned forward and clasped her small childish hands. Her brown eyes filled with large tears, clear like a baby's tears. "Isn't it simply terrible?" she whispered.

Mrs. Barton did not answer. Nothing could be as terrible for this girl as it was now for her. There was nothing in common between them. The girl moved quickly and fell on her knees by Mrs. Barton's chair.

Mrs. Barton shrank back. "No," she said, "no—I don't want to know anything about you."

The girl rose slowly. "You mean—you really want me—just to go away?"

"Please," Mrs. Barton begged, "please—just go away."

"But Tigger said—"

"Please," Mrs. Barton cried, "please, please!" She buried her face in her hands and began to weep aloud, her whole body shaking.

Beside her the girl stood quite still. Then Mrs. Barton felt a touch on her shoulder.

"Don't cry," the girl said. "You don't have to cry. I'm going away. I wouldn't have come in the first place if he had not told me I must. 'You get there,' he told me, 'at twelve o'clock. She'll be home from church about then.' 'They won't let me in,' I told him.

So he tore a leaf out of his little notebook and gave it to me. I was to give it to the old man at the door. Then I was to wait for you and when you came in I was to wait for you to ask me who I was. And I was to tell you and when we'd both got acquainted I was to give you his Christmas present for you."

Mrs. Barton took her hands away from her face. "His Christmas present for me?" she exclaimed.

"I've kept it ever since he went away," the girl explained. "He bought it the Saturday afternoon before he went. I was with him. It took a long time—nothing was good enough for him to give to you. 'It's got to be just right, Tiggress,' he says. That's what he calls me."

"You aren't married to him?" Mrs. Barton gasped.

"Certainly not," the girl said quickly.

"Then," Mrs. Barton said, gathering her dignity. "I should only like to ask why you are here."

"I told you. Tigger told me to come and give you his present," the girl said calmly. "Here it is. And I'll give it to you and go away." She opened her little brown bag and took out a small package.

"Open it," she said. "I want to tell him how you like it."

Mrs. Barton hesitated and then opened it. Inside a small satin-covered box was an old-fashioned locket of filigreed gold set with pearls. Inside the locket on ivory was painted Ranny's face when he had been a year old.

"That's where my baby picture of him went!" Mrs. Barton exclaimed. "I missed it when I was looking through his baby book."

The girl took an envelope from her bag. "Here it is," she said. "He told me to be sure to give it back to you."

Mrs. Barton took it without seeing it. She was gazing at the baby face in the locket. "Wasn't he the sweetest baby!" she murmured. "That little gold ruff on top of his head—Oh, I'm glad to have this—it seems to bring home to me again—my baby—"

"That's what he said it would," the girl said coolly. Her eyes

201

meeting Mrs. Barton's were so large and cool indeed, that Mrs. Barton felt vaguely angry with their look.

"Isn't he sweet?" she demanded, holding out the ivory painting.

"Yes, he is," the girl said dispassionately.

"Maybe you don't care for babies," Mrs. Barton said.

"Don't I!" the girl said succinctly. "I've always said I wanted ten."

"I had only the one," Mrs. Barton said. "Ranny's father was killed in the first World War.

"Tigger told me all that," the girl said. "It's a pity you didn't marry again and have some brothers and sisters for him."

"I wouldn't have thought of it," Mrs. Barton cried hotly.

"Tigger told me about that too," the girl said quietly. "But it would have been better for him all the same." The dimples in her brown cheeks straightened. "Maybe I'd have married him then. Maybe he'd have been free."

Mrs. Barton snapped the locket shut.

"What do you mean?" she demanded. "Ranny has always been free."

The girl shook her dark curls. "Oh, no, he is not free," she said, not sadly, but with a sort of childish wisdom. "He's bound to you, Mrs. Barton. Everything he does he thinks first of how you would like it. Then mostly he doesn't do it."

"That's absurd," Mrs. Barton said sharply. "Why, you said just now he—he proposed to you."

"Yes, but—I could see he did it—in spite of you—and if you didn't like me he might be—sorry."

"Is that why you wouldn't marry him?" Mrs. Barton asked.

"I don't want to marry a man who belongs to anybody else," the girl said calmly. Again there was neither pain nor reproach in her voice.

Mrs. Barton sat up straighter in her chair. "If I have had an influence on my son—" she began.

"Oh, I wouldn't mind influence," the girl said cheerfully, "but

202

you're—you see, you're selfish. You've made him think he owes it to you to keep you from being—lonely and all that."

Mrs. Barton felt the blood rise slowly up her cheeks from her neck. "Has he talked to you about me?" she asked with anger.

"Oh no," the girl said. "Well, I mean, just enough to explain things to me. When I didn't want to come here today he said you'd be—you might even kill yourself if—you thought he wasn't coming back. He said you'd told him you were afraid because your father had done it—he said it kept him—worried."

"My son seems to have confided to you all my private affairs," Mrs. Barton said.

"No, only because you've made them his," the girl said. She put her bag down again on the chair which she scarcely half filled, and again she clasped her small brown hands. "Of course I told him the truth," she added.

"The truth?" Mrs. Barton repeated.

"I told him that it wasn't that you loved him so much that made you the way you are. It's your being afraid of yourself—without him."

Mrs. Barton rose. Her knees suddenly began to tremble. "You had better go away, I think," she said. "After all, who are you? A common girl my son picked up—the way all men seem to do—with girls like you."

But the girl went on gravely. "I wasn't picked up. I was sent to him on my job, you understand, to interview him on a murder case. I'm a newspaper reporter. He wouldn't tell me a thing, either. I liked him for that. So, when he asked me to lunch I went—and tried some more. And still he wouldn't tell me anything. So I liked him some more."

"What was the case?" Mrs. Barton demanded.

"The Pratt murder case," the girl replied.

"But that was three years ago," Mrs. Barton cried. Ranny had known this girl secretly for three years! It was because of this girl he had not wanted to marry—not because of her!

The girl jumped up and put her firm little hands on Mrs. Barton's shoulders and pressed her into her seat. "Sit down," she said, "and don't say silly things."

Mrs. Barton looked at her with severity. "Has he wanted to marry you—for a long time?"

"He says ever since he first saw me—three years ago."

"Three years ago?" Mrs. Barton echoed. "But that's ridiculous—you're a child."

"Twenty-two."

"When was it that he first really proposed to you?" Mrs. Barton asked. This was why he couldn't love Alicia!

The girl hung her head. "Do I have to tell you?"

"Not if you don't want to," Mrs. Barton said. "Still, having told me so much—"

The girl laughed again and now suddenly she sat herself on the arm of Mrs. Barton's chair.

"Aren't you ashamed?" she cried. "You told me yourself not to tell you anything!"

Mrs. Barton hesitated. Then suddenly she laughed, too. It really was absurd, this young girl talking to her! "You seem to have told me a good deal in spite of that," she said.

The door opened and old Henry stood there. He blinked his eyes at what he saw and Mrs. Barton was immediately ashamed of the intimacy of the young girl on the arm of her chair. She looked at him sharply.

"What is it, Henry?" she asked.

"Madame, the dinner," he replied. "The turkey is getting dry."

The young girl jumped to her feet. "It's time I was going," she said.

"Wait," Mrs. Barton commanded, "where are you going to have your Christmas dinner?"

"Oh, at Child's, I guess," the girl said hardily. "They give you a swell Christmas dinner for a dollar. I have a dollar. Saved it!"

"Haven't you a family?" Mrs. Barton asked.

The girl shook her head. "Orphan," she said brightly. "I was brought up in an asylum. I guess that's why I say I want ten children when I get married. It wouldn't seem like home to me without a lot."

"You don't stay in an orphanage, surely?" Mrs. Barton inquired.

"Oh, no," the girl said. "They send you out when you're seventeen—they get you a job, of course, I didn't like mine and I found another. But they do the best they can."

"Henry," Mrs. Barton said clearly. "Put another place at the table. Miss—what's your name?"

"Jenny," the girl said. "Jenny Holt."

"Miss Holt will stay for dinner," Mrs. Barton said.

"Yes, Madame," Henry's voice was a sigh of amazement as he closed the door softly.

"Is Holt your real name?" Mrs. Barton demanded.

Jenny shook her head. "It was the next name on the H's," she said. "Harrison, Holmes, Holt, Hutton, and so on."

"Haven't you any idea who you are?" Mrs. Barton asked.

Jenny laughed and shook her head again. "Child of a doorstep," she said cheerfully.

Mrs. Barton pondered this for a moment. "Well," she breathed. "It's amazing—simply amazing!"

But she rose and led the way upstairs to take off her things. And once upstairs on an impulse she did not understand, although she had planned to direct the young girl to the guest room, she pointed to Ranny's room instead.

"That's his room," she said. "You can go in and wash and take off your hat if you like."

"Oh, thank you," Jenny said.

She went into her own room and shut the door and sat down. Then on the table Ranny's eyes looked at her tenderly over the bit of holly.

Selfish, she thought. Yes, I suppose it's been selfishness—to be afraid to live without you. The young eyes suddenly seemed alive

205

and her own eyes brimmed with tears. "How shall I make it up to you?" she murmured. The blue eyes smiled back at her steadily for a long moment. "Of course I can," she said to them—"of course I will."

. . . But before old Henry nothing could be said and the necessity for formality simply made Jenny silly and gay. To this brown-eyed gaiety and childlike mischief, who could fail to respond? Mrs. Barton found herself laughing and making remarks that mystified old Henry to pain. She saw bewilderment in his eyes and it only seemed funny to her again. When Henry left the room Jenny put out her soft little brown hand and patted Mrs. Barton's diamond-ringed fingers.

"Tigger didn't do you justice," she said caressingly. "Why, he simply doesn't know you and I shall tell him so."

Mrs. Barton was grave in a moment. "What do you mean?" she asked.

"Tigger always said you were delicate and sort of severe, you know," Jenny explained. "He's afraid of you—really."

"Afraid of me?" Mrs. Barton repeated.

"Yes, really he is," Jenny said earnestly. "But you're a scream, really, Mrs. Barton. Why, you have a wonderful sense of humor. I'm not afraid of you at all."

Mrs. Barton put down her fork and sat quite still for a moment. Then she leaned over and touched Jenny's cheek.

"You must tell my son he needn't be afraid of me, my—my dear," she said.

Old Henry came back in the room with plum pudding at this moment. It was blazing away so hard that the sprig of holly in the top had caught on fire and was blazing too, every berry a jewel of fire.

"Oh," Jenny said in ecstasy, "it's the first time in my life I've ever seen a plum pudding whole—and burning!" She ate two large helpings, and the hard sauce was as smooth as cream.

In the library over the coffee cups before the fire Mrs. Barton felt suddenly comfortable and relaxed as she had not in many days. She had eaten heartily of the excellent dinner, far more heartily than usual but somehow she felt she was going to digest all she had eaten.

"Do you know," she said to Jenny, "I don't believe I have laughed since Ranny went away. I hadn't thought of it, but I don't believe I have. There hasn't been a thing to laugh at."

She looked at the bright brown eyes that were always brimming with laughter, she now saw, and suddenly she laughed again. Then she touched her eyes with her lace handkerchief. "I don't know why I'm laughing," she confessed, "but it just seems good to laugh. After all, Ranny is alive." She put the handkerchief down. "You do feel that, don't you, Jenny?"

"I know he is," Jenny said firmly.

"But how do you know?" Mrs. Barton whispered.

"If he were dead—I'd know—the minute it happened," Jenny said.

Mrs. Barton leaned forward. "You love him," she said.

Jenny nodded. "With all my heart," she said simply.

Mrs. Barton put out her hand upon Jenny's folded hands. "Then why, dear child, will you not marry him?" she asked.

Jenny's eyes filled with tears. "I'm plain—afraid to," she said.

"Jenny, please!" Mrs. Barton said. "If he loves you—the best? If I—want him to love you the best?"

They were looking with utter gravity into each other's eyes.

"I am asking you to marry my son," Mrs. Barton said gently.

"You're almost as good as Ranny is at it, too," Jenny said.

Suddenly they were laughing again and Jenny jumped up and hugged Mrs. Barton. "I'm really tempted by you, you precious thing!" she exclaimed. "I said no to Ranny as easy as could be but it's lots harder to say it to you. I'd love to have you for my mother. Oh, how I have wanted a mother! They were good to me in the asylum—but it's not the same."

"Then," Mrs. Barton said, her arms about the soft warm child, "will you let me be your mother?"

Jenny drew away a little, just enough to look into Mrs. Barton's eyes.

"You mean it?" she demanded.

"With all my heart we mean it," Mrs. Barton said, "Ranny and I. Dear child, come and live with me and make it—home—for Ranny."

Jenny kissed her cheek. Then she drew away and stood by the table, her hands to her cheeks. They were very rosy cheeks now and her eyes were shining.

"But I'd want to keep on with my job, Mrs. Barton—until he comes back."

"You shall keep on with it," Mrs. Barton said.

Jenny straightened herself. "I'd want to pay board and room."

"Of course," Mrs. Barton said respectfully.

Then Jenny took an uncertain step backward and leaned against the great carved table. "Mrs. Barton, am I—would you say—I was engaged to Tigger—now?"

"I should certainly say so," Mrs. Barton said gently.

The atmosphere in the room changed. The older woman felt it first because it came of course from the younger one. There was sort of glory in it. There was a light and it came from Jenny's eyes. There was music and though it was only the sound of the chimes next door, playing instead of the hour a Christmas carol, still it was an unearthly music.

"We must send a cable to Ranny," Mrs. Barton said softly. "We'll have to send it to the War Department, of course, but maybe they'll let it through when they see what it is. What shall we say, Jenny?"

"Tell him," Jenny said faintly. "Tell him . . ." She shook her head and her voice failed.

Mrs. Barton smiled. "I shall say 'Your Christmas present received.' And then I shall say, 'And approved.'"

Jenny nodded.

"What else?" Mrs. Barton asked.

208

Jenny thought hard. "Just tell him he's engaged," she said. "Sign it with your name—and Tiggress. He'll understand."

Mrs. Barton laughed again. She had a feeling that somehow from now on her life was going to be full of laughter. She had really made up to Ranny—for everything.

Death and the Dawn

"THERE'S NO PLACE TO PUT HIM, Doctor," the nurse said. "The wards are full."

"Put him in a private room," the surgeon said, stripping off his white coat.

"Private rooms are full, too, except that semiprivate where old Mr. MacLeod is. And he's under an oxygen tent—not expected to live through the night. His family is standing by."

"This kid won't bother him. He'll not be waking tonight," the surgeon said. He had his topcoat on now and his hat. It was midnight, he was tired, and he slammed the door after him.

If ever he wakes, the nurse thought, looking at the kid. He was the reckless type, blond hair worn too long, sharp thin face, long thin body, thin to the bone, the kind that was always getting smashed up in car accidents. Under the heavy white bandages the young face was somber. Nobody knew who he was. There had been nothing on him to tell who he was. The car was stolen—at least the owner had not yet been identified, except that he was not this eighteen-year-old boy. Eighteen—seventeen—maybe only sixteen, he could be any age. He was unconscious when they brought him in, and bleeding. Lucky for him the town had a hospital—not every small town had one.

"Put him in Twenty-three," the nurse said to the orderlies.

They wheeled him away and she followed. The hospital was quiet at this time of night. Not even a baby cried. In an hour or two and before dawn the calls would begin, bells ringing, sick people sighing and moaning and babies waking each other up.

Twenty-three was quiet, too, except for the hissing of the oxygen. The small night light was on and she could see old Mr. MacLeod lying there. She'd take a look at him before she went out.

"Be careful of the boy's head," she told the orderlies.

"We know," the older one said. "We saw him brung in."

"Nothing left of the car," the other one said.

They lifted him on the bed with big gentle hands and straightened his arms and legs.

"Anything more, Miss Martin?" the older one asked.

"Nothing, thanks," she said.

They went away and she pulled the sheet and the thin cotton blanket over the boy. He was breathing but not too well. She took his pulse. It was fluttering but that was to be expected. No sedatives, the doctor had directed, after the last injection.

The telephone rang in the hall and she went to answer it. One nurse on the floor wasn't enough at night but that was the way it was. There weren't enough nurses. Mr. MacLeod ought to have a nurse with him. And now this boy—

"Hello," she said softly.

"Miss Martin?" A clear, carefully calm, voice and she recognized it.

"Yes, Mrs. MacLeod."

"I can't sleep, of course. None of us can. Would you just see if—"

"Certainly."

She put down the receiver and went back to the room. The boy's breathing was a little better, but she did not look at him. Mr. MacLeod was lying perfectly still. She was not sure about him. Was he

211

breathing, this old, old man? She felt for his pulse and could not find it. She ran back to the telephone.

"Mrs. MacLeod?"

"Yes?"

"You'd better come."

"Immediately."

She called then on the house telephone for the intern on duty.

"Doctor, I've sent for the MacLeod family."

"Oh—it's the end, is it?"

"I'm afraid so."

"I'll be over. Have the hypodermic ready."

"Yes, Doctor."

She arranged the small tray, the needles on the white sterile cloth. None of it was any use except perhaps to bring an old man back for a moment to say goodbye. But it was the rule, and only a doctor could break it. She carried the tray to the room and set it down noiselessly. The old man had not moved. Neither had the boy. But the boy was breathing better.

She adjusted the oxygen tent and increased slightly the flow of oxygen. She turned on a side light and brought in two extra chairs. When Mrs. MacLeod had been told yesterday, in the doctor's office, that her husband could not live beyond the next day, her face had turned as white as her hair. Then she said, "I ask only one thing— that when the end is near you call me. I shall not leave the house."

These had been the instructions from doctor to nurse. "When you see the end is near, you are to send for Mrs. MacLeod."

The intern came in, a short stout young man with a round kind face.

"Ready, Doctor," Miss Martin said.

"Good. I'll just check. Take the tent off."

The nurse took away the tent and the doctor checked quickly.

"He's very nearly gone. As soon as they come I'll give him the hypodermic."

"It's here," Miss Martin said.

"Not that it will stay him much," the doctor went on. "Half an hour—maybe an hour. Who's the other patient?"

"Accident case."

"Hm—too many of those nowadays."

"Yes."

It was commonplace talk, concealing the knowledge of death—death of the young, death of the old.

"Shall I come in?" It was Mrs. MacLeod at the door.

"Come in," the intern said. "I'm just about to give him a shot—a boost, you know. You'll be able to talk."

"Thank you, Doctor."

She was composed, an aging figure, short but strong, her face controlled. Only Miss Martin noticed that her small compact hands were trembling as she took off her hat.

"Sit down, Mrs. MacLeod."

"We're all here," Mrs. MacLeod said.

"Come in, come in—it can't hurt him," the intern said.

They came in, the son, a tall young man, his plain face anguished, his wife a slender blond woman who was crying behind her handkerchief, and the daughter, pretty and young, and dark like her father. Miss Martin knew them all, George, Ruth and Mary. It was a close family, anyone could see. The children had come every day to visit their father. They had decided together for the operation. It had been successful—that is, it had prolonged his life for three months in this narrow room.

"What about that fellow?" George asked, nodding toward the other bed.

"He's unconscious," Miss Martin said. "There's no other place to put him. Hospital's full. You can just forget him."

She was rubbing Mr. MacLeod's skeleton arm with alcohol. The intern plunged the needle into the loose skin.

"You should have as much as a half hour, Mrs. MacLeod. I'll be just outside the door."

"Thank you, Doctor," Mrs. MacLeod said.

She waited until doctor and nurse were gone and then, at her

213

look, George and Ruth sat down near the bed. Mary came and knelt by her side.

"We're all here, Hal," Mrs. MacLeod said in her clear voice. "George and Ruth came over for supper tonight. We had lamb stew, the way you like it. The garden is coming in nice now. I pulled some little carrots this afternoon for the stew. It was good."

"We had lemon pie for dessert, Dad," George said. "Ruth is learning to make pie like Mom's. I didn't tell her she had to, either, did I, hon?"

"Sure not," Ruth said. She had stopped crying but her lips were quivering.

"Ruth is one good little cook," George went on.

"Better than I was at her age," Mrs. MacLeod said. "You remember the first pie I ever made, Hal? Burned on top and raw on the bottom! It was cherry, too—your favorite. I could have cried. But you laughed and said you hadn't married me for a pie maker."

"The cherry tree will be full of cherries again this year, Dad," Mary said. She leaned her elbows on the bed, her eyes fixed on her father's face. "When they're ripe George must spread the net over it for you. The starlings are already waiting."

George laughed. "Those starlings, Dad! They never learn. Remember how they come every year and sit on the net and stare down at the cherries inside? You said you could almost hear them cuss. Well, it'll be the same this year as ever."

Mary spoke, her voice very soft. "Cherry pie and picnics. That's when summer begins for me."

"I like picnics, too," Mrs. MacLeod said. "Old as I am, there's something about a picnic. We got engaged at a Sunday school picnic—your father and I."

"Dad, remember the time we had a Fourth of July picnic at Parson's Lake?" It was George again. "You showed me how to cast and the very first time I caught a bass. I yelled for everybody to come and see it."

"I love the summers," Mary said, in the same dreaming voice, "but when autumn comes I am glad, too. Remember the hickory

214

nut tree, Dad? And I liked school, I really did. Don't make a face at me, George, just because you didn't!"

"Now you two," Mrs. MacLeod said, trying to laugh. "Can't you ever quit arguing?"

On the other bed, the boy's eyelids quivered, but no one noticed. He did not know himself that his eyelids quivered. Deep in the caverns of his brain he heard voices echoing.

"We had such good times when we were little," Mary said. "Sometimes I wish I were back there again, Mom, with you and Dad."

"Hush," Mrs. MacLeod said. "He wants to say something."

They leaned forward, their faces etched in the light, their eyes fixed upon the old man's grave face. His lips moved, he sighed, he opened his eyes and gazed at them, one face and then another.

"Dear," Mrs. MacLeod said, "it's lonesome at home without you. When the dishes were washed tonight we thought we'd come over."

She stopped to listen. He turned his head toward her.

"Martha . . ." It was his voice, a sigh, a whisper.

"Yes, Hal, I'm here, we're all here, the children wanted to come too, just to talk."

She nodded toward them.

"Little Hal and Georgie said to tell you hello, Dad," Ruth said quickly. "They're in bed. I have Lou Baker sitting with them. She's the girl next door, a nice girl. Little Hal said as soon as you come home he wants you to see his new tricycle you told us to get him for his birthday."

"He's thinking about Christmas already," George said. "He asked me yesterday if you'd get him a horn to put on the tricycle."

"I love Christmas." It was Mary's voice dreaming again. "Every Christmas I think about all the other Christmastimes that I can remember—our stockings hanging up on the mantel, yours and Mother's at the end, Dad, and George's and mine between. And the carol singers in the night—Oh, how lovely the music was outside the window when I was warm in bed!"

She sang softly, "What child is this, who, laid to rest . . ."

215

In the other bed the boy's eyes were half open. He turned his head, not seeing, but the voices were clear now. He heard singing.

"I remember . . . everything," Mr. MacLeod said.

"Christmas Day," Mrs. MacLeod said, her yearning eyes upon his face. "It's always pure happiness. I never believe in company at Christmas. It's enough to have us all together. And now we have little Hal and Georgie."

"Mary will be getting married one of these days," George said. "And there'll be more of us."

"But we'll not be changed," Mary said. "Dad and Mother are our parents, forever and ever. We're your family, Dad. Even our being grown up can't change that."

"I hope I can be as good a father as you are, Dad," George said.

The boy could see now. His eyes were open. He saw the other bed. An old, old man was lying there, and around him—people.

"Good children," the old man said drowsily. He seemed half asleep.

"How you two always knew exactly what we wanted!" Mary's voice was tender. "I remember the doll I had when I was nine, and the ring I found on the tree when I was fifteen—my first ring, but how did you know I wanted an emerald?"

"It was a very small one," her mother said.

"It had a little diamond on either side, and I still have it, and I still love it."

"I had skis when I was twelve," George said, "but I don't know how you knew I wanted them, Dad, for I never told you. I was afraid they'd cost too much. That was the year I had my appendix out."

"Dad always listens, especially around Christmas," Mrs. MacLeod said.

"But how did you know that for graduation I wanted a shock-proof watch almost more than I wanted my diploma?" George asked.

"Or that I wanted a trip to California?" Mary asked.

"We . . . knew," Mr. MacLeod said. His voice trailed off. His eyelids fluttered.

The boy on the other bed turned to see the people better. That hurt, that hurt something awful. Where had he been going when he hit the truck? Nowhere, nowhere at all. He just couldn't stand it any more. He couldn't stand anything any more. He was running away from nobody, from nowhere to nowhere. Loafing around the streets, because nobody cared what he did—he couldn't remember anybody who had ever cared. Christmastime—he couldn't remember.

"Next Sunday is Easter," Mrs. MacLeod was saying. "The daffodils are up and the Easter lily is in bloom. It has six flowers on it this year. I think the most it ever had before was three, wasn't it?"

Mr. MacLeod made an effort. "Five," he said distinctly.

"There now," Mrs. MacLeod said proudly. "He remembers better than I do. It did have five, one year."

The boy on the other bed listened. Easter. He knew the word. People dressed up and went to church. But what for?

Mr. MacLeod's eyelids fell. Mrs. MacLeod nodded and George went to the door.

"Come in, please, Doctor."

The intern came in on tiptoe and bent over Mr. MacLeod. He felt his pulse. It was still. Then he felt a few wavering beats. He shook his head.

Mrs. MacLeod's face went white but her voice was still clear. "You'd better be getting home to bed, children," she said. "You need your sleep—you're young. I'll stay a while with your dad."

They looked at each other, knowing. Ruth tried not to cry again. "Wait till you get out of the room, honey," George had told her.

"Good night, Dad," George said. "We'll see you in the morning."

"In the morning, darling Dad," Mary said. She leaned over her father, all her tenderness in her face. "In the bright, bright morning," she said.

Her father's eyes opened, but he did not speak.

217

They were gone then, the three children. The intern hesitating, followed them.

From the other bed the boy watched the two old people. Gosh, they were old. What would happen now? He felt like crying but not about them. He felt like crying about himself because he had never had a father, because his mother had died when he was little, because he had no family. That was the trouble with him—he had no family. You could be born and grow up with a lot of other kids in an orphanage and you thought you were all right but you weren't. The old woman was talking to the old man.

"Hal, all this remembering—and you and I have more to remember than the children. You've been a good husband, Hal. A good husband makes a happy wife. I don't mean just a good provider. You're that, of course. But the man you are, you've made me a happy woman, Hal. And out of our happiness together, the two of us, we've made happy children."

She paused, controlled her voice and went on. "I never pass by that little piece of woods where you asked me to marry you that I don't see us two standing there, you taking my hand." His hand was searching for hers and she clasped it in both of hers.

"Here I am. Oh darling—darling—darling—"

Her voice broke at last but she bit her lips. "Oh God, help me—"

Then, her voice strong again, she went on. "I'll always see us standing there in the woods together. I'll never pass by without seeing us—"

"Martha." Her name scarcely broke the stillness, but she heard.

"Yes, Hal? I'm here. I shall stay right here."

He opened his eyes suddenly, he saw her and he smiled. "A good—life . . ." His voice trailed into silence and his hand loosened upon hers. His eyelids closed.

Now anyone could see the old man was dying. The boy wanted to cry. He hadn't cried since he was a kid and a big boy had hit him on the head. He didn't mind being hit, he was used to it, but not from that boy. And he had cried because he had liked to think the boy was maybe like a brother if he'd had one.

Mrs. MacLeod was crying, too. Tears rolled down her cheeks. After a few seconds she put down her husband's hand. She opened her bag and took out a small book with a leather cover, and she began to read aloud in a low voice, while the tears kept rolling down her cheeks.

"The Lord is my Shepherd, I shall not want . . ."

The boy heard the words. It was something in the Bible. In the orphanage Sunday school he'd heard that. But it hadn't meant anything. It was just words. People said words and it didn't mean anything. Now suddenly he knew what it meant. It meant the old man needn't be afraid, even though he had to die.

"Yea, though I walk through the valley of the shadow of death, I will fear no evil."

You don't need to be afraid, that's what the old woman was saying to him. You have a family, she was saying, and we love you. She would always remember that piece of woods, she told him, and how they stood there, he and she, long ago, and he'd asked her to marry him, and she did, and they loved each other and that's how the family was made, he and she and then the children, and George's children—and Mary's, some day. . . .

The boy lay back on his pillow. His head was hurting him but it didn't hurt too bad. He didn't feel like crying any more.

"And I shall dwell in the house of the Lord forever," Mrs. Mac-Leod was saying.

She closed the book and sat for a long, long moment. Then she got up and leaned over her husband and kissed him on the lips.

"Goodbye, my love," she said, "until we meet again."

She went to the door. "I'll go home now, Doctor," she told the intern.

He came in. "It's all over. You've been very brave, Mrs. Mac-Leod."

"I haven't been brave," she said. "And it isn't over. The life we began together will go on and on—eternal life."

"Yes, indeed," the intern said without listening.

She went away then. But the boy knew what she meant. He

219

lay thinking, staring up at the ceiling. He had never before known what life was for or what it was about, but now he knew. It was simply to love someone so much that you wanted to live together and make a family. It didn't matter any more that he'd never had anyone to love him or to love. He could make his own family. *from here*

"Hey, young man!" The intern leaned over him. "How long have you been awake?"

"Not too long," the boy said, "maybe half an hour—"

He smiled a big smile but the intern was upset. "It's too bad, your seeing all this."

He pressed the bell and the nurse came in.

"Get a screen here, nurse!"

"Yes, doctor."

So they put up the screen and soon two men came with a stretcher and took the old man away and the boy said nothing. He knew just what was going on anyway. The family was together in the house that was their home and they'd be getting some breakfast, likely, and George would tell his mother not to mind for she still had them and the little kids. But all the same she'd never forget the old man—never, never. That was sure, because they loved each other and always would.

Peace came into the boy's heart. So now he knew why he had been born. And he wasn't going to die . . . only sleep. . . .

He woke late. The room was clean, the screen was gone. The other bed was empty and made up with fresh sheets. The sun was shining through the window. He was alone but for the first time in his life he was not lonely. He didn't have to live alone ever again. He could make a family, now that he saw how it was done. He'd get a job, find a girl, a nice girl. A girl could be nice. The old woman must have been a nice girl. He could see the old man, too, when he was young—a tall, skinny kid, standing there in the woods, asking the girl to marry him. And she'd said right away she would. He'd find a girl like that, someone who would be good to the kids, someone who would know how to cook and how to trim a Christmas tree. A tricycle! He'd wanted a tricycle something awful when he was a kid. It was the first thing he could remember about the orphanage—the tricycle he never got. You had to have parents for things like that. And kids—you could have kids of your own. Lucky old man, dying comfortable like that with all his kids there to see him off! You wouldn't mind dying when you'd had everything to live for—

The nurse came in, looking starched and clean. "How about some breakfast, young man?" she said in a bright voice.

He laughed and stretched himself.

"I feel *good*." he said. "Give me a real meal, will you? I'm plenty hungry!"

The Silver Butterfly

THE MAN BEGAN to speak.

"I tell you of my mother . . ."

I closed my eyes in the hot darkness of a summer's night in Hong Kong. There I had been sent upon a mission. It was to hear the true stories of men and women who slipped over the border of mainland China. This man had refused to enter my room unless it was dark. He did not want me to see his face, only to hear his voice, his words, as he went on.

The words ceased to be the spoken words of a man, the voice ceased to be the voice of a man. They were instruments, revealing to me in the harsh new light of today, a well-remembered scene. My imagination, living through the instruments, recreated the past. A village by the Yangtze River, and how often I had seen such villages, each a cluster of the brick-walled, tile-roofed houses of central China! On the street among poorer houses there was a gate opening into a walled compound. Inside the compound were the courtyards of the landowner, rich by village standards, possessing perhaps twenty acres of land, which was perhaps twenty times what the other men in the village owned, individually. This was his father and he was rich in more than land for he had a concubine, perhaps more than one, but at least one.

"She was my mother," the voice in the darkness said.

Ah, here was the story. She was his mother. In the old days the tie between mother and son was very close among the Chinese. Young soldiers, village boys snatched from the quiet dusty streets and forced into military service, would cry out for their mothers. *"Wo-tih Ma! Wo-tih Ma!"* Thus, when they were dying in the battles of revolution they cried aloud for their mothers. Once on the streets of Peking, when students had revolted against the local war lord and had been shot down by the soldiers, I had heard them cry for their mothers.

"I had a brother," the voice in the darkness was saying. "He died when he was five years old, before I was born. My mother always loved him better than she loved me. I know that because whenever she saw a little child about that age, a boy, she coaxed him to come to her and she fed him sweets. And I was the child of her old age. She was more than forty years old when I was born and it was her disgrace to be so old and still giving birth. She fought for me, nevertheless. She made my father treat me well, as well as he did the children of his wife. She would not let him forget that whatever she was, I was his son. I remember that she was good to me. I owe her a debt, so long as I live."

The voice was silent, a silence seeming very long, but perhaps not more than a full minute.

"Then the new people came in. My father was accused, as a landlord, and by his tenants. They could not have forgotten all that he had done for them, how he had forgiven them his share when the crop was poor, how he had helped them settle their disputes. But when the Party members took control of my village, their job was to teach the people to hate. If the tenants did not demand the execution of the landlords, they too would be punished. So, good and bad, the landlords had to die. The new order must be established, we were told. My father was hung up by his thumbs on the tall dragon tree in our main courtyard and then was flayed to death.

We, his family, were compelled to watch this. Then we were separated, my half brothers and their families dispersed. My wife and I and my mother were moved into a small mud-walled one-room house which had formerly belonged to our gateman. I was given work to do as a bookkeeper for the co-operative, since I have some education. They were called co-operatives at first before the communes came. I had also to work many hours digging in the riverbank for the foundation of the pillars upon which the great bridge was to be built. You remember the cities facing each other there at Wu Nan?"

"I remember," I said. "Even in those days there was the dream of a bridge connecting the cities. It remained a dream. The river there is wide and swift."

"It is wide and swift," the voice agreed. "And the soil of the banks is clay and in the dry season it is like rock. I had never done such work before. My wife worked with me. She also had never done such work before. We were so tired at night that we seldom even spoke. And all day long my old mother was alone in the house. She could not understand what had happened. After she saw my father die, she was never the same, you understand. Her brain was muddied, as one muddies a clear pool."

"I understand," I said. The words the voice used were *"hwen, t'ou hwen liao"*—memory vague, thought confused.

The voice went on, quiet, gentle, patient. "Our problem was food. We had not enough to eat. Since my mother could not work, she had no food ration. Therefore my wife and I were compelled to share our food with her. It was not enough. We were always hungry, and my mother could not understand why she was hungry. She would say to us, 'Can you not buy me a little piece of pork?' She had been accustomed to good food, pork or fish every day and as much rice as she wished. Now we did not see these dishes, and pork we had not more than once a month and then only a fragment. We gave it to her, but she was still hungry and she thought we were to blame. We could not make her understand that we had only what food was given us. 'Why do we not buy a small pig?'

224

she asked. 'We could feed it and then eat it ourselves when it is fat.' In the old days this was easy."

"I know," I said. "Every farmer had his own pig in those days, and chickens and perhaps a water buffalo or an ox."

"All these have been taken from us," the voice said. "We share, you understand, but this means we have nothing. Our wages are not given to us in full. Some is kept back, on deposit we are told, but we do not know where. Even the peasants, our former tenants, who were expecting so much after the landlords were killed, have nothing. The commune took away what little they had and gave nothing in return."

The voice broke off abruptly to cough. "You understand I am not complaining."

"I understand," I said.

The voice went on. "Of what use is it to complain? We can only bend as the reed bends when the wind is strong. We can only wait for the wind to die so that we may stand straight again."

"The wind will die," I said. "Go on and tell your story. I do not want you to be caught here."

"The time came," the voice said, "when even the house was taken from us."

The long pause came again, and when the voice spoke it was in a lower and more mournful tone. "Let me be honest. If the house had not been taken from us, I do not know what we would have done. I had to be very careful. I was suspected because I was the son of a landowner. The sons of peasants and tenant farmers are trained in Communism and put in charge. Communism is all they know. They have no other learning. For this I do not blame them. They, too, are helpless. But had I made one misstep, I would have been killed, and my wife and mother with me. I had to think, night and day, of such a misstep. And my old mother, understanding nothing, put me in danger again and again. When we were away and some young official came by to spy on us, she received him as a guest, as she would have done in the old days, and she used our few ounces of tea leaves to make tea for him, or she

225

added water to the rice my wife had set aside for our one meal of the day, and made a bowl of gruel for the guest. I was then suspected of hoarding. We were desperate, my wife and I. It is possible that had this gone on, we might have forgotten ourselves and put my mother to death, not from cruelty but to save us all. We might have done it. It has been done by others."

"I can quite understand how it might happen," I said, "though in the old days it would have been impossible. The son would have been considered a monster and he would have been stoned to death by the villagers."

"Were there such days?" the voice inquired. "I have forgotten them. We have all forgotten them. Now we have the commune. They let us stay on in the small house until the new commune building was put up, but they took away our cooking utensils. We were compelled to eat in the central mess hall, and my wife was made one of the six cooks in the communal kitchens. My work is heavier than before—in the office in the mornings and digging in the afternoon. At night we must attend commune meetings until eleven o'clock. But I speak only of food. We have meal tickets, my wife and I, and my mother was not given a meal ticket, because she was not able to work. I went to the commander, a young man of twenty-one, the son of our village barber. He had joined the Party now and our lives were in his hands. All the commanders are young and of peasant families. They are overzealous in trying to please their new superiors, whom they fear. We all fear someone.

" 'Your mother must work,' the commander said in a big voice.

"I told him that her brain was muddied. He said that even such a person could be of use. She could work in the nursery where the children are kept. So I took my old mother there, and for this reason I was able to get her a meal ticket. We were better off than before, so far as food goes, for my wife being one of the cooks, she could snatch a mouthful here and there, as all the cooks do. She can even wrap a bit of rice for me in a lotus leaf and hide it in her pocket.

"Things might have been well enough for such times as ours if

226

it had not happened that the nursery was in our own old great house, where my mother had lived her woman's life. She was too muddy in her mind to know this and yet by half-forgotten instinct she remembered her way around this house. True, it looks very different now. The trees have been cut down, and the gardens are ruined. It has been used for many purposes, at first a headquarters for the Party and after that for a basket factory, and after that barracks for soldiers. Now that it is a nursery it would be hard to remember that once it was comfortable and even beautiful in its own country way. You have seen such houses."

"Many times," I said. "They are very beautiful, as you say, in their own way. They belong to the earth upon which they stand, and they have been shaped by generations of the same family."

The voice trembled slightly. "So it was with our house. My mother, I said, did not remember and yet she had not forgotten. Her poor brain made her believe that she was now reduced to being the lowest slave in this house full of children whom she supposed somehow to be the many children of our family. She followed the directress from room to room, telling her that once she had been mistress in this great house and that now she should not be a servant. She should be respected and allowed to sit in a chair by the door, in the sunshine, and others should bring her tea.

"The directress is a young woman, herself the daughter of a peasant, and she was impatient, as well as terrified, not only because my mother had been of the landlord class but also because she feared the retribution she would suffer if the old woman did not do her work well. She was angry because such a stupid old woman as my mother was assigned to help her. Still, I cannot say she was cruel—only impatient and afraid. All young men and women are that way now. They are forced to go very fast. But everything that is done is at a cost to the people."

The long pause fell again.

"My friend," I said. "It is very late."

The voice began immediately.

"Still, we might have got along, except that one day a little boy

227

of five years, or thereabouts, was brought into the nursery, crying. He was frail and sickly and the moment my mother saw him, she thought of her son who had died young. She began to love this child, and this was her great crime. She could not hide her love and this was her great danger. Love is forbidden us. We are taught that love is a bourgeois weakness and destroys the whole purpose of the nurseries. Children must grow up thinking only of the group, not of any individual, not even of themselves. By the time children have been in the nursery for about four years they have learned what is called collective living. They learn this easily, but still sometimes the little ones cry at night for their mothers. This is a problem not yet solved. If an older child cries he can be punished. As it is, the only solution so far is work. The three-year-old children pull weeds and the older ones carry stones. They learn chants which teach them how to think. If one disobeys, they must do extra work.

"The boy whom my mother loved was of course among the disobedient. He had never worked, and he could not keep from crying. My mother tried to help him carry stones, but this was forbidden, and she was threatened with being sent away. This frightened her for by now she loved the child very much. She stayed away from him in the daytime, but at night she crept to him in the darkness and took him in her arms. She carried him to a corner in the fuel shed and there she held him until he slept. It was of course a great unkindness to him, for though she comforted him and made him happy she weakened him. He tried even less than before to do his work, and she, my mother, fell into a dream of confusion. She imagined herself a concubine again, with her little son, and that all the great household hated them, so that she had no friends—not one.

"One day when she was sweeping the floor of the fuel house, which was part of her work, her cloudy brain cleared for a moment and she remembered that when she was a concubine she had been given some jewels, and once during a riot she had hastily hidden them in a moment of fear in this very shed behind a brick in the wall and had forgotten them. As though she walked in her sleep she now went to that place and found the jewels as she had left them, but covered with dust. There were three pieces. I do not know what the two were. They were of no value or I would have heard what they were. The third piece was valuable. It was a butterfly of filigree silver set with small good pearls. The workmanship was very fine. I saw it myself when she was put on trial. She took that piece and hid it in her bosom. All this was told at the trial.

"The next day it happened that the boy cut his hand. It was a bad cut. I saw that, too, at the trial. It was slashed in the palm. He had been given a sharp tool to dig weeds. We had had no rain for many weeks and the earth was like iron. The tool slipped as he pressed upon the handle. He was taken to the infirmary, of course, and raw disinfectant poured into the wound. There are many sick children, there are always many, and the attendants are harassed and busy and no one had time to comfort him. My old mother crept to him and led him away and no one paid any heed among so many children. She led him to the fuel shed and there, behind the bundles of reeds, she showed him the silver butterfly to comfort him. 'See how pretty,' she whispered. 'This is your butterfly. I will keep it for you, so that no one can take it from you, but it is yours. We will look at it every night. Here, take it in your hand.'

"The child had never seen a beautiful thing. He stopped crying and held the butterfly. He looked at it and smiled. This my mother told quite plainly at the trial. We were surprised that she remembered so well. Every night they looked at the butterfly. She told him of course not to speak to anyone, but he was a child, and how could he help telling another child? The butterfly was discovered. As a matter of fact, the child persuaded my mother to let him keep it, just for a day, and having it in his possession he showed it secretly to another boy, who told the directress. Those who reported such deviations were rewarded with a bit of sugar. The authorities were called. The little boy was compelled to tell the truth. For truth he was beaten severely. The sin was that he should want something that the others did not have and could not have. He had become a deviationist. He was then not quite six years old.

"The authorities now fell upon my mother. They demanded the truth from her and she gave it quite simply. No one believed her. Five years ago she would have been killed for such deviation. Now she was only sentenced to be denounced at the next meeting of our commune. To be denounced is nevertheless very hard to bear."

The voice broke off. There was the sound of a stifled sob. I waited. What was there to say? The voice went on again.

"On the day of the meeting I hid myself in the crowd. There I waited. I knew what was to happen. I had seen it often before. But this was my old mother. She was led out of the inner room and she stood before us. Her hands were tied behind her. The young commander shouted her crime in a loud voice. And we who stood about her were required to shout at her, too, to accuse her, to shake our fists at her and denounce her. This must go on until finally we must demand her life. And I—I—had to shout the loudest of all. They were all watching me to see whether there was any sign of love in my voice for my mother. I had to shout more loudly than any of them. She kept smiling, all the time. I think she could not understand any of it. She turned her head this way and that, smiling, not understanding. She did not see me. I stayed as far from her as I could.

"The worst was when she was compelled, as all are when denounced, to walk down from the dais and through the crowd. And the crowd must strike and slap her cheeks and kick her. My mother walked through the crowd, her hands tied behind her back, and they slapped her cheeks and struck her shoulders. She fell down, for she was very thin, and in her youth her feet had been bound and she could not walk well even when she was strong. Now she had no strength. When she fell, it was time to kick her. Everybody was watching me and I was afraid. I stepped forward to do what I had to do. In that moment she looked up and saw me. She recognized me. When I saw that she knew me, I tried to look angry.

230

She was bewildered for a moment, and then she smiled. She understood . . ."

The voice wavered and fell.

"Is that the end?" I asked.

"No," the voice said, "but there is an end. It seems that when she was released, she went back to the child. It was evening. He was lying on his cot alone. The others were eating their night meal in the mess hall. The boy too had been beaten, he too had been denounced by his own age group. They are taught so. She took him in her arms and held him. She coaxed him to come with her to the shed. You may wonder how I know this. It is from my wife. She had stayed in the kitchens during the meeting to cook the evening meal, she said, a pretense, but it served. While the people of the commune ate their supper she stole away to the nursery. She saw my mother come in and put her arms about the child. My mother talked to the child softly. She said something like this.

" 'You see, my child, I am now a burden to my son. He is obliged to strike me. I cannot help him by living. I see this. . . . So come with me, my child, my little one. Let us go to a better place.'

"The child's lips were swollen and purple, but he spoke quite clearly. 'Where is the silver butterfly?' he asked.

" 'Come with me,' my mother said. 'We will go to the river. There are many butterflies there. They gather at the water to drink, live butterflies, real ones.'

"My wife watched my mother lead the child away. She followed them through the twilight, down to the river's edge. My mother took the little boy in her arms and he clung to her neck and put his head on her shoulder. She walked with him out into the quiet water. There was no wind that evening and no waves. From behind a clump of willows my wife watched. My mother walked into the water until it covered her head and the child's head and she did not step back. That was the end."

"And your wife?" I asked. "She did nothing?"

The voice replied. "My wife is a kind woman. She did nothing."

The silence was long now. Who could speak?

Yet even silence must come to an end, else it cannot be borne. "What of the bridge?" I asked.

The voice spoke again and to my surprise, it was a different voice, though surely the same man. The voice was suddenly calm.

"The bridge is finished. It is strong and very wide, like your American bridges. It has four lanes, two from north to south, two from south to north, so that vehicles and people travel both ways at once."

"Some of our bridges have six lanes," I said.

The voice was quick to reply. "I hear that two new lanes will be added also to our bridge."

"Remarkable," I said, "especially when it spans such a river. We have no river so swift or wide. You must be very proud of the bridge."

The answer came bravely.

"Oh yes. We are proud—of the bridge that is. But—"

The voice broke off. Silence mounted between us again, this time a barrier not to be broken. For he was gone—to hide in some secret refugee room in the city, or to return to that from which he had escaped?

Who knows?

Francesca

MAXWELL COOMBS WAS SITTING in the library of his comfortable house waiting for his wife, Francesca. It was a small room, pleasantly designed with a large window looking down a lawn that sloped into a brook. Shrubs skillfully placed hid the fact that there were neighbors on three sides. Neither he nor Francesca could have lived happily without neighbors, but they did not want to see them whenever they looked out of the window.

That is, he supposed that Francesca felt as he did. He could not be sure from one day to the next. She had been fairly constant in character for the last two years, during which time she had been the star of the Broadway hit, *All-Time High*. He had during these years become used to living with a woman whom he knew to be his legal wife, Francesca Coombs, née O'Malley, but who was not at all the Francesca he had married. Nor for that matter had he married the Francesca with whom he had fallen in love.

The Francesca whom he had first seen was the ingenue in *The Golden Bell*. He had noticed her because she was the only endurable item in a wholly vile play. He had mentioned her casually in his notice, written shortly after midnight, and then had gone on to say in his own solid and devastating fashion how bad the play was. After he had written the notice he had turned it in and gone to bed to sleep, he had supposed, until his usual noon breakfast.

Instead he had been waked before ten o'clock by a clear loud voice, shouting his name from the downstairs hall. The murmur of his housekeeper explaining that he was invisible was as effectual as a whistle against the wind.

"He can just get up," the young voice declared. "He ought not to be able to sleep anyway—not with that conscience of his!"

He had lain in his bed for a moment, groaning as he always did when he was waked, and then he had got out of bed, had staggered into a bathrobe and flinging open the door he had bounced to the stairwell.

"Mrs. Bailey, who is that person?" he demanded.

The young woman had answered for herself. "I am Francesca O'Malley, and I am not a person!" she had called up the stairs.

He looked over the bannister upon a face as fresh as a primrose, and he grunted, "Well, what do *you* want?"

"You reviewed the play!" she accused.

"Of course I did," he declared.

"Men like you ought to be shot!" she flung up the stairs at him.

"People who put on such plays ought to be chloroformed," he retorted. Then it permeated his sleep-dimmed mind who she was. "Here, you," he cried.

"What are you kicking for? I didn't pan you. In fact, I said—"

"How dare you not pan me?" she cried passionately. "Do you know what you've done? You've made them all hate me—and they were my best friends before—"

"If you have such best friends," he began, but she would not let him finish.

"If you had only panned me, too!" she wailed. "Then the play could have closed decently with everybody still fond of everybody. If you only know how we've worked. And now we have to watch the author for fear he'll take a dose of sleeping pills. It's his first play."

"I have also to make my living," he said a trifle grimly. "And I prefer to tell the truth—if I can. You were good, see? The rest of it was rotten."

She swallowed hard and sat down on the bottom step. He watched her while she opened her handbag and refreshed her already blooming face. Mrs. Bailey stood by dubiously silent.

"Mrs. Bailey!" he called.

"Yes, sir?" Mrs. Bailey had a stiff neck and found it difficult to look up at him.

"Set the table for two." he ordered.

"Not for me, thanks," Francesca O'Malley said with chill in her big voice. She rose promptly to her feet.

"For you and me," he said. "Please! Let me explain."

She wavered. "If I weren't so hungry," she said uncertainly. "I suppose you know you've taken the bread out of my mouth? Why, I've been counting on that play for six months." She opened her bag and found her handkerchief and blew her nose.

"Let me give you a good breakfast," he pleaded. "Mrs. Bailey is wonderful with bacon and eggs— Wait, have you any more of those tiny sausages, Mrs. Bailey?"

"Yes, I have, sir, but I was keepin' them," Mrs. Bailey said somewhat unpleasantly.

"I'd fancy them myself today," he declared. "Now please, Miss O'Malley, just sit down and make yourself happy. I'll be down—"

The end of it had been the most delightful breakfast he had ever eaten. He had entirely agreed with Francesca's accusation that play critics were worms and had promised to find her a good play and had wondered if there were ever such glorious eyes in a human face as her big brown ones—or, for that matter, a face to match the eyes and the hair of browned gold. She was a trifle too tall—for the stage, that is. Luckily he was tall, too.

He had kept all his promises. He had found *Quest for a Heart*. By the time it opened and he had been able to praise it proudly in his column, they were engaged. They were to be married on Christmas Day. Francesca had set the day so that she would never forget the anniversary, she said, no matter what she was playing. The remark had meant little to him at the time but it had gained significance during the four years they had now been married. She had been playing the part of Clemence for three months by the time Christmas came and he felt vaguely that he was not marrying Francesca at all, but a shy reserved young woman from Maine, very honest and direct and somewhat humorless, whose name was Clemence Partridge.

He had even complained about this. "Hey, Fran," he had exclaimed somewhere in their brief three-day honeymoon, "lay off the act, will you? Be yourself, honey." She had opened wide grave dark eyes at him, from whence the light of youth seemed to have fled.

"But this *is* me, Max," she had insisted.

He could not explain what he meant and after some further effort he gave up and resigned himself to finishing his honeymoon with Clemence. Since then she had played *Madame Chenery* and when that failed, as he had told her it must, she went straight into *All-Time High* where she was now the triumphant star. He had been embarrassed by Madame Chenery. The play had developed something in Francesca that was the exact opposite of Clemence and he was not prepared for it. He was not sure it was permanent, but certainly it had had its piquant moments. If she had only kept the something for him, he might have found it altogether exciting, but she applied it to her most casual contact with other men, and he always felt like apologizing to them—or else knocking them down. He had tried to quarrel with Francesca while she was Madame Chenery, but she had smiled at him mysteriously from under her half-drooped lids. "But this *is* me, Max," she had insisted.

One night he had even suggested that it was time they had a baby. At this she had yawned and patted her pretty mouth. "I doubt I shall ever want a child," she said frankly. He had been horrified and amazed at this. Children had always been in his scheme of things, and he reminded her that when she had played Clemence she had actually clamored for a child, saying that she would never be fulfilled without it and so forth.

She shrugged the memory away. "That was then and this is now," she said.

Thank God Madam Chenery had not lasted long. He rather liked the present Linda, in *All-Time High,* a brisk competent fashionable young modern. At least he was used to her.

He heard the front doors open and close and her sharp quick footsteps ran upstairs. He had left the library door open, thinking she would come in and find him and impress upon his lips the swift warm kiss that he had come to accept as Linda's. It was a change from the sultry clinging variety that he had nevertheless enjoyed from Madame Chenery. That she had not stopped, that she had sped upstairs to her own room, meant that she was not thinking of him at all. Had he not been the understanding husband that he compelled himself to be, he would often have been hurt over such forgetfulness. He had been so foolish once as to complain of it and she had turned on him. "But if I don't think of you, what will you do—beat me?" So she had demanded.

"Darling, no," he had replied. "But somehow I expect you to remember that I'm around."

"Most of the time I do, don't I?" she had asked.

"Most of the time you are charming," he had agreed.

"Well, then remember those times," she had said with Linda-like bluntness. Then because she really loved him she said, "You ought to hate me—but you may as well know—there will be lots of time between now and our deaths when I don't think of you." The dimples came out at both corners of her mouth. "Goodness, maybe even when I'm old and dying I'll be thinking about how to die perfectly!"

He saw a dream dawning in her eyes as she spoke and he broke it. "Please, Francesca, don't anticipate *that* curtain!" She had laughed and there had followed one of their most satisfying intervals.

The silence in the house became absolute. He sighed, rose slowly and dragging his feet a little, he went upstairs. There he tried the door of Francesca's room. They had never shared a room because she had said she did not feel that an actress and a critic should be compelled to sleep together. She was sure, she told him, that there would be times when he wanted to be quite free to say what he thought of her performance and at those times she wanted to be quite free to hate him, without having to face the fact that he was her husband.

The door was locked. He sighed again, and then put his ear to the panel. He heard her voice murmuring but was not able to catch the words. Then her voice rose and he could hear her clearly,

"Am I not a woman? Do I not bleed if I am pricked? Weep if I am scorned?"

"Oh Lord!" he muttered.

Her voice subsided again, and after a moment he tapped at the door. "Darling?" he called cheerfully.

The silence held and then she answered. "Yes, Max?"

"May I come in?"

She replied to this by flinging the door wide. "Max, I've found the most wonderful part!"

He stood on the threshold staring at her. She had stripped the lace scarf from the bureau and had wrapped it about her head. From its creamy folds her dark eyes looked out tragic and fathomless.

"But Linda—" he stammered.

"Oh, she's boring me," Francesca declared. "Those smart young women are really so shallow, Max."

"But the box office—" he said in consternation.

"Oh, the play can go on," she answered. "Verna is crazy to get me out." Verna Leigh was her understudy.

He came in and sat down on her pink taffeta chair, and she flew to remove him. "Not there," she exclaimed. "It's ripping and I'm saving it to show the decorator. Think of it—why, it was only when I began to play Linda—I used my first week's pay to do my room over—remember?" She steered him into a carved English-oak seat.

"I should think it would help if I ripped a little more," he remonstrated.

"No, because she'll ask me, and I do like to be honest," she said fervently.

A somewhat stunned look came over his face. "Do you, darling?" he said.

Seeing the look she cried indigantly, "You know I do, Max Coombs! Why, I always act exactly as I feel."

"I'm sure you do," he agreed. "Where's the play?"

She took a bundle of typed sheets from the bed and handed it to him with both hands. He looked at the name on the first page and grunted.

"That old dope!" he muttered.

"He isn't old," she retorted. "He's scarcely forty-five, not fifty, anyway."

"A dope," he repeated firmly. "That last thing of his was treacle."

"This is divine," she maintained.

He ran his experienced eyes through the sheets. By the third page he had found her. This was his future wife! He chased her speeches down and loathed her increasingly—a dramatic, soul-laden, self-pitying female, crabbing against the universe because she wasn't born a male—that was what it amounted to—following the fad of the moment to put women under a microscope and find out what was wrong with them. As if what was wrong could be diagnosed from women alone! He resisted the impulse to hurl the sheets across the room. Instead he said in his coldest critic tones, "I hate to contemplate what I shall have to say about this play."

He saw the handsome red fly into her cheeks and then she paled. "Maxwell Coombs, do you know what people are saying about us?" she demanded.

"Don't know and don't care," he replied.

"They're saying that you are so jealous of my success that you can't give a good notice to any play I'm in!"

He forced a mild laugh, but she did not smile.

"Do you know what is going to happen?" she demanded again.

"I never know what is going to happen," he replied somewhat feebly. She was walking about the room in approved Linda fashion.

"Producers will soon be afraid to have me star their plays," she said fiercely.

"Honey, you make me proud but I know I'm not that important," he replied, in a pretentiously humble voice.

Suddenly the Linda wilted out of her. "Damn you, you are!" she wailed. She crumpled at his feet and folded her hands on his knees and placed her adorable chin on her hands and looked at him out of Francesca's own eyes. "Please, Max—please don't hate the play! Anyway, give it a chance!"

Looking into those eyes he found himself snatching at an idea fluttering in his brain like a bird that had come down the chimney.

"Look here," he said slowly, putting salt on its tail.

"What?" she asked docilely.

He felt obliged to kiss her and then after that to kiss her again and again, and then to comment upon the peculiar radiance of her hair in the afternoon sunlight, all the time mindful of the bird.

She took part wholeheartedly and entirely to his satisfaction in this interlude and then she said, "Weren't you about to tell me something?"

"Haven't I been telling you that I love you?" he demanded.

"Oh that," she said, dimpling. "But I mean—"

"You mean something practical," he said accusingly. "Actually, my love is the most practical—the most real, the most—"

But he stopped, having learned that when a moment had ended, it was over, and he could only look forward to another. At least she was still comfortably on his lap, her arm around his neck. He returned to the bird with the salt on its tail, and examined it.

"I have an idea of my own," he announced.

She kissed him. "Produce it," she demanded.

"That is just the idea," he said. "I am going to write a play, my dear, for you, and we will produce it together, you and I, and what a play that will be!"

She was so silent that he looked at her face on his shoulder. "Hey," he demanded, "what's going on under your thatch?"

She sat and smoothed the thatch with expert fingers. "But can you write a play?"

"I've been telling people how to write them for an increasing number of years," he reminded her.

"Ah," she said, with a world of doubt.

He pushed her off his knees. "Look here, just for that, young woman, I am going to write a play for you and around you, and sew you up for the rest of your life in such a success that you'll never want to play anything else."

"Promise?"

"Promise!"

"Meanwhile?" she asked.

"Oh, I'm used to old Linda," he said disrespectfully. But he was already planning how he would bury her.

. . . The play was inspired—there was no use in pretending it wasn't. He had begged, borrowed and stolen time from his job, he had got Benny Wales to write his notices, and daily he gnashed his teeth over the softness of Benny's hand. All sorts of trash was creeping into Broadway because he was not there to cleanse it. But he let it creep, and learned to avoid his own column and then not to read the papers and at last not to do anything except put some food into his mouth when he felt himself beginning to break in the middle and to drop on his bed when his brain refused to work any longer.

It was the hardest work he had ever done until he knew what he wanted. Then it was the easiest. What he wanted was to discover the Francesca he most loved, develop her into the woman he had dreamed of for his wife, and then hold her there. Talk about Pygmalion! He was Pygmalion and she was the marble, waiting to be carved, and his tools were edged and shining words.

He spent solid weeks dreaming her up, and it was to the living Francesca's credit that she did not ask him when he was going to begin to write or, when he did begin, how he was getting on. She went about her business, a curiously docile Linda, waiting for her change of self.

And when he had dreamed her up, when he saw her plain, his love, his wife, he asked her one day, "Mind if I called my woman Francesca?"

"Not if it helps," she said.

"It does help," he said. "I'm so crazy about her that I keep calling her Francesca, anyway."

She smiled sweetly at this, and he went to put the smile into the play. He left out a great deal, of course, but he put a lot in. He put in Clemence and Madame Chenery and Linda, and he put in himself, a big stubborn unchanging fellow, who was looking for his wife. And he found her in an undiscovered Francesca, a girl that had looked at him sometimes out of Francesca's eyes, had spoken, rarely in Francesca's voice, but whom he had never been able to hold and to keep. In the play he did hold her and he did keep her, and she bore him a child.

When the play was written, he took it to Francesca.

"Shall we read it together?" she asked.

He shook his head. "I couldn't," he confessed. "I couldn't bear it if you don't like her—it."

She said gravely, "I couldn't pretend."

"I know," he said.

She read it alone that evening while he gnawed his thumb in the library, and kept himself half drunk with rage by reading over his column in the old newspaper under the direction of Benny. Tomorrow he'd go back to his own healthy blistering of trash on the stage. He was stayed for a moment by thinking again of his own play. Did all of the writing fellows care as much as he did? He was bemused for that moment by the compunction of a man who had stepped on much small life in his path. Then he hardened again. No, if his play was no good, by the strictest standards of his own and Francesca's, too, he would never let it see the light of Broadway. He'd be sure as everybody ought to be sure that the play was worth the life of those who brought it into being. But it would break his heart—because he had fallen in love with his Francesca and he wanted her to live forever. He threw the papers on the floor and sat out the rest of the evening.

It was midnight when she opened the door and he knew at once. Linda was gone. In her place was this tender woman—a woman, not a girl. He was sick of girls—party girls, he called them. He had made his own Francesca a round-limbed grown woman, female without being oversexed, feeling and unpretending, sensible and sensitive, warm-tempered and generous, child-loving but loving not only her own children.

She came into the room and stood with the play clasped to her breast. He went up to her and took the sheets away and dropped them on the chair. "Why, Francesca, you've been crying," he said softly.

She nodded and the tears welled to her lashes again. "I couldn't help it," she said humbly, "It's because you've made me—exactly as I want to be. Oh Max, it's a great play! Thank you, Max—I want to play it—forever."

He took her in his arms, and held her in close silence. Forever? So she had spoken the eternal word! Then he knew better. There was no such word—not really. Forever is a dream word. It might mean a very long time, but it was not forever. Holding her tight in his arms, triumphant that he had won her, he began to plot how he could keep her.

. . . The play went into rehearsal. She slipped out of Linda gratefully, as from a garment grown too small. "I'm glad to get rid of that woman," she declared.

But she did not wait for an instant before she took on his Francesca. She lived with his play, talked about it, slept with it under her pillow so that, she said, it could creep into her brain. Her enthusiasm infected the news and the gossip, and the enthusiasm of

243

other people increased her own, until he began to be half afraid of what he had done.

"Suppose the play isn't so good?" he said to her uneasily one night. "After all, you and I—we aren't exactly impartial."

They were going to bed late, too late, after fourteen hours of steady rehearsal that day.

She flew at him. "That's just like a critic," she declared. "Beginning to pick on a play before it even—Why, I suppose you'll pick it to pieces in your own column!"

"Benny will take the column for me that day," he said, "and Benny is soft enough to be trusted. Honey, it's for your own good— I can't see you destroyed."

She burst into tears, and he tried to comfort her. But she refused his comfort. "It is too late," she insisted. "I am already committed. I've made myself into your Francesca—clear through—"

She suddenly stopped crying and looked at him with something new in her beautiful eyes.

"What is it?" he asked half frightened.

"Yes!" she repeated. "I am your wife. Max darling . . ." Her voice fell to a whisper.

"Yes, dear?"

"I want to have your—child."

. . . He was frightened. He told himself that he had committed the worst of all follies to allow her to begin having the child he wanted so much at the very time when she was opening in the heaviest part she had ever played. But there had been no refusing her. Her healthy body responded, and there was something almost religious in the ceremony she made of going to the doctor and confirming the child's life on the day that the play opened. She was wholly confident after that. The curtain went up on the most flawless, the most profound performance, Benny said, going mad the next day in the column, that the stage had seen, at least in his generation.

Max, sitting in the shadowy corner of a crowded box, had given instructions that he was not to be spoken to during the performance. With each succeeding scene he was more terrified. What had he done? He had made Francesca to the measure of his dreams, but she had lifted his dreams beyond the measure of himself. Laughter roared from beneath and he laughed, and then out of silence, sobbing, and the tears stung his eyes. He spoke to his unborn child. "Look here," he muttered to that small shaping spirit, "you've got to help me!"

. . . But when his son was born the next summer, he had strong doubts that anything so minute could be of much use. True, growth could be expected, but it would obviously be years before the little blob could express himself with anything like clarity and conviction. He looked at Maxwell Coombs, Junior, with reproach.

"I didn't know they came that small," he objected.

Francesca opened her tired eyes at this. "He is not small," she retorted. "He weighs eight and a half pounds. Give him to me!"

When the nurse had obeyed, she held the baby in the crook of her left arm and with the finger of her right hand she pointed at Max.

"See that?" she asked the sleeping infant. "That's a critic—Don't you ever pay any attention to him! Criticizing you, the first thing!"

The play was taking a vacation. Nobody could bear the thought of a substitute for Francesca. When she opened again after six weeks she was more beautiful than ever and the critics said that they felt obliged to mention the fact that if possible the whole performance was better than it had been. Max himself that day tore to pieces a slight thing called *The Lady and the Orchid,* and it sank through the floor the same night.

At home the baby thrived under the ministrations of his mother. A nurse was hired in order that Francesca could get her morning's sleep, for Max Junior was an early riser by nature and habit. But the rest of the day, until he was tucked into his crib at night before she went to the theater, he was served by his adoring mother. This devotion might have amazed even Max, had he not detected in it a carry-over from Francesca in the play. But this discovery he hid from everyone, and even resproached himself for, as an evidence of his unpleasant critical mind. He set himself to enjoy his life as he never had before even in his enjoyable existence, and certainly Francesca was more beautiful and more completely lovable than she had ever been. He almost believed that she was his Francesca. Perhaps he had done the inconceivable thing—perhaps he had unlocked her real self.

But he could never be entirely sure. The play went on in fabulous triumph, and they all went with it. In the rich atmosphere of their joy and content, the baby grew with the same fabulous quality, began to creep, to walk, to talk. He adored his mother and made no bones that he preferred her to his father, and Francesca returned his love completely. Max resolutely held his place in the triangle, but he admitted that his son was an unrelenting competitor.

Sometimes, waking in the night, he told himself that it was all too happy to last. The day would come, the hour would arrive, the very minute be there, when she—Then he made himself go to sleep.

But it came, on a morning in March, when the play was nearly three years old and the baby nearly two. Francesca yawned when she woke up and he heard something new in the yawn. He was shaving himself and trying to be as quiet as possible because he had sneaked the door open into her room so that he could watch her in the mirror as she slept. Now he saw her sit up in bed, push back her hair restlessly, put one foot out of bed and then the other. "Hello," he called tentatively. "Feel all right?"

She yawned again. "Yes—I think so—"

He put down his razor, wiped the soap off his chin and came in. "I shouldn't have waked you."

"You didn't exactly," she said indifferently. "I was awake—nearly. I was thinking."

A cold chill danced on his spine. "Thinking?" he repeated.

She sat on the bed, like an angel on a cloud, in her filmy nightgown, with her hair around her shoulders. "Max, you know . . ." She paused. "You won't be hurt?"

He shook his head. "Even if I am, I want to know."

"I'd hate to hurt you—"

"Don't be silly. I'm made of plastic."

She laughed and tossed her hair back. "Max, I'm getting a little tired of the play—Oh, not the play, but doing the same thing over and over."

Well, here it was. He took it at one swallow. "I don't blame you," he said politely. "It's been going on a long time. Do you have a new play in mind?"

She looked at him from under her lashes. "Why don't you write one?" she suggested.

"What would you like?" he countered.

She reflected. "Oh—something entirely new—maybe a newspaper-woman or something of an executive. Lots of charm, of course."

He was revolted at the idea of such a woman. "I don't think I can write another play," he said.

"Don't be silly," she said sweetly. "Of course you can. Why, lots of the notices said you were a born playwright."

But he shook his head with decision at that. "It's because the critics are my rivals," he declared. "No, my Francesca, I can't. I wrote myself out on you. From now on I shall merely destroy other plays."

He remained unyielding when in some anger she declared she would go to Hollywood.

"We can go along, Maxie and I," he said philosophically.

But that was not the end. When it was announced that Eunice Frame was to take the part of Francesca, plays swarmed about her at once and she chose rather quickly *Lady Susan,* which was already a hit in London.

Max read the play and was compelled to admit against his will that it was good, and while he thought Lady Susan a snob she had her points. Privately he supposed that he could endure her for a season or so, and he settled himself for the change.

Rehearsals however did not proceed smoothly. "I played Francesca too long," his Lady Susan complained. "I can't seem to get into the part."

She was difficult for some days and inclined to be irritable. Maxie cried a good deal, and Max spent more time with him, and tried to soothe him by explaining to him what the life of an actress is.

He was not sure that he made himself intelligible to his son, however. After all, Maxie's vocabulary was less than a hundred words as yet, and did not include the word temperament although of the quality he had his full and healthy share.

"Look here," Max said one night to Lady Susan, after some weeks. "I think the boy's coming down with something."

He was in the library and she had just come back from the dress rehearsal. She paused on her way upstairs. "Oh dear, I hope not—just when I think I've really swung into the part at last!"

"That's good," he said. "Let's have a look at him together."

They went upstairs, and he saw that she had really got into Lady Susan. Her voice was changed, her words more clipped, she held her head high like a restless mare, she hunched her shoulder slightly in her excellent tweed suit. He sighed and opened the door. The nurse was gone, but the night light burned. He turned it up a little and they bent over the child's bed. Maxie opened his eyes and stared at them.

"Hello, old fellow," Max said comfortably.

He gave his father a half smile and then he stared at his mother. His eyes widened, his mouth quivered.

"Why, Maxie, old chap," she said, "what's wrong, eh?"

It was Lady Susan speaking. Maxie gave her one look of burning hatred and burst into screams. Max caught the little boy in his arms and lifted him out of his bed and held him against his shoulder.

"There, there," he murmured.

"Why, he's afraid of me!" she gasped.

"No," Max said, "only afraid of Lady Susan." He held the sobbing little boy close.

"But—but how silly," she said weakly. She sat down on the bed.

"Not silly," Max said steadily. "It's a bit tough on both of us—getting used to not having Francesca."

She sat looking at them after that, a strange expression on her face. "Don't bother about us," he said half lightly. "He'll get used to it, too, when he's older."

"Meanwhile?" The word broke from her.

"I'm always the same," Max said simply.

"You're blaming me," she cried.

"No, my darling," he said.

The little boy was quiet now, curled in his arms, his face turned away from her.

Max took pity on her. "You see, darling, little children have to be sure of what we are."

"But I am the same—to him," she insisted.

"He has to know that," Max explained patiently. "He has to see you the same and hear you the same—and that, of course, you aren't."

There was a long silence after this. He rose and put the child back in his bed and turned down the light and they went out. When they were in the hall she said abruptly, "Leave me for a bit, will you?"

"I'll be in the library," he replied.

He sat there not reading, wondering and waiting, and in a little while—no, it was a long while, a full half hour—the door opened. Francesca stood there in her old blue chiffon robe, her hair down, ready for sleep.

She came and curled into his arms, where lately the child had lain. "I took a good hot bath," she said drowsily. There was nothing clipped in her words. "I didn't know how tired I was."

"Don't think I want you to be anything except what you want to be," he said in alarm. "It wouldn't work out if you pretended for me or for Maxie either. We'd know. Besides you'd be no good at it."

What had gone on in that half hour she had been alone with herself? Would she ever tell him?

"I'm not pretending, silly," she replied amiably. "It's just that I'm not going to be women that my own baby cries at. I'm going to be—myself. When the curtain goes down, it goes down on the rest of them and I'm coming home—always me."

"But this," he said, lifting up the wide filmy sleeve, "this belongs to Francesca."

She laughed. "Oh, you old smarty," she cried. "You made Francesca just like me." That was all she would tell him.

Nevertheless he was astounded at her cleverness. He was searching for a suitable word of admiration when she put her fingers on his lips.

"Listen!" she cried softly.

It was the baby, crying again. He prepared to get up, but she pushed him down. "No, let me!"

Through the open door he saw her flying up the stairs in a soft blue cloud, and the next minute the crying had stopped. There was murmuring, then he saw her coming downstairs, and then she was at the door. She stood there clasping the child and his arms were tight about her neck.

"He's not afraid any more," she said softly.

Max sat gazing at them with all his heart in his eyes. "Now I see why the old fellows kept painting mothers and babies," he said.

He admired them for a moment. "Nice composition," he remarked, and then went over and took his wife and son into his arms.

DATE DUE